LAST STAND

ROBERT CIANCIO

First Edition

Fulton Books, Inc.
Meadville, PA

Published by Fulton Books 2020

This is a work of fiction. Names, characters, businesses, places, events, locales, and incidents are either the products of the author's imagination or used in a fictitious manner. Any resemblance to actual persons, living or dead, or actual events is purely coincidental.

ISBN 978-1-64654-504-9 (paperback)
ISBN 978-1-64654-605-3 (hardcover)
ISBN 978-1-64654-505-6 (digital)

Printed in the United States of America

ACKNOWLEDGMENTS

First and foremost, I would like to thank my beautiful and wonderful fiancée, Melissa, for her support while writing this book. She pushed me and gave me the motivation to finish it and pushed me to have it published. Without her, it would not have been completed.

Next, I would like to thank Bill Everts, a close friend and mentor, for planting the seed which led to me wanting to be an author. Without his encouragement, it would not have been started.

I would also like to thank my family, Bob, June, and Cari, for providing me the education, love of books, and work ethic that was needed to not only undertake such a task but the fortitude to finish it.

And finally, I would like to thank my hero when it comes to writing. D. J. Molles, author of the "Remaining" series, is a self-published author that took a dream and made it into reality. Thank you for doing what you do. It helped me move forward into what I hope is a new career path.

PART 1

THE JOURNEY HOME

Going by my past journey, I am not certain where life will take me, what turns and twists will happen; nobody knows where they will end up. As life changes direction, flow with it.

—Katrina Kaif

PROLOGUE: A RONIN IS BORN

Ronin—a warrior with no lord or master during the feudal period (1185–1868) of Japan. A warrior became masterless from the death or fall of his master, destined to wander the countryside in search of purpose.

"Dude, What the fuck?"

"Hey brother. Glad to see you too."

"I was afraid you were dead. Come on, let's walk. Tell me what happened."

1

My morning started with a cold nose to the back of the head.

"Shit, Fred. Go lay down. It's too early for this shit!"

Fred, actually Freddy, was my cat. She was a Heinz 57 mutt, and when she decided it was too late for me to be sleeping, she woke me up by sticking her cold nose into the base of my neck. I tried to go back to sleep, but it was futile. Once I was awake, that was it—I was up.

I rolled over and petted the purring bundle of fur. Freddy was sixteen years old and had been through every good and bad thing that had happened to me since I got her. She was my only living contact in the house. I had been single for some time and had no kids. So when I got home from work, having that fur ball to greet me at the door was very important.

I got out of bed and looked at the clock. Nothing, not even flashing mode. I picked up my cell phone and again saw nothing. I walked out into the living room of my one-bedroom apartment and found that all the power was out. There was no TV, no lights, nothing was working.

I looked out the window. It was light out, but I couldn't tell what time it was. There were several of my neighbors walking around my apartment complex. I lived in Laurel, Maryland, and had lived there for about ten years. The neighborhood was quiet, and the people were fairly friendly, but I was a loner and didn't associate much with my neighbors.

I was a police detective in a municipality just outside Washington, DC. I had been a police officer for twenty-five years, half of which had been with a sheriff's department in Pennsylvania. When I started in police work, I looked at the job as though we were modern-day samurai, protecting the people of the village from the rogues and bandits of society. I had done everything from patrol to SWAT and was currently the Investigations Unit Supervisor for my current department. But today, I was on day one of a two-week vacation. I had taken some time off just to chill out a little and get away from the office. I was starting to get tired of my job. Society was expressing a deep hatred for the police and criticizing us for everything we did right or wrong. I was losing my faith in the human species and was beginning to take more time off because I was just not caring about the job or the people anymore. I had always heard that when you start to feel like that, it's time to look for another job. For now, a couple of weeks off was all I could muster. A job search just wasn't in the cards yet. Soon, but not right now.

I recognized a few of the people walking around as being from the neighborhood. I decided to go out to see what was up. I got dressed and walked outside. It was the beginning of March, but was surprisingly warm for this time of year. It wasn't unbearable, but comfortable. The sun was out, and the humidity was low. It was a nice break compared to the bitterly cold winter we had just had. People were wandering around, talking to each other, but everybody seemed to have confused looks on their faces.

I walked up to one guy who lived in the building next to mine. I think his name was Andre. Andre was an African American, in his late twenties. We spoke when we saw each other, but it was just in passing conversation. He always struck me as being a good guy.

"Hey man, what's up?"

"I don't know," he said. He looked puzzled. "It's sunny out, doesn't look like it rained at all last night, and I didn't hear any rain. But nobody has power."

"Yeah, nothing in my place is working either," I said. I walked over to my patrol car and hit the unlock button on the key fob, nothing. I was starting to get a little nervous. My mind was starting to run with ideas about what could be causing the power outage. I didn't want to jump to conclusions, but I had read stuff about EMPs, and I was hoping beyond all hope that this wasn't that. I walked back over to Andre.

"All right, brother, I'm heading back in. If you happen to hear anything from anybody, let me know, okay."

"No problem," he said as he waved at me.

I went back to my apartment and closed and locked the door. My apartment was still cool inside, but without power, the outside temperature would soon heat up the inside of my place. I sat down on my leather fat guy chair and started to ponder the possibilities. Could the electricity just be out? If it was, why did my cell phone not work? Why would the car not unlock? I was starting to think that maybe the EMP scenario was the most plausible explanation for what was going on. An EMP event could have been caused by a high-altitude nuclear strike, or a huge solar flare. Either way, it was bad. If this was a true loss of the power grid, who knew how long it would take to get things back up and running? It could take years. My concern started to grow. Freddy jumped up on to the arm of my chair. Her purring was a welcome comfort and small distraction from my thoughts.

I decided that I needed more information before I jumped to any conclusions. I went into my bedroom and went to my closet. I kept a safe inside the closet where I kept my off-duty pistol. Once inside, I took out my 1911 with its holster. I had always wanted a custom-built 1911 and had this one built for me the previous year by a small, one man show gunsmith in Kansas. The gun was not only beautiful, but I had also designed it to be what I thought a true combat 1911 should be. It was chambered for .45 caliber, had a light rail, front cocking serrations, with the words "Hunt Custom 1911 A-1" engraved on the side and a matte finish to limit glare. The grips were polymer from *VZ* grips, and at twenty-five yards, it would pound nails. With today's mentality, I catch a lot of grief about carrying a "dinosaur gun." But my thoughts are that if it's okay for the Marine's MEU and Delta Force, it's good enough for me. I strapped it on with two extra magazines, and once I covered it with a button-down shirt, I went for a walk in the neighborhood.

It was starting to get hotter out. The sun was up, and the cloud cover was minimal. There were a lot of people wandering around. They were talking to each other, moving around, doing the same thing I was, which was trying to find answers to their questions. I could see smoke rising from someplace in the distance but was unable to tell exactly what it was. Nobody seemed to be getting the answers that they wanted. As I moved around, I saw several cars along the roadway that had just coasted to a stop, unable to start or turn over. There was nobody in the immediate vicinity of the cars, so I assumed the drivers had walked home or went somewhere to try to get out of the heat.

As I continued to look at the plumes of smoke in the distance, it dawned on me what they could be. I got a sinking feeling in my gut because I believed I knew what they were. I saw a guy I didn't know looking in the same direction. He was maybe sixty years old and had a small schnauzer running around, between his legs.

"What is that?" I asked, pointing in the direction of the smoke.

"Both of them are planes. They just fell out of the sky. I was out walking my dog…I've never seen anything like it. They just crashed."

"How long ago did it happen?" I asked. He didn't answer me right away. He had a complete look of disbelief on his face and surprise in his eyes. It took him several minutes to answer me. He just kept staring at the smoke.

"About twenty minutes ago," he finally said. He looked at me with a mixture of hurt and confusion. "All those people are dead. They just fell from the sky. Buddy, do you know what happened here?" He hoped for some explanation.

"No, I don't. But I think everything is going to be okay," I said as I put a hand on his shoulder. "Why don't you go back inside? It's starting to get a little warm out here." I looked him in the eye, trying to convey my best imitation of strength and control. I believed he was in the first stages of shock and needed a rest. I guessed that seeing two planes full of people crash in front of his eyes might have been more than he could take. I thought to myself that if this was what I thought it was, this guy wasn't going to make it past the first few weeks.

I continued to walk around and take in as much information as I could. Nobody seemed to have power. There were cars stalled out all over the streets, and two planes had just fallen from the sky.

My thoughts immediately went to an EMP but not the solar kind. This was an NEMP (nuclear electromagnetic pulse). An NEMP was caused by somebody setting off a nuclear bomb two hundred to three hundred miles above the earth. I am no nuclear physicist, but basically, when the bomb explodes, the explosion fries all electronics. I decided that I had seen enough. I turned back toward my apartment, and went back home.

I had watched several programs on *Discovery* over the years that dealt with apocalyptic events. After about a week, the everyday citizen starts to run out of food. All power is gone, so freezers can only keep things cool for so long; frozen food starts to go bad, and canned food gets used up. There is no power to pump water, and the normal person does not stock water, so they run out of liquids to drink. After week one, citizens begin to panic and raid the local grocery stores. What can be bought will be if the stores set up a cash only policy. What can't be bought will be stolen. After week three, citizens begin to resort back to primitive behavior. They begin to form gangs and start to rob their neighbors for food and water. Eventually, they will resort to killing each other if that's what it takes to keep themselves and their families alive.

As I walked back inside my apartment, I noticed that the temperature was starting to go up. It wasn't uncomfortable yet, but I could tell that it was warmer inside than when I left. I unholstered my 1911 and set it on the table beside my chair. Freddy immediately jumped up on the arm of my chair to greet me. I had been gone maybe an hour, but she acted like I had been gone a week. As I sat there petting Freddy, I thought about what I was going to do.

2

I decided that my best option for now was to bunker in. I wasn't a hundred percent sure an NEMP had caused a power outage, or maybe I was just in denial. I had to figure out what I needed to bunker in successfully. First was food and water. I wouldn't consider myself a prepper or survivalist. We had a couple of pretty heavy storms in Maryland recently, and the power had gone out for several days. A few years ago, Hurricane Sandy hit, and the power was out all along the eastern seaboard. In some places, it had been out for weeks. Because of this, I decided to get myself prepared for the next big storm.

I had about twenty-five gallons of water stored in cases in the closet. I also had about four weeks of *Mountain House* camp food. I also had a camp stove with several canisters of propane fuel. So I was set for food and water, at least for a little while anyway. I also had two ten-pound bags of cat food for Freddy.

The next thing that I needed to consider was shelter and heat. Well, I was bunkering in so that was a no brainer. I was in my apartment so I had the shelter. The heat—well, it was the start of the spring into summer season. Heat wasn't going to be an issue either. The only problem with my apartment was that it wasn't very defendable. It was a one-bedroom apartment that had two windows and one door. They all opened onto one patio. So at some point, if somebody tried to come in through any of those entry points, I was screwed for a retreat. I would need to fight my way out. If the power didn't come back on within the next couple of weeks, I was going to need to rethink the bunkering in idea. As I said earlier, at some point, I expected neighbors to start turning on each other.

The last thing that I was worried about was security. I had my 1911 and about a thousand rounds of ammunition for it. I also had a *Rock River* .223 that I had decked out with Magpul furniture, an Eotech dot sight, a flashlight, and a laser setup. *Rock River* .223s had been chosen by the ATF as their go to rifle several years ago. The *Rock River* rifles were the only rifles to pass all the tests that the ATF threw at them. The barrel and trigger were both Wilson Combat competition parts, and this rifle was spot on at three hundred yards. I also had about three thousand rounds of ammunition for it. Lastly, I had an assortment of knives, to include a custom-made Bowie survival knife that I had made by a knife smith in Texas.

I went back to my closet and pulled out my rifle bag. I got out the .223 and a bag of batteries. I put batteries in all the attachments. My concern was that the Eotech was an electrical piece. A check confirmed that it was shot. It came off; iron sights it was. I then checked the laser. It too was a no go, so off it came. One good thing was that there was less weight on the rifle. The old adage was, ounces equal pounds, pounds equal pain. When I checked the flashlight, for some reason, it worked. I'm not sure why, but it did. That was a plus.

I had an *Eberlestock* G-4 Operator Ruck-sack. It was loaded with your normal survival gear: 3,500 calorie food bars, *Mountain House* meals, fire starting supplies, water containers, first aid kit, ammo, etc. It also had a flashlight, headlamp, and a light for my 1911. I checked all of those, and they worked. I'm not sure why the flashlights still worked, but I wasn't going to complain.

I loaded all my 1911 magazines, six in all. I also loaded all my .223 mags. Those totaled nine. I was set for now. All I could do now was to wait to see what happened.

Over the next few days, things didn't really change too much. I went out on small recon walks to see how the rest of the neighborhood was handling things. Of course nobody was really prepared, but the reality of what was going on hadn't really had the time to settle in on them yet.

One of my neighbors whom I spoke to occasionally was an avid camper and backpacker. I suspected that he was handling things a lot better than most. Prior to the event, I had seen him walking around preparing for a trip. He had a lot of the expected gear. Things like Maxpedition bags, hiking boots, and general clothing I only really saw in camping and survival magazines. So I expected that he would fare better than most. I saw him using his grill to cook what food he was eating, as were most of my neighbors. Grills were going pretty much around the clock.

As the first week passed, I could sense things starting to heat up. I could hear and see neighbors starting to get into arguments.

"Come on, man, can't you spare some water?"

"Come on, brother, just some canned veggies?"

"What am I supposed to do about my kids?"

"Man, fuck you!"

These types of conversations were starting to happen more and more frequently. I tried to avoid contact with anybody because I didn't want to be caught up in an argument. I may have had the food and water to spare, but how could I be sure? I didn't know how long this thing was going to last. I needed to make sure I had enough for me to get through as far as I could.

At about the end of week two, I decided to recon the grocery store down the road from me. I moved down the road until I could see a crowd of people who had gathered in the vicinity of the store's parking lot. I moved off into the field around the store. It was lined with decorative pine trees which would give me some cover and concealment. I moved the last fifty yards or so to the store through the trees. When I got to the edge of the field, what I saw was chaos. There was a huge crowd of maybe two hundred people in front of the store. Citizens were shoving and pushing each other and fights were breaking out. People were begging the managers to let them in so that they could get food for their families. The store managers were only letting a few in at a time, but only if they had cash.

How management was tallying up the price of the goods, and what people got, I wasn't sure. As people came out of the store with a few bags of supplies, they were attacked by others in the crowd and their supplies were stolen. Then the inevitable happened. I heard gunshots. Who fired I couldn't say, but the crowd scattered and people began to run. As the crown parted, the area where the shots came from, I could see the body of a young woman with blond hair on the ground rolling around in obvious pain. Pandemonium broke out, and people started to force their way into the store, rushing past the managers and other store employees. Fights broke out all through the crowd with everybody trying to take whatever they could in an attempt to sustain themselves for a little longer. I didn't want to be a part of any of this. I backed into the tree line and made my way back to the apartment.

As I walked into the apartment I was greeted, as usual, by Fred. She was purring, and rubbing up against my legs. She had no idea what was going on. Ignorance is bliss. I was hungry, so I cooked up a scrambled eggs and bacon *mountain house* meal using the propane and camp stove combination. Breakfast for dinner was one of my favorite things. It wasn't too bad considering it was cooked in a bag with hot water.

It was the end of week two, and as I sat in my chair, I started to ponder my next move. The electricity didn't seem to be coming back on. There was no difference in the functionality of any of my electronic items, and things were starting to heat up around the neighborhood. I had already seen somebody get shot. People were starting to steal from each other, and arguments were breaking out amongst neighbors. Soon, my safety was going to be harder to ensure. As I thought about my options, I soon fell asleep, listening to the little internal motor of the furball beside me.

I jumped awake. I didn't know what time it was, but it was getting dark out. I could hear arguing just outside my door. I grabbed my 1911 from the end table beside me and moved to the door. As I looked through the peephole, I could see my neighbor, a fifty-year-old black male who I knew worked for a construction company before this event. He lived across the courtyard from me. We spoke several times a week, but I didn't know his name. He was a small-statured, quiet guy who worked hard and never bothered anybody. Now he was in an argument with a guy I didn't know. The second guy was also a black male, about 185 pounds and he was irate. He also had a bat. All of a sudden, the second guy swung his bat striking my neighbor in the shoulder. As the thug swung the bat a second time, I threw open my door.

Several thoughts were running through my head. *You need to ignore this and let it play out. Don't get involved. The world is different now.* But I'm not like that. I'm a cop. It was ingrained in my DNA to confront aggression and to protect those that can't. Batboy swung a third time, knocking my neighbor to the ground.

"Drop the fuckin' bat!" I yelled. My front sight aimed center mass.

"What? You gonna shoot me? I don't think you got the balls… cracker!" You could see the contempt in his eyes.

"That's not something I think you should bet on," I said as I stared at him. He lifted the bat up and started to walk toward me, rage and anger in his eyes. He kept repeating over and over.

"You ain't got the balls, cracker."

"You ain't got the balls, cracker."

Each time he said it, I ordered him to drop the bat, but he kept walking toward me. He was about four feet from me when he raised the bat to swing it at me. I pressed the trigger four times, *ba-bang, ba-bang*. Two double taps, center mass. Batboy stumbled back and landed against a wall. Blood immediately started to drain from the holes in his chest and shirt. He had a look of bewilderment on his face, like he couldn't believe that I had just shot him. He had been warned. He slid to the ground, dead.

I changed out the partial magazine for a full one, placing the half-used mag in my pocket. I scanned the area for any more threats. Once I was sure there were no more, I walked over to where my neighbor was lying on the patio in front of his door. I wish I could have remembered my neighbor's name, but for the life of me, I couldn't remember what it was. I looked him over and saw some blood on his head.

"Brother, are you okay?" I asked. He grumbled a little, rubbing his head and shoulder.

"He got me good a couple of times, but I don't think anything is too serious." He looked over at the body lying beside his apartment door. "Man, if it wasn't for you, that could be me lying there with a bashed-in skull. Thanks, man." He reached out his hand to shake mine. I extended the courtesy and holstered my 1911.

"Brother, things are getting bad here." In my world, bat boy was just another casualty caused by the event and society's decline into primitive behavior. I knew an attack on me, in my apartment, was not far off. I made the decision at that moment that I needed to leave. I knew this decision had been coming but had hoped to avoid it. Bunkering in is fine if you're in a rural area that is easier to defend, but living in a metropolitan community opens you up to the possibility of attack. I decided that humping my way back home to Pennsylvania and the friends I had back there was my best alternative.

"Listen, brother, I'm getting out of here. I'll be gone by tomorrow morning. I've got extra food and water in my apartment that you can have. Once I'm gone, it's yours." I reached out my hand to shake his again. "Be safe," I said as I helped him up and headed to my apartment to prepare to go.

3

Once I decided to leave, I had a very difficult decision to make and a more difficult thing to do. I couldn't take Freddy with me. I was heading to Indiana Pennsylvania which was approximately 240 miles from Laurel, Maryland. Taking a sixteen-year-old cat in my rucksack was an unrealistic thing to even consider. I couldn't leave her in the apartment. If I did, she would suffer a slow painful death from starvation and dehydration. She didn't deserve to go out like that. I had her declawed when she was a kitten, so leaving her free to roam would have been a death sentence for her as she had no way to defend herself. She had been an indoor cat her whole life, so even if she had her claws, she would not have known what to do to survive. I truly believe animals have the same feelings that we have. I found Fred when she was weeks old. I am all that she has ever known. She would have missed me, and that's the cruelest thing that I could have done to her. The decision needed to be made. Putting her down was the best, most humane thing to do for her.

I went into my bedroom where I had a small .22-caliber subsonic pistol. It was a single shot and, with the subsonic ammo, made virtually no sound. It wasn't good for much except plinking. I decided that I would wait until she was asleep and do it while she was sleeping. She had been having problems with her hearing and was missing a lot of things lately. There were times when I came home from work, turned off my alarm system, unlocked the door, walked in, and started to put my bags down before she heard me and realized that I was home. I knew that I could do it without her even knowing what was coming.

I decided to take the time to get my gear ready. I pulled my ruck and my *High-Speed Gear* battle belt from the closet. As soon as I put my ruck on the floor, was normal for Fred, she had to get involved and see what was going on. She had her nose buried in each of the compartments and sniffed each of the items I took out to check as if to say, "What are you doin', Dad? Come on, let me see what you got in there." I teared up as I watched her play. I couldn't believe I had to do what I was going to do. For me, it was like euthanizing my child. I had to remind myself that it was the most humane thing I could do for her.

My ruck weighed about eighty-five pounds. I had all the normal "bug out" stuff in there. I had shelter, water, gun cleaning gear, first-aid equipment, ammo, and a fire-starting kit. I also had gear that could be used to obtain safe drinking water and food, things like traps and a water straw. There was probably some stuff in there that a bush crafter would say that I didn't need. The way I looked at it was that this bag was an INCH (I'm Not Coming Home) bag and I needed to have the things in it that I needed to survive not just a bush craft outing but also a combat situation. The world as I knew it was collapsing, and people were starting to kill each other for food and water. I wasn't going to be able to come back. Once I left, that would be it. I was saying goodbye to Maryland.

I checked my battle belt. I had loaded all the rifle magazines with ammo. That was 240 rounds. I put the mags in their pouches and put an additional three hundred rounds in my ruck. That gave me 540 rounds of .223. I had also loaded all my .45 mags. That was sixty-four rounds. I put them in their pouches and put an additional two hundred rounds in the ruck. That gave me 264 rounds of .45. I then checked my knife to make sure it was sharp and ready to go. Lastly, I checked my holster to make sure that it was working as it should and was attached securely.

I then filled my sixty-four-ounce stainless steel *Klean Kanteen* and sixty-four-ounce army canteen with water and put them in my ruck. I checked my food. I had about a ten-day supply of food. There were several *Mountain House* meals, beef jerky, trail mix, thirty-five hundred calorie trail bars and miscellaneous food items. To supplement my food supply, I also carried in my ruck a conibear trap, two rat traps, and a slingshot that shot arrows. These would help me hunt and trap for food as my trip progressed. I realized that things would be slim and that there would be days that I couldn't eat. I also hoped that I would find places to scavenge for supplies and food.

Once my gear was checked and double-checked, I went back out into the living room carrying a candle that smelled like apple pie. I poured myself a glass of water and sat in my chair holding the .22 in my lap. Freddy knew it was getting close to bedtime. She made her rounds, checking the front door and all the corners of the apartment. She then made her way into the bedroom to check things in there. She made her way to her litter box and then finally to the kitchen where she had her evening snack. Tears began to flow as I watched her do her thing. She had been with me for so long. When I got sick fifteen years ago and almost died, she was with me while I recovered, helping me deal with the pain of surgery. When my wife left me, Freddy was there to comfort me. When I came home from a bad day at work, she was there to do something funny to make me laugh. All the times that I had needed her, she was there for me. She never knew how important she was and never asked for anything in return. I had to keep reminding myself that this was the best thing for her.

As her rounds came to an end, she jumped onto the couch and curled up in the corner. It was her sleep spot. I waited for about an hour. My ex-wife had nicknamed her Wheezy because when she slept, she would wheeze. It was kind of like a snore and funny as hell. There were times when it got loud enough that it was almost disruptive when I was watching TV. When I heard her wheezing, I knew it was time.

I was still crying as I got up and walked over to the couch. As I had hoped, she didn't hear me. I crouched down beside the couch and put the barrel of the .22 behind her left ear. I wanted it to be quick and painless. I figured that the brain would be the quickest and most painless way to that end. I was careful not to touch her because she'd wake up. I closed my eyes and took a deep breath. There was a knot in my throat the size of an apple and a pain in my heart that I couldn't even begin to describe. Mustering all the emotional strength that I could, I pulled the trigger.

The only noise I heard was the bolt slamming forward on the pistol. She never heard or felt it. She never moved. When I opened my eyes, she was in the same position as when she fell asleep but with some blood running from her nose. I put my head down on the couch beside her and cried harder than I had ever cried before. I don't know how long I cried, but eventually, I fell asleep, lying beside the best friend I had ever had.

I awoke to the sound of thunder. I'm not sure how long I had been asleep, but I still felt drained. The candle I had lit earlier was still burning but was half gone at this point. I looked at Fred and teared up as I petted her for the final time. She had been a great cat, a great pet, and a great friend. I stared at her for a few more minutes until another crack of thunder brought me back to the here and now. I moved over to the door and looked through the peephole. It was raining, and it was dark. I decided that now would be a good time to go. With the rain, most people would stay inside. I could move around and avoid contact with as many people as possible. I didn't have an abundance of ammo, so avoiding a long shoot-out or drawn-out confrontation was the smart thing to do.

I opened my ruck and pulled out my map of Laurel city. The city of Laurel actually sat on four counties in Maryland. It was located on the points of Prince Georges, Anne Arundel, Montgomery, and Howard Counties. However, the town of Laurel was located entirely in Prince George's County and was almost midway between Washington, DC. and Baltimore. It started out as a factory town because it was located around the Patuxent River. Its industrial capabilities continued to grow and reached a pinnacle when the Baltimore & Ohio Railroad was built in the middle 1800s. The city had now become a commuter town for both Washington and Baltimore workers. Laurel was known as what it commonly referred to as a "company town" because the schools, businesses, and houses were all owned by the company businesses in the area.

When the civil war started, Laurel was divided. It was not uncommon to find sympathizers with ties to both sides of the conflict. Even so, due to the large number of southern backers, union soldiers were used as security patrols for the railroad.

After the Civil War, around the late 1800s, manufacturing became less important and Laurel became a suburban town. Since the railroad was so close, residents commuted to jobs in Washington and Baltimore. The Laurel Park Racetrack was a thoroughbred racetrack that opened its doors in 1911 and was still open…until the event happened. It was even mentioned in the book, *Seabiscuit: An American Legend.*

On May 15, 1972, Governor George Wallace, the governor of Alabama, campaigning for the presidential nomination of the Democratic Party, was attending a rally in the parking lot of the Laurel Shopping Center. Arthur Bremer, an unemployed janitor, shot Wallace. The shooting paralyzed him. And before the September 11 hijackings, many of the hijackers used Laurel-based hotels as places to meet and plan the hijackings. They also worked out at a local Gold's gym. A common phrase in Maryland seems to hold true. "All things move through Maryland."

I also got out my maps of Pennsylvania and placed them and the Laurel City map into a waterproof map case. I pulled out my Frogg Togg rain suit and put it on over my clothes. I had on a pair of green *Wrangler* Ranger cargo pants, a black *5.11* tactical shirt, and a pair of *Danner* Acadia boots. I was very product loyal. *Wrangler*, *5.11*, and *Danner* had served me well for several years.

As I said, I wanted to avoid confrontation as much as possible so preventing people from seeing exactly what I had, would keep their curiosity down. My *Eberlestock* ruck had a rifle scabbard built into the back of the pack. I placed my AR15, barrel down, in the scabbard. I then strapped on my battle belt, knife, and thigh ride pistol holster.

Once my gear was on, I attached my surefire light to my 1911 and placed it into its holster. I pulled the rain cover over my ruck and slung my pack, grabbed my boonie hat, and moved to the door.

I stopped and went over to blow out the candle. I looked around at the home that I lived in for ten years, scanning all my possessions, all the material things I had worked so hard to acquire. The TVs, furniture, movie posters on my walls, all the DVDs, everything was worthless now. I was leaving everything to essentially rot away or be stolen by somebody else. It amazed me how everything was gone in an instant.

I went over to the couch one more time and said my final farewells to Freddy. I blew out the candle, went to the door, and turned the knob, walking out into the unknown.

4

The rain was painful and was blowing almost sideways. It blew straight into my face and felt like hundreds of little needles poking at my skin. The rain and clouds were so thick that it was almost completely dark outside.

I knew the area around my apartment pretty well. I knew which way was north and moved in that direction. As I had hoped, the weather ensured that the streets were clear of people. My pack was heavier than I would have liked, but all the camping trips and repacking had taught me what could be eliminated without taking out what I felt was important. The pack was heavy, but it only contained the necessities, at least what I felt was necessary for my current mission parameters, which in this case was to get home.

The average person can move through the woods with gear and make about six miles a day. I was guessing that I could do about four, maybe five miles a day. By roadway only, Laurel to Indiana, Pennsylvania, was approximately two hundred and forty miles. At five miles a day, that would take me forty-eight days of travel. It would take me a little over a month to get home. That was if I followed the roadways and didn't stop anywhere for an extended period of time. Traveling cross country would eliminate miles, which would cut some time, which would eliminate days.

I moved as fast as I could without risking injury. My plan was to follow roadways until I was able to get out of town. Then I would move into the woods and navigate by compass the rest of the way. I would move throughout the day and rest at night. I wasn't going to set up full-blown camps each night. I wasn't in a SERE (survival, evasion, resistance, escape) type situation, but once again, I wanted to avoid detection as much as possible.

I negotiated around apartment buildings and what was now boarded-up businesses. It took me about an hour to get out of town. I had reached the outskirts of the city limits and was entering wooded territory. Once the chances of running into anybody had dropped, I pulled out my AR15, charged a round, and slung the strap over my shoulder. The rain had not let up and was still coming down pretty good. I decided to stay with the highways and move along the wood lines that ran perpendicular to the roadways, staying hidden among the trees and using them as cover. This would keep me out of town as much as possible.

Shortly, the sun started to come up, but with the rain, it stayed gray out. Once I could really start to see, I would be able to move a little easier and, subsequently, faster.

There were cars everywhere, stalled out all along the roadway. I needed to be careful. Cars stalled in the roadway, could also be used as ambush spots for people looking to attack travelers. The abandoned cars sat at all different angles, left to rust where they sat. It was the beginning of the third week into this thing, so the drivers had already left, looking for some shelter or a way to get home.

After a couple of hours, the rain stopped, and the sun finally started to shine. I had been on the road now for about three hours, so I decided that it was a good time to take a break. I looked around the wood line for a decent-sized tree. Although it had been raining, the ground under a big tree would be fairly dry.

I was able to find a large pine tree, with an abundance of soft, brown pine needles under it. I dropped my pack, dug out my army canteen, and took a couple of long pulls. The sun was out strong now, so I decided to also dig out my sunglasses, which I had in a pouch strapped to the outside of my pack. I would get hot and sweaty as it was, but the rain suit would have made things worse, so I took it off and repacked it in my ruck. I was starting to feel hungry, but I really needed to watch my food consumption, so eating now was out. I also decided to change my clothes. I took off the civilian clothes I had on and changed into *5.11* real tree camo pants and shirt. I folded my civilian clothes and placed them into a waterproof bag and put them into my ruck. The real tree camos would be my primary clothing for the rest of this trip.

The birds were out now, singing to anyone or anything that would listen, oblivious to the new world. I sat and listened to them sing, relaxing for a few minutes under the tree.

After about a twenty-minute break, I repacked my canteen and shrugged my pack back on. The humidity had started to get thick after the sun started to dry up the rain. As I walked, my mind started to wonder, and I started to think about things. I thought about my parents, and how now, after the fact, I was happy that they weren't around anymore. They would have never been able to survive something like this. My mom, June, was a great woman with a heart of gold, but she was never able to understand the evil that the human species was able to inflict on each other. She would not have understood the need to defend herself, and what people would have done to take what she had. Dad, his name was Bob, just never believed something like this could happen. When he passed away, he still had the farm I grew up on. I had talked to him several times about using the space and the land he had to store and grow food that he would need to survive something like this. But he just never took the initiative to do it. For their sake, I was glad they were gone.

My sister, Cari, had died in a car accident about a year after my parents had passed. She bought herself a scooter and was on her way to work when somebody in a Dodge truck, who wasn't paying attention, ran into her. The driver of the truck had been doing about seventy miles an hour when he hit her. The doctors said she had died instantly, so she didn't suffer.

I never really felt alone. Even though my immediate family was gone, I still had family left. The only family I really had now were my best friends Josh, Mike, and their families. I met both of them when I worked with the sheriff's department.

Indiana, Pennsylvania, is roughly located in the center of Indiana County and can be found just east of Pittsburgh. In 2013, Indiana became part of the Pittsburgh Metropolitan Area and established itself as the "Christmas Tree Capital of the World." The National Christmas Tree Growers Association was founded there, and a large number of Christmas tree farms can still be found in the area. Until this event took place, Indian University of PA was located there and was the largest employer in the area.

For years, the biggest industry in the area was coal mining, but mines began to close, creating an ongoing economic difficulty.

Indiana was also the hometown of veteran and actor, Jimmy Stewart. Although he left the town right after high school, the town had continued to support his career. A museum was built in his memory shortly before his death, and a bronze statue of Stewart could be found at the county courthouse.

Josh, Mike, and I were all deputies and had worked together on the SWAT team. We had all spent a lot of time together. We worked together all day and then hung out at night and on weekends. We watched out for each other at work and also had each other's backs out of work. I had gotten so close to these guys over the years that I looked at them like brothers.

In 2006, I decided I wanted more out of my career and wanted to try working in a place that saw constant action. I heard that a department in Maryland was hiring experienced police officers, so I applied and got the job. The rest, as they say, is history.

As I walked, I continued to think about Josh and Mike and soon lost all track of time. When I finally came back to the present, I realized that the sun was starting its downward arc. I wasn't sure how far I had traveled, but it would be night soon. I figured I was somewhere along Route 95, maybe five or six miles from Laurel. I walked off into the woods and looked for a place to set up a camp. I did a recon of the area and found a small cluster of pines several yards from the roadway that would be a good site for a camp. It was about fifty yards from a small stream that I could use as a water source and provided some cover for light discipline.

I dropped my pack and got out my canteen. I took a long drag on the water and finished off the two-quart canteen. I opened my pack and took out my cloth tarp that I used for my shelter. It was a ten-by-ten camouflage nylon tarp that worked great. I used five fifty cord to set it up in a quick and easy lean-to style shelter that would protect me from the rain if it started to come down again, but I expected it to be nice out, as I saw no clouds in the sky.

I then used a small gardening trowel to dig a Dakota firepit. A Dakota firepit consisted of two holes connected by a tunnel. You built a fire in one of the holes and fed the fire with wood pushed through the other hole. It allegedly kept the light and smoke created by the fire to a minimum, which would limit the possibility of being seen.

I gathered some wood and kindling and fed it into the pit. I had a ferrocerium rod, also called a fire steel, but I decided to just use a lighter. I didn't need a large fire for heat; I just needed something to boil some water and heat up dinner. As soon as those tasks were done, I would be putting the fire out. It was now the end of March and was averaging sixty-five to seventy degrees out at night, so I wouldn't need a fire, but I would use my sleeping bag.

I walked down to the stream and got some water in a waterproof bag I used as a water bucket. It held about five quarts of water, which I carried back to my camp. I got out my *Klean Kanteen* and emptied the water from it, into the two-quart plastic army canteen. I then filled the *Klean Kanteen* with water from the stream and brought it to a boil. Once it cooled, I put the lid back on it and repacked it into my pack. Any water I was drinking tonight would be boiled and drank with some single-cup coffee packs I had in my food container.

Finally, I took a stainless-steel pot that I carried and put some water into it, also bringing it to a boil. Once it started to boil, I emptied half of a *Mountain House* spaghetti meal into it, letting it set for a couple of minutes. Once it was ready, I leaned back against my pack and ate dinner. Once I was done, I cleaned my pot and fork, put them away, and leaned back with my cup of coffee. The air was cooling down, and the temperature was getting nice. The birds were still singing, and I could hear small critters scurrying around through the woods. I watched the sun set and soon drifted off to sleep with my AR across my lap.

I awoke several hours later. It was still dark outside, so I'm not sure what woke me up. I sat there, not moving, letting my eyes adjust and listening for anything that seemed out of the ordinary. My only thought was how much I wished I had night vision.

I'm not sure what woke me up, as nothing seemed to show itself, and no noises seemed out of the ordinary. I've heard that if you're not used to sleeping in the woods at night, normal woods noises will keep you up, so I figured that's what it was. I tried to go back to sleep, but couldn't.

I moved off my pack and dug out my headlamp. I turned on the red light, as red light is harder to see from distances at night. I decided to make a cup of coffee, so I prepared another small fire in the Dakota pit. After the coffee was made, I put out the fire and my head lamp, leaned back against my pack, and drank my coffee. I sat there awake for several hours, listening to the nighttime noises of the forest.

The next thing I knew, the sun was coming up through the trees. I decided to get started before it got too hot, so I packed the gear I had used for the fire and the coffee, took down the cloth tarp, and packed it up. I checked my weapons, and once I was sure both weapons were loaded and ready for the new day, I shrugged on my pack and headed back to the road.

Once on the roadway, I decided that I was going to play it safe and avoid roadways as much as possible now. It was now time to start moving cross country. I checked my compass, got my North West bearing, picked a tree off in the distance that fell within that North West reading, and set out. Once I reached the tree, I'd take a reading, find another tree, and set out.

Things went on like this for several days. I'd walk through the woods, cross roadways, use the road for a while, and break for water, food, and sleep. Some areas along the roads had an abundant number of cars on them, stalled along the roads, while other places seemed baron. I needed to be careful of places that were littered with abandoned cars, as they could be used as ambush sites. I would skirt these areas and get back into the woods as quick as possible.

I was doing pretty good food-wise. I had several thirty-five hundred calorie food bars that I was breaking up into two meals a day. Water was okay, as finding little streams and runoffs was fairly easy. Boiling it ensured I'd kill any pathogens in it, but it didn't always taste that great. The key was just making sure that I stayed hydrated.

I was actually comfortable in the woods. Some of the patrol skills I had learned in the Army were starting to come back to the forefront of my memory, looking for things at wrong angles, wrong colors for the terrain, or movements of trees and bushes that just seemed out of place. I was paying attention to foot placement, weight placement, and sound discipline. I'm sure that by this time, people had reached a point of desperation that would be forcing them to do anything needed to survive. I didn't want to stumble into anybody, so I needed to resort to all the patrol tactics that I could remember.

One afternoon, I could see the sun through the trees, which indicated to me that I was coming to some kind of clearing or roadway. As I got closer, I could hear what sounded like crying, mixed with yelling. I was far enough away that I couldn't make out what was being yelled or if they were yelling at somebody. All I could tell was that they were yelling. I dropped to a knee and listened. It was coming from the direction of the clearing. I dropped my pack behind a tree. This would be my personal rally point if things went south.

I worked my way closer to the yelling, moving in crouch, being careful not to step on branches or twigs. My AR was up, in the low ready position. As I got closer, I could start to hear what was being yelled.

"Help! Somebody please! Help me!"

I dropped to a knee again. I listened for any other noises, anything that seemed out of the ordinary. I was listening for anything more out of the ordinary than somebody screaming for help. I also scanned the wood line for any movements. I was looking for anything that looked like an ambush or anything that might indicate that this was a trick. I didn't hear anything or see any fishy movements.

As I moved closer, I came to a roadway that had a fairly steep shoulder. The roadway was a secluded, two-lane country road. There were no cars or people around. There were heavy woods on both sides of the roadway. Off to my right, I could see an older model, 1950s era truck, rolled over onto its roof. It was badly damaged, with the windshield shattered, and the roof collapsed. I took another knee and scanned the wood line up and down both sides of the roadway. I listened some more but heard nothing other than the yelling from the truck. I decided that things looked okay, so I moved toward the truck with my AR up and ready.

I approached the driver-side door, but I couldn't see inside. I could still hear the yelling, which now I could tell was coming from a guy inside the truck.

"Would somebody help me! Somebody help me, please!"

I dropped to my side and pointed my AR inside the truck. When he heard me move, he looked toward the window.

"Shit, man, don't shoot me! I'm hurt. I'm stuck in here, and I think my foot's broken." He had a look on his face that was scared, pleading, and pained.

"What's your name?" I asked, never taking the rifle sights from him.

"My name's Jared, but they call me Norman," he replied.

"Who's they, and why do they call you Norman if you're named Jared?" I asked.

"They are my family, and they call me Norman because they think I look like the guy who played Norman Bates on A&E." As I looked at him, I could see the resemblance. He was skinny and had dark hair and big ears. Hell, he looked more like Alfred E. Newman from the old *Mad Magazine* comics I read when I was a kid.

"Okay, can you move at all?" I asked, a little less concerned for my safety now.

"No, man. I'm trapped in here."

"All right, stand by a minute," I said as I slung my rifle over my back and tried to pull open the driver's door. It was jammed shut, so I ran around to the passenger side and tried the passenger door. It moved a little but was also jammed. I leaned into the passenger window.

"Look, both doors are jammed. Give me a few minutes, I'll be right back." As I ran back to my pack, I could hear him pleading for me not to go. Soon, I could only hear his muffled yelling again. I slung on my pack and ran back toward the truck. Along the way, I saw a decent-sized tree that was young and green and looked like it could withstand the pressures of being used as a lever. I dug my pruning saw from my pack and cut down the tree and cleaned as many branches off as I could. I grabbed my pack and ran back to the truck.

Norman was still yelling when I got back to the truck. I thought to myself that this guy needed to shut the fuck up before every turd on the planet heard him. I took the tree and slid it into the gap I made the first time I tried to open the passenger door. I pushed and pulled with all that I had. I was able to get the door to move inches at a time. It was slow and took a lot of energy, but I was eventually able to get it open enough to get into the truck.

"Okay, Norman, how are you trapped in here? What's got you trapped?" I asked.

"My foot's trapped between the roof and the back of the seat. I can't move it." He started to move around, trying to pull himself free.

"Okay, hold on." I got my lever and worked it into a small space between the seat back and the roof. I pried and pushed until I was able to get one end of the lever as close to his foot as I could. I got my end of the tree on my shoulder and pushed up. Eventually, I was able to push the back of the seat up enough to create a space big enough that Norman could slide his foot out.

"Oh man, thanks. Thanks so much. God, my foot is killing me. Man, thanks."

"Relax, Norman, I'm not in the mood for any kissing just yet. Let's get you out of here." I threw the tree out of the truck and grabbed Norman under his arms. I pulled him out of the cab of the truck and laid him on the ground. He looked around, smiling like it was the first time he had seen trees.

"Oh man, is it good to be out of there. I'm dyin' of thirst. You got anything to drink?" he asked.

"Sure, gimme a second," I said as I got up and walked over to my pack. I took out my canteen and handed it to Norman. He drank until he had his fill.

"How long have you been in there? What happened anyway?" I asked as I knelt down to look at his foot.

"I've been stuck in that piece of shit for three days. Damn man, go easy!" he yelled as I pulled, prodded, and twisted his ankle. I was no doctor—hell, I wasn't even a medic—but from the grinding sound I heard in his ankle, I could tell it was broken.

"I was out hunting for me and my wife, which reminds me, don't forget my rifle in the truck, it's the only one I have. Anyway, I was driving home and a freakin' bear ran across the road. I swerved to miss it, lost control, and rolled this bitch. Dammit, that's the only truck we got too," he said. I wasn't sure if he was pissed at the bear or himself for wrecking the truck.

"Brother, you don't look old enough to have a wife. How old are you?" I asked as I smiled at him.

"I'm thirty-five," he said, puffing up his chest and getting a proud look on his face.

"My wife's name is Amanda, and I got a six-year-old boy too. His name's Andy. We call him Dozer 'cause he's as strong as an ox and runs around pushing everything over." The proud look on his face got more legitimate as he talked about his boy. Not as comedic as when he told me his age.

"How far from your house are you?" I asked.

"Maybe six miles that way," he said as he pointed down the road.

"Where's your wife? Do you think people will be out looking for you?" I asked.

"No, it's just me and her. I told her not to leave the house unless I was gone for more than a week. Then she was to hike it to the neighbor's house through the woods about a mile from our place. But we got enough food in the house that she can feed her and Dozer without me. I just went out to look for some meat to supplement what we already got."

"Okay, let me get some stuff to make you a splint and a cheesy crutch. Then I'll grab your rifle and we'll head out. You think you can make it home with a crutch?" I asked as I started to look around.

"Fuckin-a, man, I miss my wife and kid," he said, the excitement about getting out of here evident on his face.

I pulled my Bowie knife from its sheath and crawled back into the cab of the truck. I cut several long strips of cloth from the seat covers. Once I crawled back out of the truck, I took the pruning saw and cut the tree I used to pry open the door into several pieces about a foot long. I used one of the pieces as a baton, using it and my knife to split one of the other pieces of wood into two. I then placed a piece of the split tree on each side of Norman's leg. I finally took the cloth strips I cut from the seat to tie the splints to his leg.

Once that was done, I walked back into the woods and found a tree about the size of a man's wrist. The tree had a *Y* in it about five feet from the ground. I cut the tree down with the pruning saw and adjusted the size until Norman could use it as a crutch.

I walked back to the truck, crawled back into the cab of the truck, and used my Bowie to cut a couple of chunks of padding from the seat. I used the last strips of the seat cover to secure the padding to the *Y* in the crutch.

"Okay, Norman, this'll need to do. Let's get you up and we'll start heading to your place. You just point us in the right direction," I said as I reached out to give him a hand up.

"Damn, dude. You fixed this shit up like a pro. You know what you're doin'."

"I'm no pro. Just thinkin' on the fly," I said, helping Norman get his balance. Once he was more or less stable, I crawled back into the truck cab for what I hoped was the last time and retrieved Norman's rifle. It was a Birmingham Small Arms .270-caliber hunting rifle. It had a wood grain stock and a leather sling. It was well cared for, which always told me that the owner cared about his tools and made sure that they were ready when he needed them.

"This is a nice rifle, Norman. My grandfather had one just like it when he was alive." I looked the rifle over some more. When my grandfather, Pap Pap Dale, died, he left me his hunting rifles. The .270 was one of them. It was a shame I needed to leave it in my apartment, but I couldn't carry the extra weight of another rifle and ammo. It just wasn't realistic.

"Okay, Norman. Let's get moving. You might wanna slack around here for a few days, but I don't like bein' in one spot too long.

Let's get moving." He looked at me like I was a complete idiot. I smiled at him to let him know I was joking.

"Hey, man, what's your name? I should know the name of the guy that just saved my life."

"My friends call me Buck," I said as I stuck out my hand.

"It's nice to meet you, Buck. Thanks again," he said as we shook hands.

I repacked what gear I had used to get Norman ready for travel and shrugged on my pack. We made it to the roadway and started moving in the direction he originally pointed.

We moved along the roadway fairly slowly. I scanned all around us, checking our rear to make sure we weren't being followed. Every so often, I would have Norman stop so I could listen for anything that didn't sound normal.

"Damn, man, you are one paranoid dude," he said as he again looked at me like I was an idiot.

"No, Norman, I'm not paranoid. I just know how people have been since we all lost power. Here in the country, it might not have hit you yet, but in the city areas, they're killin' each other for a drink o' water. I don't wanna die for the gear I got on my back, but I sure as hell will kill to keep it, 'cause it's what's kept me alive so far, and it'll keep me alive till I get to where I'm goin'."

"Where are you goin' anyway?" he asked as we got up to move on.

"My best friends live up north, outside a' Pittsburgh. I'm headin' up there. We used to work together years ago, and I think that if I'm up there and not in the city, and I'm with them, my chances of survivin' this are a lot better."

"Well, if you want, you can hang with me and the family for a few days. It's the least we can do. We can fill your gut a few times, maybe wash your clothes, 'cause you do smell a little ripe." He laughed like he had just heard the funniest joke ever told.

I just shook my head and kept walking. We walked like this for another hour or so, talking, laughing a little. We would stop and take breaks occasionally, as moving with the makeshift crutch was harder for Norman than it looked. He talked about his wife and kid.

Eventually, he stopped, took a breath, and pointed a short way ahead of us at a bend in the road.

"My place is just around the corner." We pushed on. Soon, the trees along the road started to thin out and turned into a small field of hay. Through the field, I could see a small ranch-style home, made of brick and tan siding. It was well-kept and clean. I could see in the backyard which held several fenced-in areas that housed some pigs, chickens, and a couple of cows. The homestead was a small farm that was just big enough for them.

We kept walking, and as we got closer to Norman's house, the door swung open and a petite brunette came bursting through the doorway. Instinctively, the AR came up.

"Easy, Rambo. It's just Amanda." She was thin and kind of homely-looking, but it was obvious that she was glad to see Norman. She was wearing a light-blue sundress and pink tennis shoes, with her brown hair pulled up into a bun. Right behind Amanda came the biggest six-year-old I've ever seen. He was about three and a half feet tall and had to weigh a good eighty or ninety pounds. He was wearing blue cut-off jean shorts and a green T-shirt that was about two sizes too small for him. Before I could stop myself, I started to laugh.

"Man, don't laugh. I told ya we call 'im Dozer. We call 'im Dozer for a reason." Norman had a smile on his face as he scolded me.

Amanda reached Norman and wrapped her arms around his neck, kissing him nonstop.

"Baby, oh my god, I was so worried," she said in between kisses. Then she got pissed.

"Where the hell have you been?" she scolded, looking at me with a pretty evil eye. Dozer was standing behind her, with his fists on his hips, looking at me like he was going to take my head off. I was kind of afraid that he might have been able to do it.

"Baby, don't bitch at me in front of guests. I got into an accident and totaled the truck. I got trapped inside and couldn't get out. Buck here happened to come along and save my life," he said as he directed attention to me like Vanna White showing off a new car.

Amanda turned and hugged me, kissing me on each cheek. "Thank you for saving my idiot's life. I hope you're going to be staying with us for a while."

"I think I might." I said. "I need a rest, a wash, some clean clothes, and some food in my gut."

"Well, all of that we can do for ya." She grabbed my hand and walked me to the house, leaving Norman to fend for himself.

We walked in the front door to a clean and well-kept house. The front foyer had a set of stairs going up to a living room, kitchen, and a couple of bedrooms. The downstairs was a family room and another bedroom. The carpeting in the house was a light brown, almost a tan, with off-white painted walls. There were family pictures hanging up and some in frames on the end tables. It looked like any normal all-American home, but after the few weeks I had spent sleeping on the ground, it sure looked comfortable.

Amanda took me upstairs and led me to one of the back bedrooms. It was the same color scheme as the rest of the house. It held a bed, a dresser, and a closet, and had its own bathroom. As she walked into the room, she pointed at the bed then at the bathroom.

"You can drop your stuff there on the bed. The bathroom has a tub. Norman was able to rig some plastic drums outside the two-bathroom windows, so we kinda still have running water. You can take a bath, or wash up. The water'll be cool, but at least you'll be clean. We'll eat in about an hour or so. Thanks again for bringin 'im back to me." She hugged me again and walked out of the room, shutting the door behind her.

I dropped my pack on the bed and dug out my hygiene kit. It wasn't major, just some toothpaste, a toothbrush, some camp soap, a straight razor, and a washrag. The bathroom was small and basic. It had a tub, a sink, a toilet, and a mirror. The bathroom was your normal working-class bathroom, nothing extravagant. I looked at myself in the mirror. My hair was usually high and tight with shaved sides and a goatee on my face. But now, I had a full beard and a full head of hair. I used the camp soap to lather up my face and the straight razor to clean things up. I didn't shave the beard off, just cleaned up the perimeter. Once that was done, I went to the window.

There was a two-inch rubber hose running in through a gap in the window, running from a blue fifty-five-gallon drum that Norman had rigged to a platform outside. The hose had some kind of garden faucet on the end of it. I turned on the faucet, and water started to drain into the tub. I smiled at the invention. It was pretty cool.

I put about an inch of water in the tub. I didn't want to waste the water, because I didn't know when it would rain again. I crawled into the tub. Amanda was wrong, the water was actually warm. I assume from being in the plastic drum, the sun had been able to warm it up some. Taking a bath felt wonderful. Before long, the water was brown, and I was clean. I got out and dried myself with a towel that had been on the tub when I came in. I walked out to the bedroom and dug the *Wrangler* pants and black *5.11* shirt from my pack. I also dug out a fresh pair of socks.

It felt good to be naked. I'm not sure why, but it did, so I stayed that way for a while. I took my camo clothing into the bathroom, dumped some camp soap into the tub, and then ran some more water into it, again only about an inch. I agitated the water, and then put the camos and socks into the tub, agitating them as well. I let them soak in the fresh water.

I went back into the bedroom and got dressed in my civvies, to include my boots and my 1911. I picked up my AR and walked to the door. When I opened the bedroom door, the smell from the kitchen was fantastic. I must have used the entire hour because Amanda was putting the food on the table. We were having some ham, mashed potatoes, and salad.

I looked at the setup they had rigged in the kitchen, and found it as ingenious as the bathroom water idea. Norman had cut a two-foot round hole in the top off of the stove. He rigged a smoke escape, using wood stove piping, which ran to the kitchen window. Now they could actually build a fire in the stove and use it to cook using the grates in the stove.

I wasn't noticed at first, but as I stood there looking at the cooking setup, I got caught.

"Wow, you look differ'nt," Norman said, causing Amanda to turn around and look.

"Yeah, you clean up nice. Here, you sit at the head o' the table," she said as she pulled out my chair. I walked to my chair and leaned my AR against the wall behind me. Norman sat down to my right, with Dozer to his right. Dozer had still not said a word to me and kept watch over me like a hawk looking for prey. Amanda sat down on my left.

"Are you a religious man, Mr. Buck?" she asked.

"First, it's just *Buck*, no Mr. needed. As far as religion goes, I want to be. Before all hell broke loose, I read the Bible every day and prayed twice a day. When I left my place, I couldn't afford the weight of a Bible in my pack, but I have still been prayin' every night before I sleep. I don't know if he hears me or not, but I like to think he does. I'm still alive, and I'm still healthy, so my guess is he's lookin' out for me. My only problem is I can't get used to turnin' the other cheek."

"Well, Buck," she said. "I am religious. God heard my prayers about bringin' Norman back to me. So if you'd be so kind as to say grace." She clasped her hands and bowed her head.

I clasped my hands together and took a breath. I always get nervous when I was put on the spot and wasn't prepared. I was a planner and always tried to make sure I had some kind of idea what I was going to do. I never prayed before my meals, so I wasn't really sure what to say, so I went basic.

"Lord, I thank you for the food that's on the table here before us. In this world today, food will become hard to come by, so this abundance now is a gift. I thank you for giving Amanda the strength to prepare it, and I thank you for giving Norman the heart to live through the trial he has had over the past few days so that he could get back to his family. Lastly, I thank you Lord for giving me the strength and skills to have survived as long as I have, and I ask that you keep all of us safe as this tribulation continues. Amen. Oh, one more thing, Lord. Please let Dozer lighten up a little. I'm not the bad guy he thinks I am."

As we ate, Dozer did lighten up. He asked me questions about my guns and where I had gotten them. Amanda, Norman, and I talked about what was going on in the city where I had come from and what my future plans were. We discussed what we thought had happened, and I expressed my concerns about what the future held.

When we were finished eating, Amanda cleaned up the dishes in a wash basin. I offered to help but just got a look of disdain as an answer to my invitation. Norman and I moved to the living room where we lit some candles and continued to talk. After Amanda had finished with the dishes, she joined us in the living room. After about an hour, I could feel my eyelids getting heavy.

"Brother, I think it's time for me to hit the hay," I said as I got up. I walked over to Norman and shook his hand.

"Amanda, thanks for a wonderful meal." I bent over and kissed her on the cheek. With that, I walked back to my room. I put my gear on the floor, my AR against the wall beside the bed, and my 1911 on the bedside table.

I went into the bathroom and finished washing my camos, hanging them over the curtain rod. I then went back into the bedroom and lay down. I think I was asleep before my head hit the pillow. I slept all night long and into the next day until about noon. When I woke, I could hear Amanda, Norman, and Dozer outside. I got out of bed, brushed my teeth, and went outside to the back of the house.

"Morning, sleepyhead!" Dozer yelled when I walked out. I gave him an ugly face and laughed.

"Good morning, everybody."

"Morning. Did you sleep okay?" Amanda asked.

I grinned at her. "Obviously. I think I slept for about twelve hours."

She grinned back. "Yeah, you slept closer to fourteen hours."

"Holy shit, you're kiddin' me." I hung my head in shame. Norman looked at me. He had a funny look on his face. He looked like he wanted to ask me something but didn't know how. He was hobbling around on the crutch I had made him.

"What's up, brother, you need help with something?" I asked.

"Man, I hate to ask you this 'cause after what you did for me yesterday, I really just wanted you to be able to chill out and relax while you were here." He had the look of being ashamed for asking for help.

"No man, what d'ya need?" I asked again.

"Well, Amanda and I need a smoke house built, but with my foot the way it is, I just can't do it."

"No issues, I got ya. Just point me in the direction of your tools and let me know how big you need it, and I'll Git-er-Done,'" I said, doing my best imitation of Larry the Cable Guy.

Norman pointed to a small shed, telling me that all his tools were in there. Once I had all the tools and wood that I needed, I got to work. Norman wanted the smoker about five feet square, with a flat roof and about five feet high. I wasn't a carpenter by any sense of the word, but I had spent some time working for my dad's construction company, so I knew my way around a saw, hammer, and nails.

I spent about three full days working on the smoker. I'd get up in the morning and work all day, taking breaks to eat, drink, and play with Dozer, who had levels of energy I've seldom seen in a kid his size. At night, we'd eat dinner together and then sit around in the living room with candles lit, joking, talking, and laughing, almost like nothing out of the ordinary had happened. Like life was still normal.

By the end of the week, Dozer and I were rolling around on the floor, wrestling at night. He had really grown accustomed to me, and I'd really started to like being around him. My dad used to wrestle with me when I was a kid. He'd hold me down on the floor and then threaten to lick my face. It grossed me out so bad that I'd scream like I was being killed. So I started to do that to Dozer. He'd scream, giggle, and sometimes scream so hard he'd fart, causing Amanda and Norman to lose it. They would sit in their chairs and laugh out loud all night long at the two of us. I never had the chance to have kids of my own. I was married once, but it just didn't work out, and we went our separate ways. I eventually learned to use other people's kids as surrogates, filling in for what I didn't have.

Josh and Mike each had boys of their own. Before the event when we would hang out together, I let them try my chewing tobacco and sneak sips of my beer. I'd tell them dirty jokes when their moms weren't around, and sometimes I'd tell them jokes when they were around just to get a reaction from the moms. I'd do things like that because I'd never get a chance to do it with my own kids, so why not take advantage of the opportunity I had with my friend's kids?

Although I was having a good time with Amanda, Norman, and Dozer, it was time for me to move on. They now had a place to smoke whatever meat they had. Norman's foot was doing better, and he was able to move around better on it now. He still needed the crutch, but he didn't seem to be in as much pain. Before I went to bed that night, I bathed, cleaned up my beard again, and washed my civilian clothes, hanging them up to dry while I slept.

I got up the morning of the sixth day with Amanda and Norman and prepared to leave. I unpacked my ruck, repacked it, reorganizing things to get them to sit better and to take an inventory of the gear I had used.

My ammo was still good, and I still had snacks like granola bars and trail mix to eat, along with one more thirty-five-hundred-calorie bar. It wasn't going to last me for too long, but I'd need to make do. The rest of my gear was still good. I got dressed in my Real Tree camos and strapped on my belt. I also took this opportunity to clean my 1911 and AR.

When I walked out into the living room, Dozer immediately came running over to me.

"Where ya goin', Mr. Buck?" he asked with a sad look on his face, as I knelt down in front of him.

"I gotta go, buddy. I have friends and family I gotta check on."

"When are ya comin' back?" His eyes were starting to water up, which made mine start to water. I wasn't sure how to answer him, so I figured I'd just go with the truth.

"I don't think I will be, buddy. Without cars anymore, I just live too far away to be able to come visit." By this time, he was in full tears. I reached out and hugged him, telling him that I'd never forget him. I was teary-eyed now too, and so was Amanda. I got up and walked over to Amanda, hugging her, then shaking Norman's hand.

"Let me pack you some food to go," Amanda said and ran into the kitchen.

I got out my maps, and Norman showed me where his farm was located. I got my compass bearing, orienting myself to the map and the direction I needed to go. Amanda came out of the kitchen with a freezer bag of homemade beef jerky, several sealed foil bags of tuna, and a freezer bag full of oatmeal.

"It's not much, but it'll help, I hope," she said.

"Oh, it'll help a lot," I said. "Thank you."

I leaned forward, hugged her, and kissed her on the cheek. I shook Norman's hand again then kneeled down and hugged Dozer, who had worked to calm himself down. I thanked everybody again and walked out the door. I got my bearing with the compass, picked out a tree, and set off toward home.

5

I traveled for most of the day, continuously getting a compass bearing and moving from tree to tree. I moved slow and deliberate, keeping an eye on my surroundings, looking for anything that didn't fit with the normal contours of the woods. A green bush when everything around it was dried up and dead or a dead bush when everything else was green. These types of things were clues to a possible trap or ambush of some kind. I would stop occasionally to listen for anything out of the ordinary, listening for whispers, the clank of steel on steel, or a cough. It was tedious work and took a lot more time than just taking a hike through the woods on a weekend camping trip. After a while, you started to notice the weight of everything; your pack, the rifle, even the pistol on your hip felt like it weighed a ton.

Things went like this for several days, with a couple of breaks a day for water, and a snack. Then, when I'd stop at night, I'd eat a bigger meal. Eating at night before I slept would help keep me warm at night while I was sleeping. I was setting up quick lean-to shelters with my tarp and not much else.

About the fourth day, as the afternoon was progressing, I noticed that it started to get darker, and the temperature was getting cooler. I could tell that it was going to rain. I started to look around for some thicker tree groupings. The more trees there were together, the easier it was to set up a shelter and avoid the rain.

I looked ahead of me and saw a cropping of huge rocks. I walked over to them and started to look around for some kind of overhang that coupled with my tarp could make a pretty serious shelter. I couldn't believe my luck, but I found a cave. I had always been told that you should never use a cave for shelter, as animals also used caves for shelter. But it looked like a pretty serious storm was moving in, and I didn't want to be caught in the storm, so I decided to take my chances.

I switched on the flashlight that was attached to my AR and started to search the cave. It wasn't a cave that went underground for miles, turning into a labyrinth, but it was just a big indentation in the rock that went back maybe twenty to thirty feet. There were no tracks or scat droppings of any kind, so I figured that I would be okay to stay there. In the northeast, especially in the PA and Maryland areas, I knew from experience that black bears were prevalent and I needed to start being more aware of the possible dangers.

I dropped my pack and immediately went out into the woods for kindling and firewood. Even though it was going to rain and the temperature was going to drop, I knew that I would only need a fire for cooking dinner and coffee, nothing more.

I found some old man's beard, some small twigs, and some larger dry wood. I wrapped it all in my shemagh and carried it back to the cave. Using my lighter again, I started the fire. The fire kit I had contained several lighters. They were light and inexpensive and were literally life savers. I also had the ferrocerium rod, but I wanted to keep that for later. I heated up water for dinner and coffee. By this time, it was raining outside, so I took my *Klean Kanteen* outside to the mouth of the cave and set it up to catch the rain water. This would be good, clean water that I would not need to boil.

I decided that I was going to stay here for a couple of days, get some rest, do some hunting and trapping, and try to supplement the food I had left, which wasn't much more than a few pieces of jerky, some oatmeal, and the packs of tuna.

In the morning, my plan was to take out the two rat traps and the conibear trap that I had and set them up to do what was called passive hunting. I also had the slingshot that used arrows that I would use to do some active hunting. But for now, I was going to get some sleep. I took my tarp and unwrapped it, enough to give me some cushion on the cave floor. I placed my pack at an angle against the cave wall to use it as a makeshift pillow. I unwrapped my sleeping bag and soon drifted off to sleep.

I woke up the next morning and checked the coals of the fire. They were still warm, and with some TLC, I was able to restart the fire so that I could heat up some oats. It was still cloudy and drizzling outside, so I decided to stay in and stay dry. I'd hunt and trap when it quit raining.

I lay around the cave all day with nothing to do but think. Out here in this cave, things were quiet and peaceful. I wondered how things were everywhere else. How violent had the world become?

We were about six weeks into this event. The most vulnerable would be the elderly, children, and those who needed medication to survive. The medications needed to live would eventually run out, not just in their own homes but everywhere, and there was no longer any type of transportation that could resupply the things needed like medication and food.

Hospitals and nursing homes have generators, but they would eventually run out of the fuel needed to run them, and the machines needed to keep people alive would shut down, and the people attached to them would die, if they hadn't already.

Those people with illnesses like diabetes, who needed medication to survive, would soon run out. If they had enough to last a while, it would need to be refrigerated, but without electricity, it would soon lose its potency and go bad.

This event, this NEMP, would eventually end up killing hundreds of thousands of people. They would die of medical complications, lack of medication, and starvation. Because without the knowledge of how to hunt and grow their own food, and the inability to go to the grocery store to buy their food, people today are lost. Hundreds of thousands of people would die because of their reliance on technology. With these morbid and depressing thoughts running through my head, I soon drifted back to sleep.

A crack of thunder and a lightning strike brought me back to the here and now. It was still raining outside, but I could see that the sun was starting to go down. I decided to skip dinner and just have a cup of coffee. I relit my fire, made my coffee, and went back to sleep.

I woke up the next morning, and it looked like it was going to be a better day. I gathered some firewood, lit yet another fire, and heated up some oatmeal. Once my belly was full, I dug out the rat traps, the conibear trap, and the slingshot. I slung my AR and set out. I had a couple of MRE peanut butter packs that I was going to use to bait the rat raps.

It was no longer raining, but the ground was still wet, and water was dripping from branches and leaves above me. I found a tree that had a branch about face level. I used some generic string to tie one of the rat traps to the branch. I set the trap and baited it with peanut butter. I found a similar tree a few yards away and set up the second rat trap the same way. If I was lucky, I'd get a squirrel or two.

I then began to look around for a game trail. I found what looked like several small animal paths leading off in the same general direction. I followed one of the trails, which led to a small stream. I made four stakes that I could use to secure the trap, setting it up a foot or two from the stream along the game trail. I had also brought along a piece of jerky that I had soaked overnight in water to soften it up. I used the jerky to bait the conibear trap. Again, if I was lucky, I might be able to catch an opossum or raccoon that I could then use to make some jerky of my own. Once I was done with that, I set out to actively hunt with the slingshot.

I went to one of the other game trails, sitting and waiting for something to come along. Nothing did, so I decided to move around a little. I hunted for about three hours, walking, stopping, and watching, but I had no luck. It was about noon by this point, so I went back to the cave to take a break. I unpacked the oatmeal and made some more oats. Oatmeal was pretty much all I had left. I had a few pieces of jerky left, but I was saving that for dinner.

It started to rain again, so I relit the fire again and chilled out in the cave for a few hours. After the rain let up, I slung the AR and went out to check the traps. One of the rat traps produced a squirrel, but the other rat trap and the conibear trap were empty. I left them there, thinking that they may produce something overnight.

I stayed in the woods about two hundred yards from the cave. I used a sharpened stick to dig a hole about a foot or so deep. I placed my hands on the squirrel's body and thanked it for its sacrifice. I also thanked God for delivering it to me. I then gutted and cleaned the squirrel, burying most of the guts and skin in the hole. That way, if predatory animals smelled the scraps, it wouldn't bring them to the cave where I was sleeping. A couple of pieces of the intestine I kept to use as bait for the conibear trap.

I went back to the cave, put the guts in the empty oatmeal bag, and buried it in my pack. I then put the squirrel on a stick, seasoned it with some pepper and smoke-flavored powder, and roasted it over the fire. It tasted pretty good. It was starting to get dark out, so I kept the fire going and relaxed, leaning up against my pack. I wasn't tired so my thoughts turned toward Josh, Heather, and their boys, Bill and Chris.

I met Josh when I started working as a sheriff's deputy. We soon became friends, and our friendship grew over the years until I was spending my days off hanging out with him and his family. Soon, his family became my family. I wasn't afraid to say how much I loved them all. I hoped with all my heart that they had all survived this thing and were doing well. Josh had also spent time in the military, and was my assistant team leader when we were on the sheriff's department SWAT team. He was smart, tactically oriented, and would be able to protect his family if the need arose.

Mike was also married. He and his wife, Mia, had a boy. Tony was twenty and was away at college. I hoped he was at home when this all went down. Mike was also a sheriff's deputy, but we had met several years previous when I was at college and on the college shooting team. Mike's dad, Mike Senior, was my shooting instructor. I met Mike Senior's family at that time and soon became a friend of the family. The whole family was shooters and participated in the shooting sports. Mike Senior taught shooting skills, tactics, and reloaded his own ammo. Mike Junior was SWAT trained and also had a tactical background. I'm also sure that Mike would have been able to take care of his family if need be.

The cool thing was that everybody lived in the same community, so they were all together and would be able to support each other. I wasn't sure how bad things were up there though. Indiana,

Pennsylvania, was a four-square mile town, but there was also a college that had a lot of students. The area surrounding the town was mostly farmland, with smaller towns sporadically placed throughout the county. The community where Josh, Mike, and Senior lived wasn't quite country, but it also wasn't a town or city either. There were several miles of woodland around the area which could provide the community with meat if people were taking the initiative to hunt. The only problem was that this area had a lot of hunters who would also be hunting to support their families. With that many people hunting, eventually the available meat would dwindle down, and meat would be hard to come by. I hoped that Mike and Josh were able to take control of their area and get everybody to work together. They were both leaders, and if they were left to it, they could keep people alive.

Before I knew it, I was sleeping. I slept all night, and when I woke in the morning, the rain had broken and the sky was clear. I decided to stay one more day and set out again in the morning. I grabbed my AR, my slingshot and the arrows, and set out to the remaining rat trap. It was empty, so I cut it down and moved it several yards away to another tree. I cleaned off the old peanut butter, tied it to a new tree branch, and rebaited it with fresh peanut butter. I also reset the other rat trap on a new tree, with fresh peanut butter.

I then went to the conibear trap and also found it empty. I took it apart and moved it to another area where the tracks seemed fresh. I reset it, baited it with pieces of the previous night's squirrel guts, and set out to do some active hunting again. I hoped that the animals had stayed low during the last couple of days of rain and that they would come out now when it was nice.

On this day, I was lucky. After about an hour, I saw a rabbit moving through the trees munching on some greens that were sprouting up through the brush and leaves on the forest floor. I was maybe ten feet from it. I notched an arrow in the pull string, pulled back on the slingshot band, took aim, and shot. I hit the rabbit right in the rib cage. It squirmed around, screaming, trying to get away, but at the angle that I shot from, it had stuck the rabbit to the ground. I pulled my knife, grabbed it around the waste where the arrow was, and severed its spinal cord. I again gave thanks to it and God. I decided to clean it here, so I went through the same process as I had with the squirrel from the previous night.

By the time I finished cleaning the rabbit and had carried the carcass back to the cave, it was lunchtime. I roasted the rabbit over the fire and ate until I was full. After lunch, I lay back against my ruck and took a short nap. After I woke, I decided to go check the other traps. It was getting later in the day, and I wanted to take the traps down if they had not produced anything. I wanted to wake in the morning, pack my gear, and set out. I didn't want to worry about going to get the traps before I left.

I got to where I had set up the rat traps and they were empty, so I dismantled them and put them in my cargo pocket. When I got to the conibear trap, I was glad to see that I had trapped a rather large groundhog. A conibear trap breaks an animal's neck when it is set off, so the groundhog was dead when I got to it. I had to be careful when I set these things up because a dog can easily be killed if it inadvertently sets off a conibear trap.

I again gave thanks and cleaned the groundhog, buried the guts and fur, and took it back to the cave where I roasted it. I cooked it longer than I should have so that it would dry out more. I could eat it over the next couple of days as either jerky or I could add it to water and make a quick stew. I put the groundhog meat it the bag that had held the oats and stored it in my ruck.

By the time this was all done, it was getting dark in the cave. The majority of my gear was packed, my water containers were full, and I now had some food to last me for a few days at least.

I took out my head lamp and maps. I knew where Norman and Amanda's house was, and by using the topography, I had a pretty good idea of where I was now. Using the distance meter on the map, I guessed that I had maybe two more weeks of travel before I got home, maybe three if the terrain got worse.

I lay awake for several hours when I finally decided to walk out to the mouth of the cave. It was a clear, cool night, and the stars were bright and lit up the sky. I sat there and watched the sky move, thinking about how beautiful this was. I thought about how much of a shame it was that I had to experience it when the world was falling apart. It got me thinking about how far reaching this thing was. Was it just the United States, or had this reached as far south as Mexico, and as far north as Canada? Was this a strike from an enemy country, and if so, had we retaliated? These were questions that I would probably never know but were questions that I'm sure were running through more minds than just mine.

I eventually got tired enough to go back into the cave and try to sleep. I lay down against my ruck and was asleep faster than I had expected.

I woke up the next morning, feeling refreshed. I packed up the rest of my gear, slung my ruck and AR, and set out.

I traveled the whole day, never experiencing anything out of the ordinary. I tried hard to avoid towns or heavily populated areas, choosing to stay as much in the woods as I could. Sometimes, as I crossed roadways, I could see cars littering the roads.

About the middle of the second day after I left the cave, I heard a girl screaming. Not the type of scream like if she saw a mouse but a true honest-to-God scream like she was in fear for her life.

I moved in the general direction of the scream and came to a small clearing. It looked like a power line with a small tool-type shed in the middle of it. There were two men in front of the shed, holding down a pretty brunette girl that looked to be in her late teens. The men were rough-looking. They both had shaved heads, wore jeans, boots, and T-shirts. Guy one was bigger, maybe weighing in at 235, while guy two was maybe 185. They both looked to be in their late twenties, early thirties. There were two rifles lying on the ground beside where they were attacking the girl. They looked like Mini 14s that had been converted to polymer stocks.

The girl was also in jeans, boots, and a flannel shirt. She was screaming and fighting with all she could as she was being held down. Guy number two fought just as hard as he pulled down her pants. There was no way that I could let this go.

I dropped my ruck, and unholstered my 1911. I left the AR with my ruck, using some brush to conceal its location the best that I could.

I moved slowly and steadily toward the shed, coming up on the back side of it. The rape was taking place in the front. I moved around the side of the shed, coming up to the corner behind guy number two. I peeked around the corner and saw that the girl was still fighting, temporarily able to hold them off. I decided to attack and move forward. Both men were so engrossed in assaulting this girl that neither noticed me. I grabbed guy number two around the neck and performed a contact shot to the base of his head, below his right ear. Brain and blood blew out of a hole that appeared near the temple behind his left eye. As he slumped to the ground, my front sight found guy number one.

Guy number one was so busy watching the fear and agony on the girl's face that it took him a second or two to figure out what was going on. It was the few seconds that I needed to get the drop on him. I pulled the trigger. Guy number one's head snapped back as the .45 round hit him at the bridge of his nose. The bullet entered the medulla oblongata, shutting off any motor function in his body. He dropped straight to the ground. The fight was over.

The echo of the gunshots vibrated through the area, causing birds to bolt from their perches, and the insects to quiet down. All that could be heard was the echo and the young girl's hysterics.

The girl was frantically pulling up her pants, trying to back away from me.

"Sweetheart, it's okay, I'm not gonna hurt you." I put my 1911 back in its holster, putting my hands up, palms forward, trying to show her that I didn't want to hurt her.

"What's your name? Honest, sweetheart, I'm not with these guys. I don't want to hurt you." Buy this time, she was dressed again, but she was still panicked, which was understandable. She turned from me, and ran up the power line, disappearing into the woods about fifty yards from the shed. I decided not to follow her.

I went back to where I had dropped my gear and retrieved my stuff. I then went back to the two dead guys and took the time to check and see if they had anything I needed or if there was anything to give me an idea of who they were. They had no identification on them and nothing really worth taking except for their ammo.

The Mini-14 used the .223 round so I could use that. They each had a magazine in their weapons and carried a second magazine in a pocket. That gave me four thirty-round magazines, or 120 rounds. I couldn't use the magazines in my AR, so I emptied the rounds into a sock and put them into my ruck.

I couldn't leave these guys out in the open, so I drug them behind the shed, into the wood line, using brush, leaves, and rotted, fallen trees to cover up their corpses. Once I had cleaned up the area to hide what had happened, I spent several minutes just listening. I wanted to see if anybody came to investigate the gunshots or if anybody came looking for the two guys I had just killed. Once I was sure neither of those things were going to happen, I got my gear back on and set out.

I got to where the girl had disappeared into the woods. There was a path there that went in a general northwest direction, which was the direction that I was going. I moved along the path for about a hundred yards when I heard a branch snap behind me. I dropped to a knee and turned around. I immediately heard a twig snap behind me again. This time, when I turned to check my six, all I saw was the butt of a shotgun as it struck me in the face. My world went dark.

6

Charles Guntrom was a big man. He stood well over six feet tall and weighed nearly two hundred and fifty pounds but carrying the piece of shit that had tried to rape his daughter back to his barn was tough. Maybe he wasn't as young as he used to be or as young as he thought he was. The stranger wasn't a big guy, but he was stocky. He was about five foot ten and weighed maybe two hundred and fifty pounds.

Charles had lived on this farm his entire life. He had inherited it from his father, who got it from his father before him. His oldest son, Charlie Junior, had gone to Penn State University and majored in agriculture so he could take over the farm someday. That was until the blackout. Now he wasn't sure what was going to happen. Being a cabbage farmer without modern necessities was going to be almost impossible, especially without the man power that would be needed to do it by hand. There were a hundred acres of cabbage to water, pick, and cultivate. Without a tractor and only two sons, a daughter and a wife to help with the labor, the farm would soon fall apart.

And besides, his second son, Justin, never wanted to be a farmer anyway. At sixteen, he was more interested in girls and cars. In fact, his real dream had been to go to automotive mechanic school to learn how to rebuild cars. Not just to fix cars but to rebuild the classics.

His twin sister, Jennifer, wasn't really sure what she wanted to do. She was quiet and kept to herself, which Charles kind of liked because Jennifer was pretty and he had always been afraid that she would end up pregnant and married before her time. Just like him and his wife, Susan. She had been a great wife, but he always worried that Susan hadn't been happy with her life or where she had ended up.

Once Charles got back to the barn, he and Charlie Junior used a piece of tow rope and strung the unconscious stranger up from a rafter in the barn. Charles looked over the equipment that the stranger was carrying. It looked like top-of-the-line stuff. The camos that the stranger was wearing looked expensive. His rifle was military grade, and the pistol looked as much like a work of art as it did a weapon. Charles guessed that the stranger had stolen his gear from somebody else. An escaped prisoner from the local prison couldn't have gotten this type of gear without taking it from somebody else.

After the blackout, the prisoners at the State Correctional Facility Charlesville had been able to escape from custody and were wreaking havoc on the locals. Some prisoners had taken off and tried to get back home, or at least that's what people suspected, however a large group of prisoners stayed, and were working their way from house to house taking whatever they wanted. Some citizens fought back, and many of them died for it. When the power went out, the prisoners were able to overrun the prison, killing a lot of the guards and confiscating their weapons. Now the escaped convicts were better armed than most of the citizens in the area.

The town police department had collapsed soon after the blackout. The officers that were on duty stayed for a while but soon realized nothing was coming back on and had taken off to go be with their own families. Who could blame them? Family came first. The only officer that stayed to try to keep any kind of order was Bill Collins. Charles and Bill were friends and often hunted together. Bill lived in town and had no immediate family, so he did what he could. But when the convicts moved in, there wasn't much that one man could do against a large group of armed convicts, so he had retreated to the safety of Charles's farm and was living in a spare room in the house.

"Charlie, go get Bill. We need to deal with this piece of shit." He watched as Charlie ran through the double barn doors toward the house. He turned back to the stranger, who was still unconscious. There was something that didn't feel right. He didn't know what it was, but something was off.

Jennifer had run back to the house screaming that somebody tried to rape her, but when Charles tried to get any information from her, all she could do was point toward the power line. So he had gone down to check things out and caught this guy coming up the path. Charlie had inadvertently distracted the stranger, giving Charles the opportunity to knock him out with a shotgun butt to the head.

A couple of minutes later, Bill and Charlie walked into the barn. Charles would always laugh when he saw them together. Charlie took after his dad. He was tall and big. Bill was quite a bit smaller. At five foot nine and 170 pounds, he was considered normal, but beside Charlie, he looked like a hobbit. From what Charles had seen, his feet were almost as hairy.

"How's Jennifer? She calmed down enough to answer any questions?" Charles asked, looking back at the stranger.

"No," Bill said. "She's still pretty worked up. Did you happen to see anybody else with this guy?" He pointed to the stranger hanging from the rafters.

Bill went over to the table where Charlie had laid the stranger's gear. He picked up the AR and looked it over. It was a nice piece of hardware. He then picked up the 1911. He didn't know a lot about 1911 pistols but saw on the slide that it was engraved with "Hunt Custom 1911 A-1." He did know enough to know that if this pistol was a full custom, it was an expensive pistol, easily four grand.

"No," Charles answered.

"Why?" he asked.

"Oh, I don't know. She kept mumbling stuff about guys. 'Big guys, smelly guys, ugly guys,' but she was hyperventilatin', and I couldn't get anything more out of 'er. Susan and Justin are with 'er now. Once she calms down, I'll try again to get somethin' from 'er." He looked at the 1911 again. "This stuff's a little too nice to be a convict's gear, don't ya think?" he asked, more to himself than anybody else. When he got no answer from himself or anybody else, he signaled toward the stranger and asked, "What are you gonna do with this guy?"

Charles looked at the stranger for a couple of minutes. *What am I gonna do*? "Well, let's wake this piece of shit up and see if maybe we can't get some answers from him."

7

I kept my eyes closed and feigned unconsciousness. I woke up when the shorter guy was looking over my gear. The other two were watching him and didn't see me wake up. They were huge. Both guys were over six feet and big. If I had to fight my way out of this, I was screwed. I kept my eyes closed but kept them open enough that I could see silhouettes.

One of the big guys walked over to a hose and filled up a bucket with water. He walked toward me and, from about three feet away, threw the water, hitting me directly in the face. I didn't need to fake surprise, it was cold, but I jerked "awake," coughing and spitting. It wasn't a bad case of acting if I do say so myself.

The short guy walked up to me and slapped me across my face. "Wake up, motherfucker. We gotta talk."

I opened my eyes and looked around. I was strung up on a rafter in a barn. There was hay and straw on the floor, an International Harvester tractor parked in the corner, and a few empty stables along the wall across from me. The barn looked old, like it had been standing for a while, but it still looked sturdy. There were just the three guys I originally saw. Big guys one and two looked like father and son. The shorter guy didn't look like the other two, so I guessed that he was a friend, a neighbor or something. He was just too different from the other two to be related.

Big Guy number one walked over and stood beside the short guy. He just stared at me. I looked back, never taking my eyes from him. If I showed any type of weakness, I was toast. Without warning, big guy one punched me square in the stomach, just below my solar plexus. He hit me with his right hand, a righty. I might need that info for later, if I had to go hand-to-hand at some point. I'm glad I hadn't eaten anything in a while because I would have puked all over big guy one.

"You get kicks outa' rapin' li'l girls?" Big Guy yelled as he wound up for another swing.

Little Guy grabbed his wrist. Like Little Guy could have stopped him if he wanted to hit me again.

"Charles! Hittin' him isn't gonna get you anywhere. Let me talk to 'im." I almost laughed. Were they intentionally doing "good cop, bad cop," or was it an accident? I said I almost laughed, but I must have smiled for real.

Bucket Guy came running up to me and punched me across the left side of my jaw.

"You think something's funny? You try to rape a little girl and you think it's funny. Is that what you were in jail for in the first place?"

This time, I smiled and I finally spoke. I looked at all three guys.

"Look, I know you're upset. I would be too. But I didn't rape or try to rape anybody. I don't know who the girl is to you, but ask her. She'll tell ya."

They all looked at me for what seemed like a full five minutes. Older Big Guy finally spoke first.

"Go get Jennifer."

Short Guy grabbed the older big guy by the arm and pulled him off to the side.

"Charles, she's still too worked up. It might freak her out too much," he said. But now I had two names. The girl I saved was Jennifer, and the older big guy was Charles.

Charles looked at the younger big guy.

"I said go get Jennifer." The younger big guy didn't move. He kept looking from me to the short guy then back at me.

"Charlie, I said go get your fuckin' sister." This time it was yelled. A third name. Charlie. I must have been right. Charles was the dad; Charlie was his son. Now who was the short guy?

Charlie ran out of the barn toward what I assumed was the house. Short Guy smiled and looked at me with a doubtful smirk on his face.

"I hope you're not lyin'," the short guy said. Charles looked at me. He was intent on doing me harm.

"If she comes in here and tells me it was you, I'll kill ya. You understand that, right?" He moved closer and got face-to-face with me. "I will kill you, and I'll do it as slow as I can."

I could hear a girl crying. She was almost frantic. She kept pleading that she didn't want to see him. She couldn't look at the guys that tried to rape her. She couldn't go in. But I also heard what sounded like a dragging noise across the ground. Charlie must have been dragging her.

I heard another female voice pleading with Charlie not to make her do it. Charlie came through the door first, and he was dragging Jennifer by her right arm. The other female came through the door next. She was maybe in her late forties and was heavy-set with dark hair. She had an attractive face, but you could see that it had been worn out from hard work. She was holding on to Jennifer's other arm. Another guy—a kid, really—came through the door last. He just looked angry. When he saw me, he started to move closer to me. It was a slow, deliberate movement. He wanted to hurt me. But then Jennifer looked up, saw me, and stopped crying and immediately calmed down. Everybody stopped and looked at her.

Jennifer just looked at me. She didn't say a word. Everybody's attention was on her. It's funny what comes to mind when you're in a stressful situation. I thought of an old Alfred Hitchcock program where a girl was raped. She was taken to the hospital where her husband picked her up. On the way home, she pointed at a guy on the street and said, "That's him, that's the guy." Her husband pulled over and followed the guy into a parking garage where the husband killed the rapist. He went back to the car and told his wife that she'd be okay, that he'd handled it. As they drove down the road, she saw another guy, pointed at him, and said, "That's him, that's the guy." The show ended with the husband's face and the realization that his wife saw the rapist in every guy and that he had just killed an innocent man. All I could think was that she was going to point at me and say, "That's him, that's the guy."

But she didn't. She looked at Charles, whom I assumed was her dad. She then looked at me. Her face was still red. She was upset, and I could tell that she had been crying, but she was calm. She walked over to me and looked up at me. She then reached out and hugged me.

I was shocked. I had hoped that she would vindicate me, but I wasn't expecting a hug, especially after her initial reaction to me at the shed where the attempted rape had happened. I got my bearing and looked over at Charles with a "See…told ya" look on my face.

He looked back at me and then looked at everybody else, one at a time. He then looked back at me. He walked over to me and Jennifer, who was still hugging me.

"Jennifer. Baby. Who is this guy? Did he try to hurt you?" She slowly let go of me and looked at Charles.

"No. God, no. He's the reason I wasn't raped. He stopped them. He came outa nowhere and killed both of them. I owe him my life." She then got this look of confusion on her face. "Why's he hangin' here? Why's he strung up?"

Little Guy spoke up first.

"We thought he was one of the guys that tried to hurt you in the first place."

"No, there were two of them and he stopped them." She looked around frantically. I assume she was looking for something to cut me down. Charles, who was standing right there, pulled a pocketknife from his right pants pocket, grabbed the rope around my wrists, and cut me loose.

I wasn't up off the ground, so I didn't fall when he cut me loose, but it was a pleasant relief to my shoulders. I immediately reached out and hugged Jennifer. She hugged me back.

"Jennifer, right? Thank you. Are you okay?" I asked. She nodded.

"Yeah, I am. Thanks to you."

Charles reached out a hand.

"Thanks for what you did. I'm sorry about all this. We didn't know. I hope there's no hard feelings." I looked at his hand. I've never been the "forgive and forget" type of person. I've been known to hold a grudge. I always did. It was one of my bad qualities. If you did me wrong, I will never forget and I seldom forgive. But in the new society, I needed as many friends as I could get. I reached out and took his hand. It was like shaking hands with a bear.

"No, no hard feelings. I understand." Charlie walked over and held out his hand.

"I'm Charlie. Sorry about hittin' ya."

"Yeah, I got your name earlier. What about the short guy though? I didn't catch his," I asked as I reached out to shake his hand. He smiled as he took mine.

"You're no fuckin' giant yourself. And my name's Bill. Bill Collins."

The kid came over. He didn't shake my hand but gave me a head bob.

"Name's Justin, and thanks for helpin' my sister." He wasn't as big as the other two, but he was young, maybe sixteen or seventeen years old. I suspected that he had a growing spurt in him yet.

Finally, the woman came over. She didn't say anything, but I also got a hug from her. She was still clearly upset and held in a lot of emotions. Charles spoke for her.

"That is my wife, Susan, and I'm gonna assume that she's also thankful for what you did. By the way, what's your name?"

When I had initially come across Jennifer, it was the middle of the day. By the time things had come to a conclusion in the barn, the sun was starting to go down, so the Guntrom family invited me to stay. Susan said that it was the least they could do after what I had done for them and their family, not to mention how they had treated me.

They were more than happy to give me my gear back, and I was just as happy that they did. As we all walked over to the house, I could see that it was a classic farmhouse and, like the barn, had been standing for quite some time. It was a white two-story single family, and I found out as the time with them continued that it had four bedrooms, a kitchen, a dining room, and one bathroom. Although the house was clean and well-kept, the Guntrom family had not taken the time to rig modern luxuries like running water and a working stove like Norman and Amanda had. They used an outside fire to cook and had rigged up an outdoor bathroom and shower area. It looked like it worked fine now, but once winter hit, it was going to be horrible.

We sat outside at a picnic table and ate a modest dinner of pork and cabbage that Susan and Jennifer had prepared. Jennifer seemed to be doing fine, and the shock of what had taken place seemed to wear off after she saw me in the barn.

They asked me what had happened to me and how I had come to find them. I told them about Laurel and what I had seen take place there. I told them of my hike north and what I had done to survive so far, finally telling them about what had happened when I saw Jennifer and where I had covered the bodies. The general consensus was to let them rot where they lay.

As we were talking, I saw a couple of people walking in from the wood line that surrounded the farm. They were both armed, the male with a pump-action shotgun and the female with an M16. I reached for my AR, but Jennifer's hand on my shoulder stopped me.

"They're okay. That's Jimmy and Megan. They're living here with us too. They've got a room set up in the barn. They were out on patrol." I looked at her with a puzzled look on my face.

"Patrol?" I asked. My shock was less about them being out on patrol and more about the idea that a group of civilians had thought to do something like that. Jimmy and Megan were engaged and had been living together for a couple years. They were waiting to save up enough money to pay for a wedding before they got married, but the event had taken place and put a damper on that.

Jimmy was an average-sized guy with blond hair and light-brown goatee. He wore jeans and a black T-shirt and carried an old 12-gauge shotgun that looked like it had seen hundreds of hunting trips. Megan was a pretty, petite blonde. She also wore jeans but had on a light, short-sleeved button-down shirt. She was armed with the M16 rifle.

As introductions were made between me and the new arrivals, it was Charles that explained what had happened here.

"My farm sits just to the south of a small town called Charlesville, and no, it's not named after me." Charles looked at me and smiled. "It was initially called River Bend because of its location by a bend in what was then known as Snake River. I know, they weren't real original back then. Well, sometime after the Civil War, a guy named Andrew Charles settled there. He found coal, and because the area was next to a river, it prospered because there was a way to transport the coal. As the town grew and the people living there also began to prosper, they changed the name of the town to Charlesville, after Andrew.

"Anyway, there's a prison about five miles north of the town called SCI Charlesville. When the blackout happened, of course the power at the prison went out. The generators were able to keep things going for a while, but eventually, the diesel ran out, the generators stopped running, and the power went out for good.

"The prison was old, and the state had been talking about building a new prison and demolishing this one; they just never got around to it. Anyway, most of the locking mechanisms were manual key locks, so the prisoners were able to take over. Once the guards were either dead or had run away, the prisoners were able to acquire all the weapons and ammunition that the guards at the prison had at their disposal. The ones that just wanted to get out and away from the prison took off to who knows where. But the bad ones, the ones in for the big stuff, they started to work together and formed a gang of maybe fifty convicts. They've been moving all over the area, raping and pillaging. They just take what they want. Food, weapons, supplies. They do what they want 'cause there's nobody to do anything about them." He looked over at Bill. "Sorry, buddy, no disrespect meant."

Bill looked back and waved his hand.

"None taken." It was now Bill's turn to talk. He explained that he had been a police sergeant with Charlesville's department, but after the power went out, his partners took off to go protect their own families. He had some weapons and ammo at the department that he confiscated and brought here to the farm, but it wasn't much.

A few M16 rifles, some .556 ammo, a few Beretta 92F pistols, the ammo for them, and the holsters needed for the pistols.

I was told that Megan and Jimmy had been living in an apartment in town when the convicts started to move in. They got scared, packed up some gear into a couple of backpacks, and fled Charlesville. They were walking along the roadway when they ran into Bill. He was heading to the farm and knew them from town so he invited them to the house. They've all been here ever since.

Because of the issue with the convicts, they each took turns patrolling the perimeter of the farm. Megan and Jimmy had finished their turns and were done for the day. Jimmy looked over at me.

"So, Buck, tell us a little about you." Jimmy seemed like a nice guy and appeared to be truly interested in me and where I had come from.

Even though I had already told them about what had brought me to their farm, I hadn't gone into too much detail about me. I didn't want to get too personal with them yet, I had just met them, so I only told them that I had spent some time in the army and that afterward, I became a police officer.

"Oh, man, it's good to have a fellow blue blood around here," Bill said with a smile on his face. "How long are you gonna stick around? We sure could use some extra help with protection, you know, with the convicts on the loose."

"Man, I don't know, brother. I'm pretty close to home—I got maybe seventy miles to go. I wasn't plannin' on bein' here for more than a day or two. But I will pull my weight while I'm here. I'll help with patrols an' any other work you need help with," I replied.

As Charlie and Jennifer were getting ready to head out for their patrol duty, Charles spoke up. "No, we owe you, so as far as I'm concerned, your stay here has already been paid for."

"Amen to that," Susan chimed in. It was the first time I had heard her speak. She was a quiet woman but possessed a kindness in her eyes that I've seen on very few people in my life.

"Well, I appreciate that," I said, "but my parents instilled a strong work ethic in me, and I couldn't sit around and do nothin' while the rest of you work. I'll help out. I'd like to get in on the patrols. I've kinda gotten used to being in the woods."

"No problem, you can go out with me and Charles. I'll show you around the area and explain our warning system to ya," Bill said.

I seemed to have made a new friend. But that's the way it was with the police. We kind of understood each other better than anybody else.

It was getting close to 11:00 p.m., and Charlie and Jennifer were to be out until about 4:00 a.m. I would be heading out with Bill and Charles then, so I decided to hit the hay, literally.

I took one of the empty stalls in the barn. I used my tarp as a base layer over the hay and then put my sleeping bag on top of the tarp. It was really more comfortable than it sounded. As I lay there thinking about the current state of events, I was soon asleep.

At what I assumed was 4:00 a.m., I got woken up by a gentle shake awake, but it startled me. My 1911 was up and aimed at the center of Bill's face.

"Damn, dude, easy," he whispered. I yawned as I replied.

"I did go easy. I didn't blow your brains out, did I?" He just shook his head and smiled.

"Okay, I got us a thermos of coffee and a couple of biscuits. Let's head out and I'll fill ya in on how we've been doin' things."

I slept without my boots and socks on, so I got those on and laced up. I had learned in the army that you never slept with your boots on. It gave your socks and feet a chance to air out and for the blood to circulate back into your feet. Except for the time I spent with Norman, Amanda, and Dozer, I had been sleeping with my boots on. I got my belt strapped on and made sure my guns were good to go. My knife was good and secure behind my 1911. All I needed to do was fill my canteen with water, which was a quick fix.

Bill took me out into the wood line to the east of the property. Charles went to the west. Essentially, one person on patrol would move counterclockwise around the property, and the other would move clockwise. When they met, they would relay to each other any issues or problems. If one of them came into contact with a trespasser of any kind, they would set off a flare to notify the others. Anybody else at the farm would respond to that location to assist.

As we patrolled the area, I thought about what problems their system had. It wasn't bad, but any system could be tweaked and made better. The farm was huge. An entire rotation around the perimeter of the property took almost an hour.

Bill pointed out where he thought problem areas would be and where they all thought the convicts would come from if and when they found the farm. He showed me where they all would meet for their patrol briefings and where they got the water they were using for drinking and washing.

After about a two-hour rotation, we got to one of the briefing spots. We took a short break and had a biscuit and coffee. Because we were "operational," so to speak, we kept talking to a whispered minimum.

We continued our patrols for another two hours and then made our way back to the farm. When we got back, Justin and Jennifer took over. As we sat down by the cooking fire, Charles asked me what I thought of their system. Bill looked at me, waiting for my answer.

"It's not a bad system," I said to them. "The only problem I have with it is the team response to the location of the flare. Let's say we had come into contact this morning. We set off the flare, and everybody comes to where we are. It could be a diversion. With everybody at the flare, it leaves the house unsecured for the actual assault team. Everybody is there, which leaves the house open for the taking. I don't wanna come in and change what's workin' for you guys. It's just some food for thought."

They looked at me with that "blinding flash of the obvious" looks on their faces.

"Man, you're right. We never thought about that. How would you decide who responds and who doesn't?" Bill asked.

"Easy," I said. "Pick a primary team and a secondary team. The primary is out in the field, and the secondary is your reaction team. When the patrol time is up, the secondary team moves into the primary position, and a new secondary team is picked. The original primary team gets to rest."

"Nice," he said. "We have eight people, counting you. Each four-man team would need to work twelve on, twelve off. That might be a little rough."

I thought for a minute about what he had said. He was right. People would soon get burned out.

"During the day, you could just run two like you have been but just designate two as your reaction team. Everybody will more than likely be up anyway. At night, run your two two-man teams."

"Yeah, that could work," Bill said. "We'll give it a try. And hey, if it doesn't, we can always change things around until we get something that's safe yet manageable."

We continued to sit by the fire, drinking coffee and talking about the NEMP and the state of the country. I asked Charles about his meat supply and how he would get the protein he and his family needed to survive.

Charles explained that he would continue to work in an area of his cabbage farm that he and his boys could manage to manually work. It would produce enough cabbage for his family and friends that were living there. The areas not worked would eventually go bad. So a neighbor named Dave Whittikin would use the rotten cabbage to feed his pigs. In exchange for the cabbage, Charles would get a hog every other month or so. The exchange system wouldn't last forever, but for now, it would help supplement their meat issue.

They hunted as much as they could, but it wasn't always productive. Most farmers have prepper tendencies anyway. I grew up on a farm and lived in a farming community. Many of the farmers had shelves and shelves of jarred food, preserved for use later. You could jar meat, but you also needed fresh meat once in a while, and the problem was keeping meat that could be used.

What a lot of preppers thought prior to this incident was that hunting would be the answer to the meat issue. What a lot of people didn't think about was that everybody would turn to hunting. Nobody could go to the store and pick up the meat they needed, so hunting was the answer for everybody. Eventually, the supply of animals would die down. Once the population began to dwindle due to illness, age, or starvation, the animal population would slowly return. But until that happened, people needed to make due any way that they could. And for now, Charles and his family seemed to have things under control. In fact, Charles told me that Jimmy and Charlie were making a pig run the following morning so we would have fresh pork for dinner.

8

Jimmy and Charlie had made the pig run several times already, so they had no reason to think that this trip would be any different.

As was becoming the norm in our new world, no trip outside was made without weapons. This trip was no different. Charlie had one of the M16 rifles and a .357 revolver. Jimmy was carrying his twelve-gauge pump shotgun.

The dirt road that they were on was lined with trees on both sides that formed a canopy over the road way, making the temperature on the roadway cooler and shaded from the sun. Crickets were making a racket and birds were chirping.

The two friends walked the first part of the trip in silence, enjoying the sounds of nature and focusing on security and the contraptions that they each dragged behind them. They each pulled a wheeled cart with two fifty-five-gallon drums full of rotted cabbage that would be traded for the pig they were soon to have. The whole trip usually took about two hours, and eventually, they started to talk about the past few days and the "stranger" now living with them.

"So, Jimmy, what do you think of Buck?" Charlie asked.

Jimmy thought for a minute. "Oh, I don't know. He seems nice enough. He's been working hard and he really seems to know his way around weapons. He's got knowledge of security and what needs to be done to secure the house. I think he's good to have around."

Charlie shook his head. "I know, there just seems to be somethin' about him I don't like. I don't know what it is, though."

"He's spending a lot of time with your dad. Do you think that might be it?" Jimmy asked.

Charlie thought for a minute. "Yeah, it could be. Dad came to me and Bill all the time for advice before Buck came around. Now they talk about everything, and Dad trusts his opinion more than mine. It bothers me a little."

Over the past few weeks, Jimmy and Charlie had become very close. They spent what little free time that they had talking and hanging out together and, if they could work it, pulled patrol details and hunting details together. They trusted each other's opinion and went to each other for advice.

Jimmy stopped in the roadway, causing Charlie to stop also.

"Charlie, let me ask you a question. Do you know what I did before all this shit took place?"

Charlie just shook his head.

"I was an accountant. I sat behind a desk and played with numbers. I had, and have, no knowledge of farming or what it takes to make cabbage grow. Hell, I thought cabbage grew on a metal shelf underneath little sprinklers. Now whom are you going to go to for farming advice, me or your dad?"

Charlie dropped his head, realizing, as Jimmy continued to talk, where he was going with his argument. "Like I said, Buck seems to know a lot about this stuff. Your dad's concern is the safety of his family and friends. He's gonna go to the guy who knows the most about security. Bill's a great guy, but Buck just seems to know more. I'd go to him too. It's no disrespect to you or Bill. It's just a smart move."

Charlie nodded. "You know, you're right. I guess I was being kinda juvenile, wasn't I?"

Jimmy started walking again and patted Charlie on the back. "Come on, ya big baby, we got a pig to get." They both laughed as they continued their journey. They eventually made it to Dave's farm, where they exchanged the cabbage for a decent-sized pig.

Dave was an older guy who lived on the farm by himself. He didn't have any kids, and his wife had died in a farming accident about twenty years ago. Before the event, Dave had been using hired help to assist with the farm. Even though he was now doing things on his own, he seemed to still be doing well, although the drift of pigs was starting to get smaller. The three men talked for a while and then parted ways as it was getting close to noon, so Jimmy and

Charlie wanted to get back for a nap before patrol duty later that evening.

They moved some empty drums to Charlie's cart and put the pig on Jimmy's. They started out for the farm, relaxing and talking about all kinds of things. They talked about missing movies, cheeseburgers, and air-conditioning. They soon realized that the majority of their discussion focused on the things that they missed, which made them both laugh.

As they rounded a bend in the road, they looked up and saw a rather good-sized black male standing in the middle of the road. He was wearing an older-style army camouflage jacket. He carried a bolt action rifle and a .38 revolver tucked into the waist of his pants. He was big but not quite as big as Charlie.

"Hey, fellas. Where y'all goin' with that fine-lookin' pig?" The guy smiled as he started to walk toward Jimmy and Charlie. "I haven't ate any meat in a long time. It gots to be at least a day or two." He laughed at his own joke.

Jimmy acted first, pulling up the shotgun and pointing it at the guy that they both suspected was one of the escaped convicts. "You need to stop where you are, lay your rifle down, and let us pass," Jimmy said, trying to keep his cool.

The convict's smile faded. "Fuck you, you scrawny whitey piece of shit. I ain't layin' down nuttin', and I ain't gotta do nuttin'."

Jimmy kept the shotgun pointed at the convict. "Mister, I got my gun on you. I don't think you could get yours up fast enough…" A loud crack echoed off the trees, sending birds scattering into the air. Jimmy stumbled backward, a look of surprise and disbelief on his face. He looked down at his chest, disbelief turning to fear, as blood started to pour from the massive hole in his chest. He never said a word as he fell straight to the ground.

Charlie jumped and dropped the M16, causing the convict to start laughing again.

"Man Shooter, nice shootin'," the convict said, talking to somebody that Charlie hadn't seen.

Charlie heard some movement off to his left and turned to see a white male wearing jeans, boots, and a green flannel shirt step out of the brush. He was of average height and weight. He had used branches, leaves, and brush to camouflage his silhouette and he had a hunting rifle in his hands.

"Shut the fuck up, Darious!" Shooter reprimanded. He continued to walk toward Charlie and the carts. He looked at Charlie but even with the huge size difference showed no sign of fear. "Farm boy, let's get to the point. My celly and I are gonna take this pig. Now you can give it to us and walk away from here with no holes in ya, or you end up like your buddy here and we take the pig anyway. The decision is yours." He was calm and direct, like a guy ordering a pizza on the phone.

There was no decision to be made.

"Take it, just don't shoot me," Charlie begged.

Darious walked over to the cart holding the pig and picked up the handle. He looked over at Charlie with contempt in his eyes. "Pussy."

Shooter yelled at Darious again, "Darious, shut the fuck up! You talk too fuckin' much."

He then looked over at Charlie. "Oh, and farm boy, we're gonna take that M16 and the shotgun too."

Shooter must not have noticed the .357 pistol. Shooter picked up the shotgun and laid it on the cart with the pig. He slung his rifle and picked up the M16 that Charlie had dropped when Jimmy was shot. As he and Darious walked away, Shooter kept the M16 trained on Charlie.

Soon they were gone, and Charlie was alone with what was left of his friend. Charlie dropped to the ground, kneeling beside Jimmy's corpse. Jimmy was lying on the roadway, a heap of lifeless mass. His eyes were still open, and his cheeks were wet from tears that he had started to shed before he died.

Charlie held his friend and cried. He was drained physically and emotionally. The stress of a traumatic situation like he had just been through was more draining than most people would ever know.

Charlie didn't move from that spot for almost an hour. Finally, he was able to gather the energy and composure to move. He stood up and pulled the remaining cart over to where Jimmy lay. He moved the empty barrels from the cart onto the ground and placed Jimmy onto the cart.

It took him what seemed like hours to get back to the farm. Charles and Bill were in the yard, working around the barn, making repairs, and trying to keep the farm looking and running respectably. They were also the reaction team to Jennifer and Justin's patrol team. As soon as they saw Charlie, they knew something was terribly wrong.

9

I had worked the patrol and reaction detail over the night time shift, so I was asleep in my barn bedroom when Charlie got back. What woke me up was Megan screaming.

Megan had been in the house helping Susan prepare lunch and dinner for the day. When she saw Charlie coming up the walkway, she ran out to greet Charlie and Jimmy. When she saw the legs on the cart, she collapsed to the ground, screaming. A long shrieking scream of pure terror and pain.

"*No!* No! Not Jimmy!"

Not yet knowing what had happened, I jumped up, grabbed my AR, and ran out to the yard. I looked around, looking for the cause of the panic. I saw everybody standing around the cart, wracked with grief. Megan was in complete despair, hyperventilating as she cried and wailed in anguish.

I walked over to the group. I looked down at the corpse on the cart. I hadn't had the opportunity to get to know Jimmy all that well over the past few days, but he had seemed to be a nice guy. He and Megan had obviously loved each other.

"Charlie, what happened?" I asked. Charlie was still visibly upset. He was also beginning to look angry. The anger was clearly visible in his eyes as he looked at me.

Charlie started his explanation of what took place when they left the farm after breakfast. He talked about walking to Dave's farm, dropping off the cabbage, picking up the pig, and starting back to the farm. When he got to the part of the story about what had happened to Jimmy, he stopped often and needed to be pushed to keep talking. Megan obviously had a hard time listening to the details of her fiancé's death and ran into the house to get away. When Charlie was done, he walked away, clearly needing time to himself.

"What do we do now?" Bill asked, looking at me and Charles for answers. I really didn't have any answers for him. His question was a little ambiguous. Was he talking about with the body, or was he thinking about some kind of retaliation? I didn't know, and I thought that talking about anything like retaliation was a poor topic of interest. After the loss of a loved one, especially to a violent action like murder, the brain doesn't think clearly and reacts from a position of anger, not logic.

Charles answered before I did, although we were thinking the same thing.

"We need to get Jimmy buried. We can't hold off on that." We were in the beginning of May, and the daytime temperatures were starting to get higher.

"Charles, I got it. You go take care of your family," I said. "I'll come get you when I'm done. If you want to say something…"

Just then, Justin and Jennifer walked in from their patrols. When they found out what happened, Justin wanted to immediately go looking for the killers. Jennifer began to cry, although I got the sense that they were more tears of anger than sadness. Once Justin calmed down, he realized that rash retaliation at this point would not do anybody any good, so he agreed to go with Bill and take the afternoon shift of patrols so that Charlie could get himself composed and give Charles a chance to take care of everybody.

As they walked off into the woods, I grabbed a shovel and the cart with Jimmy's body and headed for an oak tree behind the barn. It was in a small corner of a field and had a nice view of the property. It was away from any water source and wouldn't contaminate any drinking water. I dug for the better part of three hours. Although it wasn't exactly six feet deep, it was close and was long enough to be able to lay Jimmy out completely.

I went back to the barn and found a generic blue utility tarp. I wrapped Jimmy in the tarp and put the body into the hole as gingerly as I could. If Jimmy was looking down on me now, I hoped that he understood that I was doing the best that I could.

I walked back to the house and let Charles know that I was done and that some kind of service could be held if they chose to do so. Megan was still worked up but had stopped crying. She was more catatonic than anything.

Charles and Susan gathered everybody and we went out to the tree. I went to the meeting spot for the patrol rounds and called in Justin and Bill. A short break for them was welcomed, and it would not have been right to keep them from the ceremony.

Charles spoke a few words to try to comfort Megan.

"I don't really know what to say." He paused for a few seconds to gather his thoughts, hanging his head low. I could hear sniffling from Susan and Jennifer. Megan was still in shock and just stared straight ahead, not really looking at anything. As he looked up, his eyes found Megan. "I only met you and Jimmy a month or so ago when Bill brought you in. In that short time, you both became family. You are now my daughter, and Jimmy was my son, so his death is as much a loss of a family member as it is a friend. His passing will be hard to bear. But with his passing comes the knowledge that he is in a better place, that God is now looking out for him, and that the suffering caused by this new world is over. Megan, I am truly sorry for your loss."

Megan walked over and hugged Charles. When she was finally able to speak, tears were starting to run down her cheeks.

"Thank you, Charles. I love all of you as well. You have all been so kind and accepting. You too have become like a family to me and…who picked this spot?" Megan asked, never taking her eyes away from the blue tarp that was wrapped around her fiancé.

"I did," I said.

She looked over at me and although no words came out, she mouthed "Thank you." With the service over, Susan and Jennifer helped her back to the house. Bill and Justin went back out to finish up patrols, while Charles and I worked for another couple of hours filling in the grave.

There was no real time for mourning. The new world didn't give you time for the comforts that used to be afforded to you. There was always something else that needed to be done.

Nobody was really in the mood for dinner and just picked at their food. There was no talking. As the sun began to set, Bill and Justin walked back in from their patrol. Technically, Megan and Jimmy would be heading out with me and Charles as the reaction team, Charles and I took patrol, and Bill and Jennifer stood by as the reaction team. The others needed to reboot, and were persuaded to just relax. Tomorrow would be another day.

At about 2:00 a.m., Bill and Jennifer took over patrol for me and Charles. Charles went into the living room of the house to catch some sleep. I stayed outside and sat by the fire. I thought about what had happened with Jimmy. Everybody died, and in this day and age, more people would die more quickly than before. What bothered me the most was that Jimmy didn't die from starvation or some illness that there was no longer medication for. He had died because there was nobody to make sure people did what was right. There was nobody to enforce rules or punish those who broke those rules. The world had become lawless.

As I sat and watched the flames lick the air above the fire, I eventually fell asleep. When I woke up the next morning, the fire had died out and the sun was coming up, but it was cloudy out and looked like it was going to rain.

Charles came out of the house with stuff to make some coffee. He lit the fire, started the coffee, and sat by the fire. There was no conversation for about twenty minutes. Finally, Charlie looked at me.

"So is there anything we can do about what happened yesterday?"

"What do you mean, 'anything we can do'?" I asked.

"Well, is there anything we can do to even things out, I guess? They took one of ours—shouldn't we retaliate? Get some kind of payback?"

I knew at some point that this topic was going to come up, and I had been thinking of a way to answer with a little compassion while at the same time, being blunt and honest about the circumstances.

"We have four adult men, one teenage boy, a teenage girl, and two women. One of which is your middle-aged wife, and the other is emotionally crushed because of 'what happened yesterday.' Going up against fifty hard corps convicts. It's suicide." Charlie was obviously taken aback by what I said. "Look, I know you're upset, fuckin' pissed even. You lost a friend, a member of your family, but we don't have the numbers for this and I've got my friends back home I'm thinkin' about. I wanna get back home to them so that I can help them survive, help them live through this bullshit." I looked at the hurt on his face as he realized that the points I was making were right. "Look, if we had more able-bodied people—hell, if we had more people—I'd think about the possibility of some kind of retaliation, but I won't commit suicide."

Charles hung his head, a look of defeat on his face.

"I just gotta do something. These assholes killed a friend of mine, and I know that they're doin' worse to the folks in town. Just because the world's harder now doesn't mean we can forget about what's right and wrong. The good people still need to believe that they can have justice when they are done wrong." With that, he stood up and walked away, leaving me to the fire, cold coffee, and my thoughts.

As I sat there, I thought about what Charles said and agreed with him. People still needed justice. I needed to see what was going on in town. I needed to see it for myself.

Charlie, Susan, and Megan were in the house, still asleep. Megan had stayed in the house that night, too worked up be alone, which was reasonable considering the situation. Bill and Jennifer were still on patrol, and Charles and I were to be the response team, but I decided that I had other plans.

I went into the house and went to the kitchen. Susan had made some biscuits the night before that nobody ate. I loaded several of those into a plastic bag, along with some homemade jerky and some ham.

I then walked out to the barn, to the stall where Jimmy and Megan had made their room. Jimmy had a small three-day Maxpedition backpack that I decided to use. My *Eberlestock* was just too big for what I was going to do.

I loaded the pack with the food and both my canteens of water, extra ammo, and magazines for the AR and ammo for the 1911. I also took my binoculars, my sun glasses, my boonie hat, my tarp, and my sleeping bag. I changed into my civilian clothes, shrugged on the pack, and walked out of the barn, right into Charles.

"Where are you goin'?" he asked, a surprised look on his face.

"I got something to do. I'll be gone in a few days, don't wait up." I set off toward Charlesville. I needed to see what was going on firsthand with the town. If it was as bad as I expected, maybe I could figure out something to do.

10

When Charles and I initially started to talk, he had said that the farm was just south of town. When I finally reached a decision about what I was going to do, I set out in a northern direction. I knew from what happened with Jimmy and Charlie that there were convicts running around in the area, so I needed to move slow and careful. I knew that I couldn't get into any type of fight or shoot-out, so I needed to make sure that I avoided contact with anybody at all cost.

It was still cloudy, but the rain had not yet started to fall. It was cooler than it had been and the humidity was low, so the hike wasn't bad and was actually kind of peaceful. It took me several hours, but I was able to make it to the outskirts of Charlesville without any trouble. A couple of times, I thought I heard voices off in the distance, but I just hunkered down and waited for them to pass. The clouds stayed out, but the rain held off up to this point.

As I got closer to where I thought Charlesville would be, I started to smell smoke in the air. Charlesville sat dead center in the middle of a valley, so all the terrain surrounding the town was on high ground. Running through the center of the town was the river. I wasn't sure what it was called now, but I think Charles said it had been called "Snake River" back in the day. I came out of the woods about a half mile from town limits, along a two-lane roadway. I decided that this close to town, it wasn't safe to use the roadways, so I backed into the woods and moved to a location on the mountainside that gave me a clear view of the town. I found a large oak tree that would provide me with some cover and shade. I used a couple saplings that were growing beside the oak as supports for my tarp, using brush and bushes as camouflage, setting up what hunters called a blind, making sure that it looked like the surrounding foliage. You would be surprised how easily something can be seen if it looks at all out of place.

My plan was to camp there for a couple of days and watch what was going on in Charlesville. Were the convicts running rampant? Were people being indiscriminately killed? How bad was it? If things looked bad and the convicts were truly running rampant, then maybe some type of plan needed to be made. If things looked okay, I would report that back to Charles with hopes that his desire for revenge would subside.

I was on the far side of the river, looking down at a bridge leading into town, the river, and an open view of the center of town. I don't know what I expected to see, but it was bad. I had read several articles before this thing happened about what to expect in the event of an EMP strike, and what I saw was exactly what they said would take place. The business section of town was desolate; there was nobody there. The buildings looked like they had been looted, with many that looked like they had been set on fire. Businesses and houses alike were burning or had been burned. I saw several people by the river washing clothes or getting water to drink.

Off to the right side of the town was a cemetery. There were several people there digging graves for a stack of bodies that were stacked in the graveyard. But it looked like the townspeople couldn't keep up with the burying details, as the stack of bodies looked like cordwood. Life for these people had become a living hell, all because the electricity had gone out and technology had failed.

It was a shame to sit here and see this town looking like it did. You could tell that at one time, the town itself had looked nice. The old buildings had a rustic look to them. They looked old but had a kind of homey look to them at the same time. But now, it looked more like London after it had been attacked by the Nazis in World War II.

I dug my binoculars out of my pack and bunkered in for a long few days. As I continued to watch the goings-on of the people in town, I could see a few people moving around, trying to keep what life they now had moving forward. Some were walking from house to house, stopping and talking to each other in the street. People were getting by in spite of the new circumstances. I watched the movements of the people around town for an hour or so, then the clouds finally broke and the rain started falling. As the townspeople cleared the streets, I moved back to my makeshift shelter. Listening to the rain beat off the tarp roof of my shelter was actually quite relaxing. The smell of a wet forest is pleasant and restful. Soon after I ate some biscuits and ham, I fell asleep and waited out the storm.

It rained all night, and the temperature dropped enough that I needed to crawl into my sleeping bag. I didn't sleep much but dozed off and on all night long. I kept thinking about what I hoped to accomplish with this little recon. What was I hoping or not hoping to see? What was I going to do with the information I got?

When morning started to rise, the sun came up with it. I could see the humidity rising as the sun warmed up the ground. The sun reflected off the wet grass, making a trillion small mirrors sparkle in the morning sunlight. I left my tarp and moved back to the large oak tree. I dug out my binoculars again and started to watch the town.

I could see several people moving around, but these people were different from the ones that I had seen the night before. These people were all men and they each had some type of weapon. One guy even had a Samurai sword. There were three groups of about five or six convicts, or at least I was assuming they were convicts, moving throughout the town. I watched as they moved from building to building, taking whatever they thought they could use.

One group was at the grocery store and carried out all kinds of canned goods, which surprised me. I assumed that by this point, the perishable stuff would have been rotten, and all the canned goods would have been pillaged.

Another group was at the NAPA store, loading hand tools and equipment into shopping carts and wheelbarrows. Group three had decided that booze was what they needed and had moved into the liquor store, taking every bottle and can that they could carry or load into a shopping cart.

As group one finished up with the grocery run, they pushed their carts and wheelbarrows uphill to a building that looked a little like a log cabin. I couldn't tell what it was, a business or a residence, but if it was a residence, it was a big house. The other groups finished up and also pushed their loot to the same building. As the confiscated goods were unloaded, the group would move out again and head to another area.

There were large groups of convicts loitering around the building, yelling, screaming and just acting crazy. What I saw going on was expected behavior. People were in need of things and would take what they needed from those that had, but I also saw something that bothered me. I guess I expected it also, as I had seen it in my apartment complex, but it was still a shock. After they were done in the business district, the groups moved into the residential area and forced their way into houses.

There had been no civilians that I could tell anyway, out and moving around at this time of the day. It appeared as though all of the civilian population were hiding inside their homes. When a group of convicts showed up, the residents were either forced outside or ran outside to escape the convicts. Anybody who tried to fight back was shot on the spot. The bodies were left where they fell and the items taken were hauled back to the wood building.

I focused my attention on the wood building as several convicts moved in and out of the two doors that were visible to me. It looked like they were fortifying the building, using the tools and equipment taken from the NAPA, to secure windows and doors. The food that had been unloaded at a side door was being carried inside, along with whatever goods were being carried back from the residences.

I wasn't just watching what they were doing, but I was looking for anybody that stood out as the leader, and he was actually easy to find. He was one of the biggest convicts there, and several of the other convicts would go up to him to report and get orders. He was a black male wearing jeans and a T-shirt that was too small for him, which I thought was more by design than accident. He carried himself with an air of confidence and leadership that I believed was earned more from fear than respect.

I needed to get more information than what I could get through binoculars. I needed to go into the town and talk to somebody about what was going on, but I also needed to be smart. I wasn't going to go in while all the activity was going on. I wanted to go in when the convicts settled down. There were fifty or sixty of them and one of me. I was greatly outnumbered, and if I got killed, what good would that do anybody?

I took down my tarp and disassembled my AR. I put the AR into the three-day pack and wrapped it all in the tarp. I would attract too much attention with it hanging off my back. I was in my normal civilian clothes so I wouldn't stand out. There is a theory called "the gray man." Basically, you wear clothes that look like normal, everyday stuff that everybody wears. That way, you don't stick out. If you're all decked out in military-style tactical gear, you stick out and become a target, and I didn't want that. So using a stick, I dug a hole big enough to accommodate the pack and then covered the pack with dirt and leaves. I was fairly confident that if somebody came by while I was gone, my gear would remain secure. I waited until dusk and checked and holstered my 1911. I also had a K-Bar Karambit knife in a sheath at the small of my back. Once I felt ready, I set out.

I worked my way through the woods and brush, down the hill, moving toward the bridge. It was the only way over to the town unless I swam across the river, which I wasn't going to do. When I got to the bottom of the hill, I stopped at the roadway to watch and listen. There were several cars and trucks scattered over the roadway and across the bridge. Once I concluded that there was no human traffic on the roadway or the bridge, I set out using the cars and trucks as cover and concealment as I crossed into town.

On the other side of the bridge, there was a 7-Eleven convenience store that had long been ransacked, emptied and destroyed. I moved past it, along a one lane road that ran parallel with the river. From what I had seen through the binoculars, a block or two past the 7-Eleven, was where the residential area started. As I walked past the houses, I could see that garbage was starting to build up. People were still accumulating large amounts of garbage as they used up what canned and bottled goods that they had. The problem with that is that with the abundance of garbage just sitting around came an abundance of rats, which carries disease. With the rats came an increased chance of sickness. With no medical facilities to help... well, you get the idea.

I walked along like I belonged there, hoping that if I was seen, I'd look like any other citizen and be ignored.

I got to a corner building and saw that the area beyond it was a wide-open park with kids' toys, swings, and monkey bars, along with benches and tables for the grown-ups. I quick-peeked around the corner of the building but saw nobody on the street or in the park. It looked like the setting sun had been a sign for everybody to go in for the night, but I needed to cross this park. I had been taught in SWAT training that slow is smooth, smooth is fast. If you tried to hurry movement, it was awkward, and the chance of screwing up was higher. In this case, running would draw attention, where walking would look more natural. If you moved slower, your actions were more fluid and were performed correctly, which in the long run was faster. So I walked slowly across the park, heading toward the residences on the other side.

When I got to the other side of the park, I stopped beside a tree and crouched down to catch my breath. I had held it the whole way across the park. Have you ever played hide-and-seek as a kid, and when somebody got close to finding you, you held your breath? Well, it was like that, but held a higher penalty if I got caught.

I could see a faint light come on in the house in front of me. I assumed a candle had been lit. I moved over to the house and up the steps to the front door. As I reached the front door, I put my ear up to a window and listened. I could hear people talking in tones that were calm and friendly. I didn't think any convicts were inside.

Slowly and as quietly as possible, I began to knock on the door. I used a slow, continuous pace and rhythm, hoping to get the attention of somebody inside. As I knocked, I looked around the area, hoping that I had not attracted any unwanted attention.

The door swung open, startling me. Immediately, my hands went up. I wanted to convey the idea that I didn't mean or want any trouble. A middle-aged man in shorts and a green Polo shirt stood in front of me with what looked like a broom handle sharpened to a point in his hands. In a whisper, I said, "I don't mean you any harm, I just want to talk."

The guy didn't seem to relax much. He kept the spear pointed at my face.

"Look, I just want to talk to you about what's going on in town. I don't want to hurt anybody." The man continued to look at me but eventually backed up and let me into his house, keeping the spear trained on me. I wasn't permitted past the front foyer, and he kept the door open a crack. There was a middle-aged woman and a teenage girl standing in the living room off to my left and a set of steps leading upstairs to my right.

"Who are you and whataya want?" he asked, keeping the spear positioned for a quick strike.

"My name's Buck. I don't want anything from you except some information." I kept my hands up. "I just want to talk to you about the convicts that moved in. See what kind of information you can give me on their activities, movements…" I let the sentence trail off to try to read the guy's expression.

He watched me for several minutes. I assume to try to get a read on me. He eventually lowered the spear some but kept it pointed in my direction.

"I'm Carl." He pointed to the women. "You guys go upstairs." The women stared at Carl then at me. "Now!" he yelled. Both women jumped and moved toward the stairs. Once they were gone, he relaxed a little. "That's my wife and my daughter. No offense, but I don't trust them being around strangers, not with the state of the world today." I smiled to show him I meant no harm to them and to convey understanding.

"No offense taken, I understand. Look, Carl, I need to know everything you can tell me about the convicts and what's going on in town."

Carl and I talked for about an hour and a half. He eventually relaxed enough to lower the spear. He told me that the convicts are most active during the day, patrolling the town, pillaging whatever they can take from the town and its people. At night, they go back to the police station / city hall building where they drink, get high, and pass out until the next morning, when they start all over again. A few of them stayed out at night for security, but that was usually just four or five guys around the perimeter of the city hall building.

That was good and bad. Good that they passed out at night but bad that it was in the police station. That meant that they had access to other weapons. I would need to confirm that with Bill, but if I remembered correctly, he said he had only brought a few M16s and Berettas with him when he left town for Charlie's house.

Carl said that the leader of the group was a big black guy that he had heard called "Outcast." He said that Outcast was ruthless. He had seen Outcast kill somewhere around ten citizens for not turning over clothing or food to his guys when they came by. It was a rule in the town that if the convicts came around, they got what they wanted. If not, somebody in the house was killed. And if what they asked for was a person, they got that too.

I asked Carl why they didn't just leave.

"Where would we go? We have no family in the state, let alone in the area. Nobody else is any better off than we are. At least here we have shelter, and as you saw coming in, we are right next to the river, so we have water. Foods short for everybody, so…" He let it trail off.

"Why did you need this?" Carl asked as I got up from the couch to leave.

"I just saw some stuff that bothered me. I just wanted to see what was going on. Carl, take care of yourself and your family." I reached out to shake his hand. He took my hand and shook it with purpose and vigor.

"You too, Mr. Buck."

When I left Carl's house, the darkness outside was complete. The only light was the moon reflecting off the river. It was cool but not uncomfortable. The sky was clear and the stars were crisp and bright, reflecting off the river like a bunch of tiny flashlights reflecting off a mirror. I worked my way back the way I had come in, using abandoned vehicles as cover. When I got to my campsite, I found that my gear was safe and secure where I had buried it. I put up my tarp for a quick shelter, reassembled my AR, and strapped on my tactical gear.

I got out my binoculars and a small notepad and pen that I kept in my cargo pocket. As I watched the convicts through the binoculars, I could see a pattern starting to emerge and I wrote down what I saw. I wasn't sure what time it was, but the sun had set about 8:00 p.m. I was at Carl's for about an hour and a half, so I was guessing that it was somewhere around 10:00 or 10:30 p.m.

As I watched the activity around the wood building, it started to resemble what the streets in the Old West must have looked like. The convicts were starting to congregate around the wood building, drinking hollering, smoking, and causing a large, scary ruckus. There were no longer any civilians on the streets moving around, I assumed because everybody was afraid to come out of their houses. These citizens were on lockdown, too afraid to do anything. The only difference between this and old west Dodge City was that there was no Wyatt Earp to clean up the town.

I watched this go on until what I guessed was around 2:00 a.m., when the partying moved inside. Some of the convicts stayed outside as security. You could still hear yelling and screaming coming from inside the building. The partying continued until about 4:00 a.m. As the sun rose, the patrol guys wrapped it up and went inside to sleep. As the day progressed, the others slowly started to come out and go in separate directions doing their own thing. I saw Outcast come out a couple of times yelling and barking orders, but for the most part, he stayed inside.

The next night, the routine was the same, except when the security crew took over, it was a different group. The originals got to party, while a new crew got stuck with patrol duties. Other than personnel, the routine was the same. The patrol guys were out all night as the others partied. Both nights, you could see a definite lack of energy and attention as the shift got closer to dawn.

From what I could see, if any kind of plan could be made to take this town back from these convicts, the biggest opportunity was around the 4:00 to 5:00 a.m. time frame. The partygoers would be passed out, and the patrol guys would be dead tired. Everyone was at their most vulnerable then. My concern was the building fortification around the windows and doors. That would be a problem.

The more I thought about this, the idea of taking over the town, I realized that it was a bad idea. It would take a small army to do this effectively and safely enough to minimize casualties to the liberators. Otherwise, it was a suicide mission, and I needed to convey this to Charles and his family.

As the sun came up on day three, I slept for several hours. When I awoke, I ate some biscuits and ham, packed up my gear, and headed back to Charles's farm.

11

I got back to the farm at around dinnertime. It was still fairly sunny and warm outside. Everybody was working to get dinner ready when Jennifer and Bill saw me and came running up to me, wanting to know where I'd been and what I'd been doing. Soon, Charlie, Charles, and Justin joined in.

I filled them in on the last three days and the information that I had. I told them about Carl, what he had told me, and what I had seen for myself afterward. I let them know about the pillaging that was being done, the assaults on the townspeople, and the terror being forced onto the citizens. I also made it very clear that I believed that there was nothing that we could do to help. I made sure that they understood that we were just not qualified, equipped, or in possession of enough people to affect any type of rescue for the townspeople.

Bill looked upset.

"Shit, they're using the hall as their base. Man, I couldn't get all the rifles out of there. They must have access to eight or ten M16s, probably as many Berettas, and who knows how much ammo. Damn!"

I looked at Bill. I could understand his frustration.

"Look, the other day after what had happened to Jimmy, Charles and I were talkin'. I don't think they should be doin' what they're doin', and I think every one of them should have a bullet in the head for it. But look around here. We would need a squad of highly trained people to do this. All we've got is six adults with one who has any type of training at all. We just don't have enough of who we need to do this."

We sat around a fire discussing the possibilities of what everybody wanted and what they thought we should do. Everybody was acting on emotion and the need for revenge. I wanted the revenge as bad as anybody else, but I knew the logistics of this type of idea and knew that it couldn't be done.

As the discussion continued, Meghan and Susan came out of the house and walked over to the fire. Meghan looked a little better, but she was obviously still grieving. She walked over and hugged me.

"Thanks for what you did, you know, picking that spot for him. It really is nice."

"How are you doin'?" I asked.

"I'm doin' better. I miss him." Her eyes started to water, but she kept her composure. "He was a good man, and I'll miss him for the rest of my life. It'll take me a long time, but I'll be okay, eventually."

It sounded very healthy. She was logical and made clear sense about how she described what she was feeling. I was no longer worried about her. I knew that it would take a little time but that eventually, she would be fine.

"What are you guys talkin' about?" Susan asked as she poured herself a cup of coffee.

Justin chimed in first. "About whether we should fuck those convicts up in town." They just weren't hearing me. Susan was the only one still thinking logically.

Susan coughed up a sip of coffee.

"First, watch your mouth. Second, 'we' who? You guys?" She looked around at all of us. "You're farmers. Bill, you were a small-town cop that dealt with maybe a call a week. None of you, except maybe Buck, has any idea what you're talkin' about. You're all idiots. It's suicide. This life is hard enough as it is. If you think I'm gonna let you…" she said as she pointed at Charles. "Or any of ya, for that matter, get yourselves killed so I gotta work this farm alone, you're nuts. No, you're not doin' it."

Charles spoke up first.

"Susan, you don't know what they're doin' to the people in town. They're killing people and stealing whatever they want from everybody. They're doing to those townspeople exactly what they were gonna try to do to Jenn." He was clearly angry.

"I'm sorry," she said. "But I'm not gonna lose my family so that another wife can keep her family. If you go out trying to save everybody, you'll all end up dead. You nuts have seen too many movies." With that, she threw out the rest of her coffee and walked back into the house.

"Maybe she's right. We don't have any clue what we're doin'," Justin said.

"Buck." Bill grabbed my attention. "What if I could round up some ex-vets, some other cops? You know some guys that have some experience and have seen some action. Do you think we could do somethin' then?"

I grabbed my head in my hands, leaning back and looking up at the sky, shaking my head in disbelief. "Look guys, I'm against this. The logistics of taking over a town is so far beyond our capabilities that with even a decent amount of manpower, it would be a suicide mission. I say we let it go and let whatever happens happen. You guys need to focus on taking care of yourselves. I'll be packin' up soon and takin' off. If you decide you're set on this, you'll be doin' it without me." With that, I got up and walked over to the barn and into my makeshift bedroom.

Some people just don't get it. They get something into their heads and they can't let it go, no matter how illogical their argument is.

That night while I was asleep, Charlie and Bill gathered up some weapons and ammo and set out on their own for town. They had decided that if they couldn't get them all, at least they could look for the two guys that had killed Jimmy.

Once they had the gear and weapons that they thought they needed and the sun was starting to come up, they set out. They were not concerned with noise discipline or ambushes, so it didn't take them as long to get to Charlesville as it did Buck. It took them a little over an hour to get there. Once there, they sat on a hilltop and, using a set of binoculars, scouted out the town.

"Would you remember them if you saw them again?" Bill asked.

“No doubt I’d remember those fuckers again. I was scared. Shit, I had a gun pointed at my face, and Jimmy’s brains all over me, but I’ll remember ’em.” Charlie kept watch through the binoculars, watching for the convicts that had killed his friend.

The two guys sat there and watched town for a good part of the day. Finally, at around two in the afternoon, Charlie sat up straight.

“There they are. I see ’em.” He pointed toward where the city hall building was. “You see the two dudes walking down the street toward the river? That’s them.” He handed the binoculars to Bill.

“Damn, Charlie, that one guy looks big.” Bill was looking at the black male, and he looked huge, every bit as big as Charlie. He had an army jacket on and carried some kind of bolt action rifle. The second guy, a white male, was wearing a green flannel shirt. He wasn’t anywhere near as big as the black male, but he carried himself with an air of confidence that could easily be seen. He also had a bolt action hunting rifle in his hands. They looked like they were heading out of town into the woods surrounding town.

“I don’t plan on fightin’ ’em, Bill, I plan on shootin’ ’em.”

“What’s your plan?” Bill asked.

“I don’t have a plan. I’m just gonna follow ’em until I get a chance to get the opportunity, then I ‘plan’ on shootin’ ’em.” Charlie said.

Bill thought about it. He had hunted these woods for a long time, so he knew the area. He figured that they had the advantage over the convicts. If they could figure out where the convicts were going, they could set up a quick ambush and take them out.

“Okay, Charlie. Let’s watch them for a while and see where they’re goin’. If we can get in front of them, we’ll set up an ambush and take ’em.”

Charlie and Bill started to work their way toward where the convicts were heading. The brush was minimal so they were able to catch up fairly easily. Once they reached the area where they had seen the convicts enter the woods, they started to follow them, keeping far enough away that the chances of being heard were minimal but close enough that they could keep an eye on them.

Bill realized that the convicts were heading toward a corn field about two miles from town. Bill had hunted the area a lot and knew it well. Deer grazed in that area all the time and would provide a pretty easy opportunity at getting some game to feed people.

"Charlie, they're headin' to Graham's cornfield," Bill said, using the farmer's first name. "We can work our way around and cut them off at the west end path. We can ambush 'em there. What dya think?"

Charlie watched the two convicts, and the direction they were going. "I think you're right." He said. "We're gonna need to boogie if we're gonna beat them there. We better get movin'."

The two friends moved off as fast as they could without being too loud. Neither of the men had any military experience, no idea about patrol tactics or tracking, but both of them had spent their lives hunting and knew how to move fairly quietly through the woods.

Graham had recently cut back the brush and trees around the field so that his tractor could negotiate the perimeter of the fields easier. Once they reached the west end path, they were able to use the brush and cut down trees as cover and concealment.

About twenty minutes after they set up, they heard the two convicts moving up the path. They were talking quietly, not paying attention to their surroundings.

Charlie had his Remington shotgun, and Bill had an M16. When the convicts were in front of them, Bill and Charlie opened up. Charlie's shotgun roared, spitting out flame and a load of double ought buck at the smaller convict's legs. Charlie thought he remembered that the convict had been called "Shooter." Shooter fell, dropping his rifle, which fell out of his reach. The big convict wasn't sure what had happened, surprise causing him to freeze where he stood. Bill opened up on him, pressing the trigger several times, striking the huge convict in the gut, groin, and thighs. He stumbled backward, eventually falling to the ground, but somehow, he was able to keep control of his rifle.

The movies always showed people flying backward, their feet leaving the ground when they're shot. But that's not how it worked. People didn't fly backward; many times they were able to keep fighting for several minutes before finally succumbing to their wounds.

Charlie and Bill kept their weapons pointed at the convicts as they left their ambush site. As they walked up to the convicts, their anger grew, the desire for revenge increasing. Shooter was on the ground, blood pouring from the wounds in his legs. He had not screamed or even made a sound. He just laid there, gritting his teeth. Charlie looked at the other guy. He thought he remembered his name being "Darious."

"You assholes remember me?" Charlie asked with contempt and anger in his voice.

"Yeah, I remember you. You're that pussy that almost cried when we took his pig. Fuckin' pansy." Shooter spat.

"Yeah, you're right. I was scared. Almost as scared as you two are now. The difference is, you're both gonna die." Without another word, he pulled the trigger on his shotgun, blowing Shooter's head off, painting the ground with red and gray brain matter.

"Wha' da fuck!" Darious screamed as his friend's head disappeared.

Charlie changed his voice to imitate Darious's voice.

"Wha' da fuck…?" Charlie mimicked, repeating what Darious had just said. "Fuck you, convict," Charlie said as he pulled the trigger again.

Bill never said a word. When it was over, he looked at his friend.

"We better get goin'. I'm sure somebody heard that."

As the two men worked their way back to the farm, the adrenaline was rushing through them. They had a hard time controlling the energy that the adrenaline rush caused. Caught up in the moment, they failed to see the skinny, nerdy-looking convict in the woods behind them.

This skinny, nerdy, white convict was the type that had never been accepted by the public before his arrest and was never accepted by the other convicts after his arrest. His name was Jeremy, but everybody at the prison, when they lowered themselves to talk to him, called him "Finger Fuck" or "Double F" when they were too lazy to say the whole thing. He had been a janitor at a middle school for several years when one of the teenage girls worked up the nerve to report him to school officials. After the investigation was over, he had been charged with thirteen counts of sexual misconduct with minors. If you asked him, the sixty-five years he was sentenced to was extreme. After all, he didn't fuck them, just touched them a little. The bad part was that he got caught.

Double F was always trying to make friends. When he saw Shooter and D leave to go hunting, he figured he'd follow, maybe get a chance to hunt with them. He had followed the other guys and was maybe five minutes behind them, when he had seen them ambushed. He couldn't believe D and Shooter had been wiped out so easily. They were two of the tougher guys in the group.

But when he actually thought about it, this was his chance to prove himself. He wasn't gonna let those two hillbillies get away with it. No, he couldn't take them out himself, but he could do something to make his status with the rest of the group better. He had a plan. He was going to follow them and find out where they went. Hopefully it was to where they lived. If it was, he could report back to Outcast what he knew and what he had found. Outcast was gonna be pissed. These two hillbillies had just killed his brother.

12

I had just woken up and was in the yard eating lunch with Jennifer, enjoying a cup of coffee, when Bill and Charlie wandered in. They looked different somehow. Stressed but hyped up. I had seen that look before on my tactical team after we had finished an entry. Adrenaline is an interesting thing. People who are not used to what's called adrenaline rushes process the overload of the chemical in different ways.

As adrenaline is dumped into the system, it gets used up and gives the host the energy and stamina to complete whatever task they were doing. Once the task is over, the excess adrenaline gets dumped into the stomach. This is what causes people to puke after a stressful situation. Sometimes, though, it's not enough to make them puke, and they just get really hyper and antsy, as their bodies deal with the unused energy. The body becomes jerky, and the eyes get wide and twitchy. These two had that exact look on their faces.

"Hey, guys…what's up?" I asked with some hesitation.

Bill looked at me like he had just stolen a cookie from the cookie jar.

"Look, you were right about not being able to take on all the guys in town. It would have been suicide and we know that. But the guys that killed Jimmy didn't deserve to get off scot-free."

"What do you mean 'didn't'?" I asked. Charlie spoke up.

"We went into town, found the two that done it, and took care of business." He said it like I should have known what they did.

"Are you outa your fuckin' minds? Did anybody see you? Were you followed back?" Questions were running through my head. I threw down my coffee and grabbed my AR, immediately up and scanning the wood line where they had exited, looking for any type of movement.

Both guys assured me that they had not been followed. They said that there had not been anybody around when they did it and they were sure that there had been no noise behind them on the way back to the house.

I was sure that they were telling me what they thought was true, but I needed to be sure myself. I always had my 1911 on, and I had my AR.

"Look, we gotta check to make sure you weren't followed. I need everybody's help searching this place. Bill, you take the north. Charlie, you take the south. I'll take west. Charles, east. Take your time—stop, look, listen." I was pissed, and I'm sure my tone conveyed that.

I entered the woods where they had exited and started doing a modified linear search, back and forth through the area adding five yards each time I started another line across the search area. I would take a few steps, stop, listen, and look, then take a few more steps and start the process over again. The problem was that here, around the farm and house, the woods were pretty thick. I could have been standing right above somebody, and if they were quiet enough, I'd never see them, but I needed to make sure that nobody had followed them.

I searched for about an hour and a half before I felt relatively sure that there was nobody in the woods. I worked my way back to the house, and when I got back, I found that the others were back and everybody was sitting around the fire eating.

"Did you find anybody?" Susan asked.

I ignored her question and looked at Bill and Charlie. I was still pissed.

"You two morons got lucky. You can't just take off and hunt other people at will. If it was just you two, fine. Whatever happens, happens. But you guys have friends and family to think of here!" I yelled as I pointed at his family. "Charlie, you've got your mom, dad, Justin, Jennifer. Bill, these people may not be immediate family, but they're your new family. Their safety needs to be paramount in every thought you have." I continued to point at each of them. "Each of you needs to put yourselves last and think about everybody else first. If you do that, you might be able to survive longer. Hell, you might just be able to survive this new shit world we're in. But if you go off half-cocked, letting selfishness, stupidity, and revenge control your actions, you'll get each other killed." I let that sink in before I continued, this time focusing on Meghan. "Sweetheart, what happened to Jimmy sucked. In the short time I knew him, I thought he was a cool guy. I know that getting revenge on the guys that did it was important, but in this new era of this country, you gotta be smart. Swallowing some stuff you may not like is important for survival."

Everybody had their heads hung, staring at the ground. Meghan had a tear in her eye, but nobody said anything. I finally spoke up again. "Charles, Susan, I appreciate all your hospitality over the past couple of weeks that I've been here, but I gotta get goin'. I got my own family to get to. I've got maybe another two weeks of hiking to get there, and I wanna get started. I'll be gone first thing in the morning." With that, I went to my room in the barn and started to get my gear packed.

Double F watched the two guys leave the woods and walk toward the house. This was awesome. He knew where the house was and who the two guys were that had killed Darious. He was going to be in with the cool crowd now. No more being fucked with, no more harassment, and no more being somebody's bitch. This was going to be great.

He watched as the guys walked up to a group of people sitting by a fire. One of them was a teenage girl, and she was hot. A little older than Jeremy usually liked, but she'd do it in a pinch. The one guy though, he looked like he could be dangerous. He was holding an army-style rifle. Jeremy didn't know anything about guns, but something about this guy looked bad. Jeremy saw the dangerous-looking guy get really animated. He looked like he was pissed off at the other two. The guy jumped up and started scanning the woods, barking orders to the others.

When they all started walking over to the woods, Jeremy decided that it was time to go. He backed away from his hiding place behind a big oak tree and worked his way back the way he had come. Once he was far enough away from the house and the people, he started to move faster, less concerned with making noise. As he got closer to the town, he started to run. He was excited about getting onto Outcast's good side. His life was about to change for the better.

Once my gear was packed, I spent the rest of the afternoon just chilling out in the barn. The afternoon and evening were cooler than normal for this time of year, so I decided to sit outside behind the barn once the sun set. I was pissed about what Charlie and Bill had done, not because they got the revenge that they did but that they left that desire for revenge control their actions. They let their emotions override common sense and disregarded the safety of their friends and family. That was what ultimately pissed me off.

I sat there staring at the sky, watching the pink and blue colors of the sky painted by the setting sun, and the beautiful countryside that surrounded the farm. As I sat there, I started to cool off emotionally as well as physically. I heard a noise to my right and saw Meghan walking over to me. She held a couple of plastic grocery bags in her hand. She set the bags on the ground and took a seat beside me. The tree where Jimmy was buried was just off to our right, so I saw her looking at the grave several times.

"There's some biscuits and jerky in the bags for your trip. You really leavin' tomorrow?"

"Yeah, I am," I said. "It's time. I gotta get to my family. They are as important to me as Jimmy was to you."

"Well, I'll hate to see ya go. You're a good guy. When are ya leavin'?"

"Thank you, you guys are good people too. I'm gonna try and leave at first light, before it warms up. I wanna get as much distance as I can under my feet before I stop for the day." She reached over and squeezed my hand. With that, she got up and started to walk away.

"Hey," I said, "I wish all of you the best of luck."

She smiled as she rounded the corner of the barn and walked back to the house. I stayed there behind the barn for another half hour before I took the bags of jerky and biscuits into the barn and went to sleep.

When I woke up, the sun was just starting to peek over the treetops. All I needed to pack was my sleeping bag; I had packed the rest of my gear the night before. I strapped on my battle belt, and press checked my 1911 to make sure it was loaded, putting it into its holster on my right thigh. I had checked all the magazines for my 1911 and AR the night before, so I knew that they were all loaded. I slung my ruck then strapped on my AR and walked out of the barn.

It was a cool morning, and there was a thin layer of frost on the ground. When I exhaled, I could see my breath, and inhaling left that cool, refreshing feeling on the back of my throat. It was going to be a nice walk, at least until the sun came out and I warmed up.

I looked around the farm and soon realized that I was going to miss these people. They had been good to me and were genuinely nice folks, but it was time to go. I wanted to get moving again. I was afraid that I'd get complacent and comfortable and not continue on.

I got my bearing on my compass, found a tree, and set off. I had maybe two weeks of travel to go, maybe less. I was excited to see my friends. It had been a long time since I had last seen or talked to them. I hoped that they were all okay and doing as well as could be expected in this new world.

The sun was coming up now, and Outcast knew that these hillbillies would be waking up and coming out to cook breakfast. When they got comfortable, he would take the first shot, letting the others know it was time to start shooting. He had fifteen guys with him to take out nine redneck cracker farmers. This should be easy.

Double F had come running into the hall yelling and screaming about Darius and Shooter and how some hillbillies had killed them and how he could point out who had shot them.

Outcast hadn't heard anything after Double F said Darius was dead. He just heard a blank hollow sound in his head. He immediately felt the urge to kill somebody and had originally wanted to take his anger out on the little child rapist, but when the little piece of shit started to scream again that he knew where they lived and how to get there, he decided that maybe letting him live was a better idea for the moment.

He couldn't believe that his little brother was dead. Darious was all the family he ever really had. He and Darius had grown up just outside Philadelphia. Their mom had been a drug addict, with heroin her preferred go-to drug. They never knew who their father was, but they looked different, so they always suspected that they didn't have the same father. More than likely, they had been addicts from the neighborhood who fucked good old Mom in exchange for a hit of heroin.

With a mom that was always high and absent fathers, both boys just grew up doing what they wanted, when they wanted. Soon, they were into a life of theft, then assault, then rape. Rape was what landed them in the state prison system. At least rape was what started it. They decided to kill some bitch that they had taken sex from when she wouldn't give it up. After they both got their shot at her, they slit her throat and left her lying along the road. But she had been tougher than they both thought. She had lived. She had been able to get up and crawl out onto the road where a passing car found her. They took her to the hospital, where she recovered and was able to tell the police who did it. They had been serving life sentences when the lights went out.

And the lights going out was the best thing that ever happened to them. Once they were able to escape the prison, they entered a new world where there were no rules, no right and wrong, no police and nobody to tell them what to do or how they should live. They could do whatever they wanted to do. And life had been good until these cracker farmer pieces of shit had ended his good time by killing the only thing he had ever loved. Now he was going to even the score.

Double F was starting to get excited.

"There they are, Cast. That's one of them anyway. The younger one killed Darius. Shot 'em in the face with his shotgun."

Outcast didn't say a thing. He just stared.

"Where's the other one?" he finally asked. "I want them both to suffer."

"I don't see 'im. He's shorter than these two. He's not out here yet. What are you gonna do, Cast?"

"F, shut the fuck up or I'll cut your kiddie rapin' throat right here." Outcast kept his eyes on the two at the firepit. They were making coffee and talking like nothing had happened, like they had not ruined the best life Outcast had ever had. After about fifteen minutes or so, something got the attention of the younger of the two. Had somebody made a noise? Had a scope reflected the sun? Whatever it was, the young one was interested in something.

It was time, even if the shorter one had not shown up yet. Outcast took aim with his M16 and pulled the trigger.

I had been walking for about fifteen minutes and had drifted off into my own little world. I wasn't really thinking about anything specific. I was just enjoying the weather. It was still cool out and the sun shining through the trees lit up the greens and browns of the forest. I loved the woods. I loved the sounds, smells, and the lack of obnoxious noise. Having lived in the city for as long as I had, the sounds of cars and constant chatter of people coupled with the gas fumes was enough to make a country boy scream. That was the one good thing about the new world: quiet.

I was following my compass and placing one foot in front of the other, kind of on autopilot, when I heard the first of the shots. I didn't really pay much attention at first, but then the second, third, and fourth shots brought me out of my trance. By this time, I was able to determine where the shots had come from. They were coming from the farm.

I started to run back as fast as I could with sixty-plus pounds on my back. I wasn't as young as I used to be, or in as good a shape. When I got to the wood line to the farm, I dropped my ruck. Charles, Charlie, and Bill were kneeling down by the firepit, firing into the wood line where Bill and Charlie had come out of the woods the day before. There were rounds coming from the woods, hitting the ground and siding of the house. I looked around, looking for the girls and Justin. Just then, Justin, Jennifer, Meghan, and Susan came running from the front door of the house. I broke from the wood line, running out into the yard, just as a round from the wood line struck Justin in the face, dropping him instantly. Susan screamed and ran to her son. As she knelt down to help him, I saw her head snap to the side, blood and bone spraying everywhere, dropping her as she leaned over her dead son, falling on top of him, as if to cover him from the gunfire.

I couldn't see any enemy yet, so I wasn't firing. When I got to the corner of the house, the guys were standing up and starting to move backward. I saw about ten bad guys coming out of the wood line. I brought up my AR and started to fire. Three rounds went off, and bad guy number one dropped.

"Don't retreat! Move forward, move forward!" I yelled, stepping forward and laying down rounds. I saw a turd wearing jeans and a red T-shirt step out of the wood line, carrying a revolver of some sort. Two rounds from my AR to his chest dropped him to his knees. A third round to the face dropped him flat.

I could hear the loud thunder of Charlie's shotgun and the crack of Bill's M16. The guys were yelling at each other, giving direction, pointing and firing at convicts as they came into view. Convicts were dropping, but it seemed like another one just stepped forward and took the fallen's spot. I kept moving forward, actually reaching the wood line, gaining a flanking position behind a large tree. I kept firing, dropping as many convicts as I could, staying crouched behind the tree. Rounds from the convicts were peppering the tree, but fortunately, none of them hit their mark. I heard a scream and looked toward the house. I saw Charles go down and saw Jennifer run over to her father as he fell, firing her Beretta as she tried to protect him.

Charlie ran over to protect his father and sister, pumping his shotgun as he moved, dropping another bad guy. Bill was crouched beside the front porch of the house, using the foundation of the house as cover, firing his M16, dropping bad guys as they exited the wood line and attempted to move toward the house.

The firing from each side continued on, with explanation points coming with the roar of Charlie's shotgun. I continued to fire from my tree, picking a convict and placing my rounds where they would do the most damage.

One convict seemed to come from nowhere, stepping from around the blind side of the tree I was using as cover. He was big. Bigger than me. He had on a set of overalls with no shirt on underneath, but I couldn't see a weapon. He was growling like a rabid animal, with anger on his face like I had never seen before. He grabbed the barrel of my AR and ripped it from my hands, pulling the sling from around my neck. He tossed it to the side and lunged at me, grabbing me around the neck with hands the size of hams, driving me backward into the ground.

I grabbed his wrist with my left hand and, using my right hand, started to punch him in the ribs. He didn't flinch. He was strong. I had spent years training in the martial arts. I had been in fights before but never with anybody this strong. I grabbed both of his wrists and moved my legs up his back until my ankles were locked behind his neck. I pinched my knees together, applying pressure to his elbows, while at the same time arching my hips and pulling down on his wrists. Normally, people let go when they feel the pressure on their elbows. This guy didn't. I wasn't getting any air, and my vision started to blur. I couldn't get to my knife, but I could reach my 1911.

I felt for the grip of my pistol. Once I found it, I used my thumb and unsnapped the thumb break. I pulled the 1911, simultaneously clicking off the thumb safety. I was still coherent enough to remember that if I put the barrel directly against the turd's side, it would take the gun out of battery and it wouldn't fire.

I was starting to blackout. I could still hear the convict growling and snarling at me. I even think I saw him drool on me. I put the barrel to his side and pulled the trigger. I saw him jerk. I pulled the trigger four more times, watching the giant jerk with each shot. I felt his grip start to loosen. He stood up and started to back away. My vision and breath started to come back, and I could see the look of fear on his face. I got a shaky, two-handed grip on the 1911 and put two .45 rounds into his face. He fell backward like a boxer that had been hit on the bottom of his chin by a hard uppercut. He didn't move.

I changed mags, reloading my 1911 and re-holstering it. I picked up my AR, re-slinging it over my shoulder. I also reloaded it as I scanned the small battlefield. I saw that Bill was down and that Charlie and Jennifer were still standing guard over their father. I looked in the direction of the wood line and saw Outcast exit the woods like a general leading a march across a Civil War battlefield. He had an M16 in his hands and was firing toward Charlie and Jennifer. The rifle either jammed or ran empty because he dropped it and pulled a Glock pistol from a holster on his left side.

Charlie was reloading his shotgun when Outcast reached him and Jennifer. With scary calm and no emotion, Outcast aimed the Glock at Charlie and pulled the trigger once, placing the shot into Charlie's forehead. Jennifer screamed at seeing her brother killed, especially that close. As I stepped from the woods, I yelled, "Hey, you worthless fuck!"

Outcast grabbed Jennifer around the neck, putting the Glock to her head.

"Who the fuck is you?" he spat. Jennifer was hysterical, crying and screaming. "Shut the fuck up bitch or I'll drop your cracker ass." He looked back at me. "I said, who the fuck is you?"

I kept the sights on Outcast's forehead. I was only twenty yards away from them, an easy shot for me at this distance.

"I'm nobody. Hell, I just met these people a couple weeks ago."

Outcast looked at me like he was confused. "Then why is you risking yo' life for them? Why you care? You could be doing anything you wants to right now. Hell," he said, motioning to Jennifer, "could be fuckin' her if you wanted to. So I ask you again, why you care?"

I pulled the trigger on my AR once. The round punched Outcast in the forehead just left of center. Blood and bone exploded from the back of his head, painting the ground behind him. He dropped to the ground like a sack of rocks. I spoke to myself. "'Cause somebody has to."

Jennifer collapsed to the ground, holding Charles's head in her lap and stroking Charlie's hair. I scanned the yard, looking for more targets, but it appeared that the fight was over. There were bodies everywhere. I walked around the yard, checking bodies, putting finishing rounds into any convicts that might need that extra push into the afterlife.

Meghan was lying in the yard with a convict on top of her. She had a knife in her chest, but he had three exit wounds on his back. At least she had taken him with her. Her eyes were open, staring up at the sky and the clouds that passed overhead.

Bill was still by the porch. He had collapsed into a praying position, shot through the chest by one of the convicts. I looked to my right and saw Susan and Justin lying where I had seen them go down at the beginning of the fight.

I walked over to Jennifer, where she was still sitting with Charles. Charlie was dead, but Charles was still breathing. He had taken a round in the chest, so his breaths were labored and bubbling with blood. Charles was on his way out. I crouched down beside Jennifer. I didn't say anything to either of them. I just sat there beside her until Charles passed. A few minutes after he was gone, I spoke to her.

"Jennifer, we gotta go." She didn't move and didn't say anything. "Jennifer! We gotta get goin'."

"Okay, I'll get a shovel." She started to move, but it was slow, like she was in a trance.

"Jennifer, we can't bury them. If we bury them and a convict got away, he can go back and get more of 'em. They'll know there were survivors and they'll look for us. We gotta let them where they are."

She looked at me like I had just insulted her.

"You gotta go get a pack together with a change of clothes, some food and water, and any first aid supplies you've got. I'll go around and pick up ammo from the ground."

Again, she didn't move.

"Jennifer!" I yelled again. "Let's go, we gotta fucking move here!"

"I'm not goin' anywhere until we bury my family. I'm not lettin' them out here to rot."

"We're not, and you will. I'm not gonna leave any trace of survivors. There's maybe fifteen of these assholes here—that leaves thirty-five or forty of them back in town. Forty motherfuckers that will track us and kill us. It ain't gonna happen. Now go get your fuckin' shit together so we can get the fuck outa here." With that, she walked away and went into the house.

I started walking around, gathering up whatever ammo I could find. My *Rock River* shot both .223 and 5.56 ammo. Contrary to popular belief, the calibers were not exactly the same and few AR rifles could fire 5.56 on a regular basis safely. *Rock Rivers* could. I was able to find maybe three hundred rounds of 5.56. I still had roughly three hundred rounds of .223, so I was okay for rifle ammo.

Outcast's Glock 21 was a .45, and he had two and a half magazines for it. I found another Beretta 9-millimeter that I took the rounds out of for Jennifer's 92 F. I picked up a discarded M16 for her also.

Once I had the ammo gathered, I went into the house and grabbed as much lightweight food stuff as I could find. Jerky, biscuits, ham, tuna packets, crackers. Anything that we could take that had minimal weight.

Jennifer came out of the house with a camping-style backpack that was a generic version of a Maxpedition pack. She was crying and still in a semi-state of shock. I could understand what she was feeling, but I needed her to get herself together. I didn't say anything to her. I just handed her the M16, two hundred rounds of ammo, and the nine-millimeter ammo.

"Let's go, we gotta get movin'."

We set out in the original direction I had gone in the morning. As we moved into the woods, I turned around and looked at the carnage that had been left behind. I couldn't believe the loss of good lives, over what? A pig? It was sad to think of the direction this world was going in. I retrieved my ruck and kept moving. As we walked, Jennifer continued to cry. I was alone with my own thoughts.

We continued to move in a northwest direction, skirting the perimeter of any type of town or city. Since the beginning of this, things had gotten pretty bad. As we skirted these towns, we could see burning buildings and bodies lying in the streets. The population in some places had obviously reached a point where other human life meant nothing to them. One town had a stack of bodies on the outskirts that people were burning because they didn't want to take the time to bury them.

Over the next couple of weeks, things were uneventful. We lived off food in our packs that we had taken from the house before we left and I continued to hunt and trap as we moved. We didn't eat like kings by any sense of the word, but we were surviving. Over time, Jennifer started to calm down and started to talk to me again.

She eventually admitted that she understood why I had done what I did with her family but that she was having a hard time thinking about them rotting away there. All I could do was let her vent because there was nothing I could do or say that would make that image easy for her to stomach.

We eventually reached the intersection of Route 56 and 594. We were maybe five miles from Josh's house. We followed 56 until we got close to Lucas Road in Homer City. Homer City was a small town in Indiana County. It had a population of maybe two thousand people. It was a small town but had a comfortable family-type atmosphere. You still had places to get groceries and any other services the residents may need. That had included everything from a pharmacy to a hair salon.

The entrance to the community we were heading to intersected with Lucas Road. I didn't want to mosey up to the place like I was supposed to be there because I looked like crap. I had a long beard, had lost at least twenty pounds, and was filthy. My plan was to approach in a nonthreatening manner and hope that I didn't get shot. We moved off into the woods and approached the community entrance from cover. When we got to the wood line, I dropped my ruck and pulled out my binoculars.

The roadway entrance was blocked off by two old cars with three guys on guard duty. One of them was armed with a bolt action rifle; the other two had AR15-style rifles. They were talking, drinking from canteens, and patrolling the area around the entrance. I tried to focus on their faces to see if it was anybody I recognized, but I didn't recognize any of them.

I was worried. Josh, Mike, and their families were my friends. I was afraid. What if they hadn't made it? What if they had been killed or had been in some freak accident and had died? What was I going to do then? These people, people who didn't know me, weren't going to take me in just because I asked nicely. The last groups that had helped me did so because I had helped them. These people didn't owe me anything. I decided that now was as good a time as any. I unslung my rifle and put my binoculars away.

"Look, I'm gonna go in first. If I get shot or something bad happens, stay put until shit cools down. Take what you can from my ruck and find someplace to go. Look for a fire hall or a police station that still has public service personnel around. If it goes well, I'll turn around and wave you in." I turned, took a deep breath, and started to leave.

"Woah, hold up. You can't just leave me." She was pissed.

"It'll be okay. I think we'll be fine. Just give me a chance to deal with this." I got to the edge of the wood line. Nobody had seen me yet. I unsnapped the thumb break on the holster of my 1911. If they started to shoot at me, I wasn't going to go down easy.

I put my hands up and stepped out of the woods and started to walk toward the cars. The guy with the bolt action saw me first. His rifle came up, pointed directly at my head.

"Stop right there. Do not move any closer or I'll drop you where you stand."

By this point, the other two guys had their ARs pointed at me. Rifle guy spoke to one of the AR guys.

"Ned, go get his guns. Check him good." I could have said no and pulled my 1911, but what good would that have done? So I let them do what they needed to do.

"Chip, if he moves, shoot 'im." Chip must have been the other AR guy. He then spoke to me again. "Who are you? What do you want?"

"My name is Buck. I'm here because I'm hoping that Josh or Mike are still alive. I'm family."

PART 2

A NEW LIFE BEGINS

The ultimate measure of a man is not where he stands in moments of comfort and convenience, but where he stands at times of challenge and controversy.

—Martin Luther King Jr.

1

"Dude, what the fuck?" Josh looked at his friend, amazed to be seeing him here, alive and well.

"Hey, brother. Glad to see you too." Buck hugged him, glad to be home. Glad to be back with people he trusted and could depend on. Josh looked good. He had lost some weight but still looked fit and ready for battle. His hair was longer, and he also had a beard now, but he was clean, and his clothes were washed.

Josh looked at Buck, still amazed that he was here. Buck looked good, thin. He had lost maybe twenty-five pounds since the last time that they had seen each other, but he looked healthy.

"I was afraid you were dead. Come on, let's walk. Tell me what happened."

Buck turned and pointed at Jennifer like he was turning letters on a game show. "Brother, this is Jennifer. Jennifer, Josh." They shook hands. "I found her along the way. I'll fill you guys in later."

The two friends walked toward Josh's house. The neighborhood looked like it had every time Buck came up to visit. There were cars in the driveways, although they weren't running, and kids were playing in the yards. If he didn't know better, it appeared as though nothing had changed.

Josh's house was a normal split-level single family home. When you walked in the front door a set of stairs took you up into the living area where you found the living room, kitchen, dining room, bedrooms and two bathrooms. Steps going down to the basement took you to a furnished basement with a third bathroom. As Josh and Buck walked in the front door, Josh called out, "Heather, come look what I found."

Heather was Josh's wife. She was a tiny brunette that was more of a firecracker with legs than a human woman. Buck always thought she had more energy than one person should have been blessed with. When she saw Buck, she ran down the steps and immediately hugged him. "Buck. Oh my god. It is so good to see you…but you stink."

Buck pushed her away. "I'm sorry, but I just *walked* from Washington, DC, to Indiana, PA. That's somewhere around two hundred and forty miles. I'm sorry, but yes, I stink." With that, he grabbed her again and squeezed her, making sure to get his armpits all around her face.

As she fought to get away, they all laughed like it was a normal visit. Buck looked up to the upstairs landing where he saw Josh's boys, Chris and Bill. They had grown since the last time Buck had seen them. They had filled out and had become teenagers. Chris had long unruly hair, and Bill's was short and neat. They both smiled.

"Hey, Buck."

"Hey, guys. You got big. Chris, you still look like a girl," he said. They both had *Sig* Sauer pistols on their hips and bolt action rifles in their hands.

"Sorry man, but we're headin' out to do some huntin'," Chris said as he started down the stairs.

"Yeah, we'll see ya when we get back," Bill chimed in as he, too, walked down the stairs.

As the two boys walked by, they both stopped to give him a hug. As they walked out the front door, Chris yelled, "Hey, Buck, you stink."

Smiling and shaking his head, Buck turned to walk up the steps. Standing at the top of the steps, he saw his other friend Mike. Mike was decked out in full gear. He was wearing a load-bearing vest and had his AR strapped across his chest, with a *Sig* Sauer P229 in a thigh rig.

"Dude, you look like shit," he said.

Buck started to laugh.

"You know, you can all kiss my ass. Now point me to where you guys take care of personal hygiene so I can take care of myself. I wouldn't want to offend your sensitive noses any more than I already have."

They had a wash basin rigged up in the backyard. Water had to be carried from a stream about twenty-five yards from the house, but it was a small price to pay to get clean. Buck changed out of his real tree camos and changed into his civilian clothes, which had been washed and packed before leaving the Guntrom residence.

Once he was clean and wearing clean clothes, he used his bath water to wash his real tree camos, socks, and T-shirt. After he hung the wet clothes on the porch railing, he worked his way back into Josh's house, where he found Josh, Mike, and Heather sitting at the dining room table talking with Jennifer. She dropped her gear on the living room floor and was sitting next to Heather, who was rubbing her back. She was crying, so Buck assumed that she was telling them about what had happened at her house.

Mike had taken off all his gear except for his pistol. As Buck crested the top of the steps, all three of them looked up at Buck.

"Damn, brother. It sounds like you saw some shit," Mike said.

Buck took a deep breath as he sat down at the table.

"Yeah. It got pretty shitty there for a while. You want me to start at the beginning?"

It took him maybe two or three hours to tell his story and answer questions. When Buck got done, he looked at Josh and Mike. They both had looks of disbelief on their faces. Buck actually chuckled. Josh spoke first.

"Man, brother, I'm glad you're here and safe. I can't believe what you've been through. Jennifer, I'm sorry for your loss. You are more than welcome to stay here, in our house."

"Thank you," she said. "I owe my life to Buck, and if you're all like him, I'm sure I'll be fine."

Mike chimed in. "I'm a better shot than he is, but other than that…" They all laughed until the reunion was interrupted by an old-fashioned dinner bell.

Heather explained that the community had been set up with a group mentality. The food was shared and distributed equally, with a cafeteria-style eating system that was set up at the pool house. It had a kitchen and grill that could be used and a room big enough that people could sit and eat. Everybody's laundry was done at once and together, three days out of the week. The clothes were carried down to the creek behind the community and washed then hung on lines beside the creek. They all explained that doing things in a group mentality made things easier and seemed to build comradery and a sense of cohesiveness.

As the group left Josh's house and walked to the pool house, Josh and Mike talked about how other things were worked. They had a hunter, scavenger unit that consisted of around eight people. Their job was to go out and scavenge for whatever they could find and carry back. Priorities were medication, food, and ammo. Secondary things like clothing, bedding, and toiletries were also high on the list of things needed. As they were out, any game that could be shot was killed and brought back to be used for feeding everybody.

There was a security team of maybe twenty people, led by Josh and Mike, that made sure that the community was safe for everybody. Patrols were conducted, and security details were posted around the development at the entrances. They were working on getting items to build walls, but it was a large, time-consuming task and was a work in progress.

Lastly, they had tried to use people based on skills and experiences that they possessed. They had a doctor and a couple of the women worked as her nurses.

Heather, being a guidance counselor, took over as a teacher and used their garage as a makeshift school to teach the kids.

Josh looked at Buck.

"Don't even ask, you're gonna be one of our security bosses."

"Okay," he said with a smile.

They all got to the pool house, and a crowd had built up outside. Buck and Jennifer were introduced as they worked their way into the hall to eat. Mike had walked off before they got to the pool and soon returned with his wife, Mia, a sassy blonde that Mike had known for years, and his father, Mike. Everybody called him Senior, even though technically, they weren't junior and senior. Buck had met Senior twenty-plus years ago when Buck had joined the ROTC rifle team and Senior was one of the instructors. Buck had been a friend of the family ever since.

After more hugs went around, they all sat down to eat. The meal was simple, venison and rice, but it had been spiced well and didn't taste too bad.

"Where's Tony?" Buck asked. Tony was Mike's son. He was in his early twenties and fit the part perfectly of a skinny college kid. But growing up hanging out with Mike, Senior, and all their friends made him more than capable with all sorts of weaponry.

"He's out with the hunters. Him, Chris, Bill, and a few other guys are on the H/S team. They should be getting back before too long."

After they got done eating, the group split up again. Senior, Mia, Jennifer, and Heather went back to Josh's house. Josh and Mike took Buck around the community, showing him how they had things set up security wise. The one entrance to the community was blocked off with a couple of cars that had been pushed down to the entrance. Cars had been moved around to as many openings between the houses as possible. It wouldn't stop anybody, but it would slow them down.

On several of the houses, they had built makeshift towers for lookout posts. Buck noticed that fires had been built at several locations around the perimeter of the community and were burning steadily. Mike explained that without electricity, that was the only way to keep any kind of light going for security purposes.

"Where are you getting all the wood?" Buck asked. "You gotta have somebody cutting wood twenty-four seven."

"No, a couple of the older people died not long after the power went out. They ran out of their meds and couldn't get any more. We've been slowly dismantling their houses, using what we can to start walls around the community, what we can't use, we burn."

"I guess ya do what ya gotta do," Buck said as he shook his head. As they walked, Buck asked questions and offered suggestions. He was kind of in his element. Once they were done with the tour, they headed back to Josh's house.

The next morning, Buck woke up early and started to get his gear together. He was planning on checking out the community on his own and introducing himself to people as he met them.

When he got outside, the air was brisk and refreshing. He could see his breath as he walked. Buck always liked cooler temperatures and loved the fresh morning air. It was like the air was fresh and clean and had not yet been breathed.

As he approached one of the openings between two of the houses, Greg turned and addressed him.

"Buck, right?"

"Yeah, I'm sorry, I forgot your name," Buck said as he put out a hand.

"Greg. Where you off to?"

"I'm just checkin' things out for myself. Seein' what's up." Greg smiled, still holding on and shaking Buck's hand. Finally, he let go.

"Okay, you be careful out there."

As Buck walked the perimeter of the community, several people came up to him and introduced themselves. They were friendly and accepting of his being there. He knew that things were harder on everybody, but these people seemed a little more at ease and looked like they had adjusted fairly well to the situation. His guess was that the community atmosphere, with jobs for everybody, gave them purpose and something to focus on other than the situation and how bad things were.

He was also able to see some security concerns and places that he believed fortifications needed to be made. He knew that Josh and Mike were working on things, but he would bring his concerns up to them anyway.

As he walked around the perimeter to the front entrance, he saw a couple of people working the security post. One of them was a pretty little redhead, who immediately caught his eye. She had long red hair, was short and petite, but walked around with a high level of confidence. She just exuded sexiness. She had on a tactical vest loaded with AR mags, an AR slung around her neck, and a Glock strapped in a thigh rig on her right leg. She was cute. Buck realized his mouth was open. He hoped he wasn't drooling on himself. Buck hadn't dated at all while he was in Maryland. He was busy working two jobs and nobody really grabbed his attention. But this girl did something for him. She looked confident, was pretty, and looked sexy as hell with all that gear on. As he approached the front gate, she turned to him.

"You must be the new guy. How are ya? I'm Melinda. Call me Mel." Buck was a little speechless and it took what seemed like twenty minutes to say anything back, but after what was in reality only a couple seconds, he was finally able to talk back.

"I'm Buck. I'm good. Nice to meet ya, Mel."

"This is Nick," she said as she pointed to her security partner.

"Hi, Nick, how are ya?" Buck asked as he put out his hand.

"I'm good. So what ya think of our layout here? It's not perfect, but it's kept us safe so far and people seem to be doing pretty good here." Nick looked around the community with a look of pride on his face.

"It's not bad at all," Buck said. "Everybody seems really friendly, and things look pretty secure. There are a few weak spots, but I'm sure Mike and Josh know what's up and are gonna take care of it. I'm just out trying to get a feel for the place and to see what's goin' on."

They stood there for a few seconds, looking out over the community. As Buck turned to continue his walk around, he threw a parting shot at Mel, making sure he had a playful grin on his face.

"Hey, if you need help seein' over those cars, come get me. I think Josh has a step stool in his garage."

"Fuck you, dork," she said with a grin on her face.

2

This was only the third day since Buck had arrived at the community. He was antsy and wanted to be out moving around. He had a hard time staying locked into the community activity. He was still getting used to being among people again and missed being out in the woods alone. He decided that he wanted to scout the area to see what kind of options the community had as far scavenging went. So after telling Josh and Mike what he wanted to do, he prepared his gear for a four- to five-day trip.

The weather had been staying pretty constant. It was the middle of May, heading into June. By this point, the temperatures were running in the mid-seventies. It was raining a lot, and it was starting to get more humid.

Buck decided to take as much water as he could carry and water purification items, as he did not want to be building fires. He didn't need to take a change of clothes or hunting gear. All he really needed was rain gear and ammo for his weapons. He asked Jennifer to borrow her pack, as it was smaller and better suited for his trip. Along with his battle belt, weapons, and ammo, he was carrying roughly fifty pounds of gear.

Once he set out, he began to remember the area. He generally remembered the countryside from when he lived in the area before, but things had definitely changed.

He was in no real hurry and had no real destination in mind. He was just out searching and looking around to see how bad things were. He stopped and rested regularly, drinking as much as he could to stay hydrated. It was hot. Buck had been out for three days working his way around the area, trying to avoid any contact with people. He eventually came to a clearing where he could see several houses and a sign that said "Dudley Manor Estates."

Dudley Manor Estates was a fairly new housing complex that had started to go up shortly before Buck had moved to Maryland. It was a series of single-family homes that usually ran anywhere between a hundred and fifty to two hundred thousand dollars. When Buck had left Indiana, there were maybe twenty-five homes in the complex. As he moved around the clearing, he could see that the size of the complex had nearly doubled.

Buck decided to wait and watch the estates for any type of human movement. By dusk, after not seeing any human movement, Buck set out again.

It was not raining, and the moon was bright. The moon provided enough light that he could move without too many problems. He worked hard to maintain noise discipline, focusing on heel, ball, toe movement, repositioning his feet if he felt twigs or branches underneath. As he moved around the perimeter of the complex, he kept his AR up, scanning in a one-eighty pattern, occasionally checking behind him for any sign of danger, checking his six as it was commonly referred to.

As he moved around the perimeter of the development, Buck saw that the houses appeared to be empty as there was no movement or activity. He decided to venture into the complex and see what he could find.

Buck moved to a portion of the clearing where the wood line was closer to a house, affording him less time in the open between the cover provided by the tree line and the house he was going to search. Moving with caution to a mid-size, single family home, Buck, with his AR up and at the ready, approached a set of double-glass patio doors. The doors had already been shattered, as he could see glass lying everywhere.

Once he cleared the doors, he entered what used to be the kitchen. It was fairly big and, at one time, had been quite nice. The kitchen table had been upended and was lying on its side. The stainless-steel refrigerator was standing wide open, with the smell of rotten food emanating from its open doors. The kitchen was separated from an eating area by a rather large bar type wall that still had plates and glasses sitting on it. The eating area was smaller but had a huge oak dining room table with five chairs surrounding it.

After moving through the kitchen, Buck moved into a living room that was furnished in all brown leather. The furniture was large-sized and overstuffed. A huge eighty-inch TV hung from the wall, with DVD, and cable boxes on a shelf beneath. Off to the left of the living room was a small half bathroom.

All through the house, Buck could see pictures of what had once been the family that lived here hanging on the walls. Family together and the individual family members stared from the pictures at him from tables and walls as he searched their house for things he could use.

Exiting the living room, Buck went down a hallway, lined with more pictures, that had a set of stairs leading upstairs to what he assumed would be bedrooms. Farther down the hall, Buck found a den/library that had a huge selection of hard and paperback books, along with a huge mahogany desk and chair. He would be back to look at the books.

Buck them moved back to the hallway and the stairs that led to the bedrooms. Upstairs, he found four bedrooms and a full bathroom. Three of the bedrooms obviously belonged to children, as the beds were twin-sized and the rooms had toys and children's belongings. The fourth bedroom was much larger and had a king-size bed, two dressers, and a second full bathroom. The house was clean, and had obviously been taken care of at one point in its life.

Once the house had been cleared, Buck decided to search the house for any supplies. Grabbing a pillow case, he went through the bathrooms first. He was able to find a few bottles of Tylenol, some toothpaste, and some antibiotics used for dogs. Most people didn't know that you could take animal medication. You just needed to take larger doses than what would be prescribed for "Fido." As he searched the rest of the house, he didn't find anything else of use. Entering the kitchen, Buck was able to find a couple of cans of vegetables and a twenty-ounce bottle of diet Mountain Dew.

Before the incident, Buck had been addicted to diet Mountain Dew, and this find put a huge smile on his face. Twisting off the cap, he took a long pull from the bottle. The crisp yet warm citrus flavored liquid tasted great going down, the carbonation tingling in his throat as he swallowed. He missed Mountain Dew…and cheeseburgers. He loved a good bacon cheeseburger.

Once he was finished looking for needed supplies, he decided to go back to the den. He also missed reading. Before the lights went out, Buck had been a vivacious reader. World War II history, action-adventure novels, and laughably, postapocalyptic thrillers. Looking through the paperback novels, Buck found a few books that looked interesting. He put them in his pack for later.

Once he was done with this house, he completed the same routine with a couple of others. There was nobody in any of the houses. The complex was deserted. It seemed odd to him that it was completely empty. He saw nobody, living or dead. It looked like everybody who had been here simply vanished.

Buck took another couple of days to work his way back to the community. It was a few hours past daybreak when he approached the front gate. Mel was working again. Damn, he thought, she was so sexy. When she saw him, she smiled and yelled.

"Hey, dork, where ya been?"

"Dork? Really? If you must know, I was out doin' some scavenging. Checking out the surroundings. I wanted to get a feel for the area," Buck said.

"Well," she said, "it's good to see you made it back safe. I'm off duty in a couple of minutes. Wanna get a cup of coffee?"

Buck had often said that if a girl was interested, she'd need to hit him in the head with a two-by-four, as he had no game and would have no idea that someone was interested in him. He wasn't sure if she was just being nice or if she was genuinely interested. Either way, he could use a cup of coffee.

"Sure," he said to her. "I'll meet you at the dinner place. Say, half an hour?"

"Sounds like a plan," she said as Buck walked away.

Buck worked his way back to Josh's house. Josh, Heather, and the boys were up and getting ready for whatever the day would bring. They all greeted Buck with smiles as he walked through the door.

"Brother, how'd your search go? I didn't think you'd be gone this long" Josh asked as he handed Bill a glass of water.

"Not bad. I didn't either," Buck answered. "I worked my way around until I found myself at Dudley Estates. It was completely empty. Nobody around. It's like they vanished. Anyway, I found a few supplies, nothing major. It might be worth another search though." He said as he looked at the boys and laid the pillowcase of goodies down on the floor.

"Do you want something to drink?" Heather asked as she put coffee on the table.

"No. Thanks. I'm meeting this cute redhead I met the other day for coffee. I think her name's Mel," Buck answered, feigning indifference.

Josh laughed. He knew Buck. He knew what Buck liked in women and knew that she was exactly what Buck liked. She was petite, had a cute little body, and was smart. She was exactly what he liked.

"She's a nice girl, man. Don't corrupt her."

"What's the story with her?" Buck asked.

Josh laughed as he answered, "She got hired with the sheriff's office a month or so before SHTF. She was on duty when it happened. She had no family to get to and lived too far from the courthouse to trek back to her house, so I offered her the option to stay here. She took it. And before you ask…yes, she's single."

Buck smiled and nodded as he headed back out the door to meet Mel for coffee.

When he got to the community dinner spot, Mel was already there, eating some instant oatmeal and drinking a cup of coffee. She smiled when she saw Buck and waved him over. He held up his index finger, signaling he'd be over in a minute and walked over to the counter area to get a cup of coffee of his own. He then walked over to her and placed his AR against the table.

"How's the coffee?" he asked as he sat down.

"It's hot and tastes like tar. So in my opinion, perfect." Buck laughed and took a sip of his.

"Boy, this could use some cream and sugar," he said.

"Are you kidding me?" she asked. "What kind of a pussy puts cream and sugar in perfectly good black coffee?"

Buck shook his head. She was giving him crap. He could see a mischievous smile on her face. He was really starting to like this girl. She *was* smart and had a hidden sense of humor. And boy, she was sexy.

They sat and talked for about an hour. She told him about her life. How she had been a teacher, how she had always wanted to be the police, and how on a whim, she decided to apply for the sheriff's office. She told him that she didn't have any kids, but had always wanted them. Her parents lived in Florida, but other than that, she had no other family.

Buck told Mel about his time as a sheriff's deputy, his time as a patrol officer in Maryland, his promotion to detective sergeant, the awards he had earned and the medal he got for saving a bank robbery suspect that tried to hang himself instead of owning up to the crimes he had committed. Finally, he told her about his walk up to Indiana from Maryland and all that he had experienced during the trip.

They talked about the situation they were now in, the things they missed and concerns they had for the future.

As they talked, Buck could feel his attraction to her grow. She was confident and coarse, but at the same time, genuine and honest. The longer they talked, the more comfortable he felt with her. He could see in her eyes that she was a good person. He had spent a long time trying to avoid being interested in anybody. As he thought about it all, he thought about how funny it was. All it took was the apocalypse to get him interested again.

3

The walk back to Josh's after his coffee date was nice. The temperature on this day was a rare anomaly and had soared, reaching the mid-nineties. Buck was in his own world and he didn't even notice how hot it was. He was thinking of nothing but Mel.

She had some other things to do before she came back to Josh's. Since she had been a schoolteacher at one time, her second set of duties included helping Heather teach the kids that were living in the community. Mel told Buck that she would find him and she would hook up with him later, maybe get some lunch or dinner if time permitted.

When he did finally reach the house, he realized that he was exhausted and dehydrated as he walked up the front steps to Josh's house. When he walked inside, Josh, Heather, and Mia were sitting at the dining room table, discussing things that the scavenger team needed to be looking for when they went out. Apparently, they decided to take Buck's advice and check out Dudley Estates.

"So," Josh said with a shit-eating grin, "how'd your date go?"

"It went fine, smartass," Buck replied. "She's a nice girl. I like 'er. But I am beat from my recon. I'm gonna get cleaned up and hit the sack for a bit if that's okay."

"Absolutely," Josh said. "You know where things are."

When Josh and Heather had built the house, the furnished basement had always been Buck's bedroom when he came to visit. When he showed up a week ago, he had naturally moved his stuff to the basement. He had noticed some other belongings there but hadn't given it much thought. He now knew that they belonged to Mel. He wasn't sure how things would work with them both just getting to know each other, but at this point, all he wanted was to be clean, get a glass of water, and take a nap.

4

When he finally woke up, the first thing that he noticed was Mel sleeping on another couch, over where her things had been the first day, he came downstairs. Buck went upstairs and found Heather working on an outline for the next school day. Heather asked him how he'd slept and asked if he needed anything. Buck assured her that he was okay.

Heather asked Buck that since he had been out pretty much since he got back, did he have any questions about how things worked in the community? She explained that everybody had some type of job as a way to contribute to the betterment of the community and that some people had a secondary job that they did to fill in and help where things may be needed. Using Mel as an example, she explained that since Mel had been a sheriff's deputy, she was used as part of the security detail. But since she had also been a schoolteacher, she helped Heather with the kids when she was needed. It was pretty much assumed that with Buck's background, he would be on the security detail and secondary on the scavenging team as needed.

As spring came to an end and summer came to life, things in the community ran as smoothly as you would expect with a group of people trying to survive after the apocalypse. Make no mistake, things were hard. Food was limited and the water became harder to find as the hot, humid summer progressed.

The hunter/scavenger teams started working almost around the clock, hunting for game and looking for anything that could be used for the betterment of the community. Dudley Estates had provided some canned foods and some other minor supplies but nothing that could be considered a miraculous find.

They made contact with another small community and had created a type of barter system with them, trading supplies that one of the groups didn't need for stuff they did need.

The security force was also working long shifts, ensuring that guards were patrolling the community twenty-four hours a day. Concerns had begun to arise with fears that with the limited food and water, normally passive, friendly people would turn violent as the need to gather supplies for their families grew more desperate.

In this new world, death was always around the corner. Everywhere, death visited the living for any number of reasons. As the loss of electricity continued, people not equipped for the stresses of living like they did in the old west started to die off. The elderly and ill, kept alive by modern medication, slowly died off as their medications ran out and the ability to resupply those medications became impossible. Without the needed medications, the natural scheme of things took over and these people passed on. The elderly and very young were ill-equipped to deal with the heat and died from heatstroke and exhaustion. As the number of people who died continued to grow, the issue of body burial became a concern. Where could they be buried? The bodies needed to be placed far enough away from the community to be safe for those still living there but also in a location where the decomposition would not interfere with the water runoff into creeks and rivers. That water was being consumed by the living, and any decomposition would make people sick, and there were no medications for the ill.

Children, who needed copious amounts of calories to support a growing body, became anemic and some starved to death. The old adage that only the strong survive was truer at this point in history than it ever had been since the beginning of the modern age. The weak just could not make it. Their end was inevitable.

Prior to the event and the loss of power, the threat of an EMP had been presented to Congress with requests for answers on how to properly protect the country from this type of attack. Studies had been conducted, and it was estimated that within the first year after a power grid failure that nearly 90 percent of the population would be dead. It had been almost five months since the EMP struck and nearly 50 percent of the civilians living in the community had died for some reason or another.

As time passed, Josh, Mike and Buck began to use the skills that they had acquired over their time in the military and in law enforcement to teach the hunter/scavenger teams patrol tactics to keep them safe when they were out doing their thing. They were also taught reconnaissance skills so that they could provide information on what was going on around the community.

The security teams were taught site survey skills to determine where the community's weaknesses were when it came to security. They were taught about fields of fire, squad movement, and urban combat tactics in case the community got attacked and there was a need for house-to-house sweeps.

The "civilian" members of the community were taught basic handgun skills as it became mandatory that anybody that was old enough to responsibly handle a gun was required to carry one. As ammo was in short supply, dry fire drills were practiced along with moving and shooting drills. The main concern was that the civilians learned how to properly manipulate their weapons and how to aim at a target if one presented itself. Although the civilians within the community had civilian-type jobs, it was felt that they all needed to provide security in the case of an attack.

But on a happier note, things between Buck and Mel continued to grow. On their off time, Buck and Mel spent all their time together. Their relationship grew until they were a bona fide item. As the days turned into nights and nights into days, a love that Buck never thought he could have grew into existence. They made love as much as physically possible, catching up on what he had missed over all the years that he had been alone.

Mel also expressed to him that she was also happier than she had ever been. The things that she had found so attractive in real men prior to the event were even more prominent in Buck. He was sweet and kind and doted on her, making sure she was taken care of and needed for nothing. As sweet and kind as he was, he had the ability to be a dangerous person. She knew about his military background, his SWAT experience and martial arts training. But with all that potential, when she looked into his eyes, all she saw was the gentleman that he was. He was compassionate, caring, and a gentle lover. He made her feel as though he couldn't live without her. She loved him more than she had ever loved anybody, and she was happy to be with him.

Jennifer had taken to the community extremely well. She started to open up to people and pitched in, doing anything she could to help out. She realized the difficulties with the community being able to provide for everybody and would often give things up so that others could have. She felt indebted to these people and wanted to do whatever she could to pay the community back.

Because she had grown up in a farming community, she had become what many referred to as a tomboy. Eventually, she attached herself to the hunter/scavenger team and, over time, came to be liked and respected by the group. Her secondary duties, of course, involved helping with the farming crops that the community had planted. She would stay after training sessions to ask more questions of Josh, Buck, and Mike, learning as much as she possibly could about patrol tactics, weapons handling, and team movement. She enjoyed the work and was good at it.

It was early evening, and Mike, Josh, and Buck had just made rounds of the community perimeter to check on the security team. There were two guys in overwatch positions on the roofs of a couple of houses, and a roving patrol was active and moving around the perimeter of the community. Everybody had ammo and water for the long night ahead of them.

Dinner at Josh's had finished; dishes had been washed and Bill and Chris had turned in early. They were getting up early to set out on a hunt and wanted to get as much sleep as they could.

Buck and Mel decided to go for a walk before they too decided to head to bed.

"How you doin, baby? You doin' okay?" Buck asked.

"Yeah. I'm doin' good. I want you to know how glad I am that I met you. You changed my life. This new world can be pretty shitty, but It's nice wakin' up next to you every day. I love you."

Buck was shocked. This was the first time the word *love* had been used.

"I love you too, baby. You know, I was single for a long time. I didn't want to be with anybody. Then when I saw you that first day at the front gate, that all changed. You swept me off my feet."

Mel reached up and pulled his head down to hers, kissing him. Buck had never really felt safe with anybody he had ever dated. He never felt safe with his wife when he was married. But when he was in her arms, he felt protected. His insecurities didn't matter, as his flaws were unimportant to her. He was safe with her. As they held each other, Buck heard a thumping sound. It was far off, but he could tell that it was a steady, rhythmic beat. It was a sound he was quite familiar with. It was the thump of a helicopter rotor.

Buck and Mel ran back to the house. Josh, Heather, and the boys had all gone to bed.

"Josh! Dude! Wake up!" Buck yelled, standing in the dining room. Josh came stumbling out of his room, running a hand through his hair.

"Man, what's up? I just fell asleep," he asked, scratching his chest.

"Did you hear the chopper?" Buck asked.

"Chopper?"

"Yea. We were out in the field, out back. I heard a thumping sound. It got louder, but I couldn't tell where it was coming from. I never saw anything—you know, lights or anything. There's not a guard unit around here is there?" Buck asked.

"Yeah, there is. There was a reserve engineer unit in Indiana and a Guard and Reserve unit in Punxsutawney. I'm not sure what they were though. There might be one around the Johnstown area too. You're sure it was a chopper?" Josh asked again, this time looking at Mel for confirmation. She nodded her head to confirm what Buck had said.

"Dude, really? I don't know what a chopper sounds like."

"Easy, brother. I'm still half asleep. Okay, do you mind checkin' with Tony and his guys? Let them know what's going on," Josh asked.

"Already done. Tony knows and is passing it on to his guys, although I suspect that they heard it too. He's gonna come get me if they hear anything else."

"Okay. I'm goin' back to bed. Come get me if anybody hears anything else." With that, Josh stumbled back to his room.

Buck and Mel went downstairs to their room. They lay on the floor, talking about the helicopter and what it could possibly mean to the community and to how things were going elsewhere.

On one hand, it meant that the military had indeed been able to at least take some precautions to protect their equipment from an EMP attack. So with that in mind, what could they do to help the public?

On the other hand, it was the military. Their focus would be keeping the country safe and rebuilding the infrastructure. Would their focus be on the people and keeping them safe?

They lay there and talked for a long time. Eventually, Buck's eyes got heavy. As Buck drifted off, with the love of his life in his arms, he was sure he could hear the faint sound of explosions and gunfire.

The next morning, after they woke up, Buck and Mel washed up and ate breakfast, which consisted of a cup of plain oats mixed with a few raisins.

Buck dressed in his woodland camos and grabbed his ruck, filling it with ammo, water, and food.

"Where are you goin'?" Mel asked. This was the second time that he had gone out on any kind of patrol. As time passed since his arrival, Buck had become one of the main leaders of the community. Most of his time had been spent with Mike and Josh, teaching everybody and helping to make sure that things were safe. Mel immediately got worried and was sure that he could see it on her face.

"I'll be fine, sweetheart. I'm gonna go out with the scavenger team today. I just feel weird about hearin' that chopper last night. I wanna head out, see what I can see. I won't be gone longer than overnight, at the latest." He grabbed her around the waist and kissed her. "I love you," he said, grabbing her butt for a little emphasis.

Mel giggled and slapped him on the arm.

"You're a perv, and I love you more."

As he turned around, Buck blew her a kiss and walked upstairs. Mel said a prayer for his safe return.

Once in the living room, Buck got with Chris, Bill, Tony, Jennifer, and the rest of the group. Once everybody had checked weapons and gear and were ready to go, the group set out.

Buck held back and brought up the rear. This was the first he had been out with the group since they had gone through their makeshift training. He wanted to see how they moved, how quiet they were, and what needed to be worked on later.

The group moved in what was called a Ranger file or a column. They moved in a line, each person approximately five feet behind the person in front of them. The point man was oriented to the front, with each person behind him, alternating the direction for fields of fire, ensuring that the flanks were covered.

Tony was walking point. Chris covered position two, covering right. A kid Buck didn't know was three, covering left. Jennifer was four, right; Bill was five, left; another kid was six, right; and finally, Buck was last, covering rear guard.

As he watched them move, he was pleased with how well they worked together. They moved slowly, stopping regularly to just listen. Their hand signals were good and crisp. Tony was a good point man. The only real problem that Buck saw was that they were a little heavy on foot, breaking a few twigs. Too many for Buck's liking. It was something that they would need to work on later.

The plan was to head to the trading community that the guys had made contact with earlier. In previous trips out, the H/S team had found a greenhouse with an abundance of planting seeds for just about every vegetable you could think of. The hope was that the other guys had some blankets to trade. Winter would be here before anybody knew it, and Buck's community would need more winter supplies like blankets and winter clothing.

The team moved through the woods for about four hours when they started to smell smoke and the unmistakable smell of burning flesh.

Tony stopped and kneeled, holding a fist up in the air. The rest of the line also stopped, kneeled, and held a fist in the air, maintaining their fields of cover and fire. Buck, staying in a crouch, moved up the line to Tony.

"What ya got, brother?" he asked.

"You smell that?" Tony asked, keeping his eyes scanning the woods in front of them.

"Yea. I started smelling it a little way back. How far is the other camp?"

"It should be maybe a hundred yards in front of us," Tony said, pointing straight ahead.

Buck gave a low whistle. When everybody looked, he waved his hand in a circle above his head. The team, knowing that this meant to bring it in, moved around Buck, maintaining a perimeter, with weapons and eyes facing out. They were good for a group of teenagers.

"Okay, listen. You guys stay here. You're the rally point. Tony and I are gonna move on to the camp and see what's up. If it's clear, I'll be back to get ya. If we come runnin', be ready."

Buck and Tony dropped their packs, only taking weapons and ammo. Tony, again, was point, with Buck scanning everything to the rear. As they got closer to the camp, the smell of smoke and burning flesh got stronger. The camp looked like it had been a small hunting camp of some kind. It was a clearing in a field, on the top of a hill, in the woods. A small single-lane dirt road led to the camp. The clearing held eight to ten mobile homes, with a slat rail fence surrounding the camp.

Several of the homes were nothing more than ash, having burnt to the ground. Buck and Tony stayed in the wood line, watching for any movement. They saw nothing. Once they thought it looked clear, Buck and Tony made their way forward. As they worked their way through the camp, they saw several bodies littering the ground.

All had been shot multiple times, and several were black char, having partially burned.

"How many people were living here?" Buck asked.

"There were maybe forty," Tony answered.

"Okay," Buck said. "Let's move trailer to trailer. Check to see if there are any survivors. Meet back here in fifteen."

The guys split up and started to check each of the remaining trailers. They found eight dead outside and three more in a couple of the trailers, but no survivors. As he was checking the last trailer, he heard Tony yell, "Buck! Get over here!"

Running over to Tony, he found him standing over a middle-aged male. The guy was skinny and scraggly, with a long beard. His clothes were ratty and worn. He had a gunshot to his midsection and a large gash on his forehead.

"He's alive, barely," Tony said before Buck could ask.

Tony continued, "It's Clark. He's the leader here." Looking around, he changed his mind. "*Was* the leader."

"Okay. Help me get him up," Buck said, bending over to pick him up. He was light and Buck was able to get him in a fireman's carry easily. "Let's go. Let's get the fuck outa here before whoever did this comes back."

With that, both men set out, heading back to the rest of the team.

5

The sun had started to set, and the community was beginning to meet at the field house for dinner. Lisa, Ben's wife, was inside finishing up the preparations of the meager rations that they had.

Mel, since her duties as the community school teacher were sporadic in nature, had started to help out elsewhere to help keep things running. One of those additional duties was helping with the cooking. People were mingling around the front door, waiting for their turn to eat and talking about anything and everything, trying to keep their minds off the problems of the day.

Mike, Josh, and Heather were in line, waiting on Mia and Senior to come down for dinner. Senior had been spending most of his days loading ammo in his shed, trying to stock up as much as possible for the security and scavenger teams. A couple of the younger kids, too young to be on any of the teams, helped him as much as they could.

When they arrived, they met up with the others, waiting their turn in line.

"How long have they been gone?" Senior asked as he got in line.

"They left around ten this morning," Heather answered. "Depending on how things go, they could be back as soon as tonight. Sometimes when they get a late start like today, they stay at the other camp and leave there in the morning. They could be back around noon tomorrow."

"Buck went with them?" Mia asked.

"Yeah, he wanted to see how they worked out in the field," Josh replied. "I think since he spent that time out in the woods coming up here, he developed a taste for it. I think he likes being in the woods. He hasn't had much time to get out there lately."

The friends continued to talk as they worked their way into the dinner area. As they sat down to a venison and rice concoction, the conversation continued. They talked about the issues the community faced with winter approaching. Even though winter always arrived, it appeared as though it was arriving quicker than any of them liked. All of a sudden, the door to the dining room flew open, one of the security guys stopping and looking around.

"Where's Doc Candy?" he yelled. Candy was the community doctor. She had been an orthopedic surgeon before the power failure, heading up the unit at the Indiana hospital. She was an attractive forty-five-year-old whose husband had died of cancer about five years previous.

Doc Candy stood up.

"Here!" she yelled. "What's wrong?"

The security guy ran over to her. Josh and Mike listened as he answered her.

"The scavenger team's on its way in. They got one shot."

Leaving their plates where they sat, Josh, Mike, Mia, and Heather ran toward the front gate, with Senior slowly bringing up the rear, the security guy and Doc Candy taking the lead.

Before they got to the gate, they could see Chris, Bill, and Jennifer leading the way. Buck and Tony were carrying somebody none of them knew on a makeshift stretcher. The two teenage team members that Buck didn't know were following them.

Doc Candy ran up to them, immediately taking notice of what injuries she could see.

"What's wrong with 'im?" she asked.

"He's shot in the side and has a massive head injury. We packed it the best we could, but he's lost a lot a' blood," Buck said as he and Tony laid Clark on the ground to be examined.

Doc Cindy pulled out a pocketknife and cut away his shirt. She peeled back the makeshift bandage and packing that had been placed over the wound, gritting her teeth at the sight of the extent of the injury.

"Okay, get him on a proper stretcher and get him to my place as fast and gentle as possible." Doc Candy pointed at the two boys. "Chris, you and Tad go to my place and get the stretcher."

When they got back, Buck and Chris lifted Clark up and placed him, as gently as possible, onto the stretcher. Buck looked at the scavenger team who were standing there waiting for some direction.

"You guys did fuckin' great. Go check your weapons, clean 'em, get something to eat, get washed up. Then do whatever it is you do to chill. You guys still say *chill*, right?"

"No, Buck. We don't," Jennifer said as she patted him on the back. Laughing, she took off with the rest of the group.

Buck stayed back and was getting ready to tell everybody what had happened when he heard footsteps. He turned to find Mel running in their direction, the obvious look of relief on her face. She had only heard that one of the team had been shot but not who it was. She threw herself at him, wrapping her arms and legs around him. He was laughing as he fought to keep himself from falling backward.

"Oh my god. I was so worried when I heard somebody had been shot," she said as she showered him with kisses.

"Baby, I'm fine. I'm okay," he said as he kissed her back.

Once he was able to pry himself free, he took her hand in his and started to explain to everyone what happened.

"Well, I told Josh about hearing what I thought was a helicopter last night. After we went to bed, I'm sure I heard what I thought was gunfire—way off and faint but gunfire. Anyway, we get about a hundred yards from this camp and we can smell smoke and burning flesh. Tony and I work our way to the camp. There are bodies everywhere, maybe eight or twelve." The group listened intently, hanging on his every word. "We check the rest of the camp, nobody. They're gone. It's completely empty. Tony said that there were maybe forty people living there. They were gone. All we found was burning trailers, and the people we found on the ground were dead. Whoever did this attempted to burn the bodies too."

As Buck spoke, Senior interrupted, "Who do we think did it?"

"Don't know. There was nobody around. The only one alive was Clark, and he was unconscious and wasn't talkin' when we found him. I didn't want to stick around and do too much snoopin' cause the damage looked fresh. I wasn't sure if anyone was still around. As good as these kids did out there, I didn't want to get too deep into shit with teenagers. We're gonna need to wait until Clark wakes up to see what happened. If he wakes up."

"Okay," Josh said. "Tomorrow we're gonna head back out there and see what's goin' on. We can't wait to see if he wakes up in order to get intel." He looked at Buck. "You up for another outing?"

"Fuck yeah," Buck said.

"Mike?"

"Yeah, I'm up. I'll let Tony know he's goin' out again," he said and walked toward their house.

The three women had gotten close as time progressed here at the community. That closeness could be seen as they all now stood side by side with their arms crossed. Heather spoke first.

"Let me get this straight. A group of forty people are either missing and or dead, and you three are goin' out with a twenty-year-old kid to try and figure out what's goin' on. Is that right?"

Mia was next.

"No, you're not going. We need you assholes here. What happens if something goes down here and you guys are out there, doing who knows what, maybe lying dead alongside the others?"

"Look," Josh said. "We need to know what's going on out there. What happens out there will start to affect us here. The more we know about that,"—he pointed out into the unknown—"the better we can protect you guys in here. It's called intel. It's how armies have been winning wars for as long as they've been around."

"We're not an army. We're a group of civilians trying to live with no food, water, or normal everyday supplies. That's what's important!" Mia yelled.

Josh put his head down. Buck knew he was right, but he was trying to win an argument with civilians that didn't understand tactics and the whole "warrior" mentality.

"Aren't you gonna back me up here?" he asked as he looked Buck's way.

"My better half hasn't said a word. I ain't getting involved with this," Buck answered as he pointed at the two irate women. "I'll see ya in the morning. I'm hungry and tired. I'm getting something to eat…then I'm gonna chill." As he walked away, Buck could feel Mel staring at him. He was going to get it later.

6

As Buck was finished washing up and was getting ready to lie down and read one of the books he had taken from that vacant house, Mel walked in. He gave her a look of "Please don't. I'm not in the mood to get yelled at."

She put up her hands. "Hey, I get where you're comin' from. I'm a cop too, ya know. I understand intel. And I understand the need for you to go out. I just want you to know that I need you here. I need you in my life. So if you do anything stupid and get yourself killed, I'll kill ya." She smiled, which made him laugh.

"I got ya. Nothing stupid."

Mel crawled into bed beside Buck. They laid there holding each other and soon fell asleep; the candle burned until it went out.

The next morning, things were not much better than they were the night before. The women were still upset, except for Mel, but the guys still felt the need to go out and gather whatever intel they could about what had happened.

As the guys got their gear ready, the women sat by and watched without saying anything. In the old days, the guys may have just left without saying anything, waiting to deal with the issues when they got home. But now, with the uncertainty of a safe return, the guys all conceded and walked over to their women, providing apologies for what they were going to be doing. When they were ready to go, hugs and kisses were given.

Before leaving for the camp, the guys went to Doc Candy's house to check on her patient. When they got there, Doc Candy opened the door before they had a chance to knock.

"Good morning, guys," she said. "He's stable. Still critical, but he hasn't gotten any worse. He lost a lot a' blood. If it's in the cards, it'll take him some time to show any improvement."

"Okay, Doc," Mike said. "We'll check on 'im when we get back. You be safe, okay?"

With that, they set out.

Once the guys hit the woods, they immediately formed a wedge. They were moving out to check on what had taken place at Clark's camp. They knew that somebody had attacked the camp and killed at least eight or twelve of Clark's people. Since they believed that there was the potential for contact with an enemy force of some kind, the wedge formation was the best formation to travel. Each of the squad members were approximately five feet apart and faced the same direction, enabling each squad member to engage the enemy from the front or the flank at the same time if contact took place.

The point position was Tony with his AK-47, since he knew where the camp was. Josh, with an AR was to his right, with Mike and his AR to Josh's right. Buck took the other side of the arrowhead with his AR and was on Tony's left.

They moved slow and steady, scanning the woods in front of them, looking for any type of movement. They were careful with fallen branches and twigs, keeping their own movement as quiet as possible.

With the slow, deliberate movement and time for breaks, it took the guys about five hours to get to Clark's camp. Unlike last time, they split up to gather information. Once they set a time frame of an hour, each guy took a side of the camp, staying in the wood line to maintain concealment.

Nobody saw any movement of any kind. The trailers had stopped burning and were just smoldering at this point. Death has a very distinct smell, and the bodies that had been left were starting to smell. After an hour of surveillance, they moved back together to exchange what little information they had obtained.

Moving into the camp, each guy moved in a low crouch, with their long guns up and scanning, moving from trailer to trailer checking for any hostile activity and any intelligence that they could gather. They found the dead bodies where they had been the previous day. They also found several 5.56 shell casings, along with a few .45-caliber casings. Scattered among the casings were several empty shotgun shells and a few casings that looked like they had come from bolt action rifles.

During the sweep, Mike stopped and let out a low whistle, calling the squad over to his location at the entrance to the camp. Once they reached him, they all took up a circular perimeter facing out for security.

"Hey, Tony, did these guys have any vehicles?"

"No. Not that I ever saw. Clark never mentioned anything either."

Mike pointed down to the dirt roadway that led into the camp. The tracks were thick, deep, and fresh. They had been made from some type of heavy-duty sport utility vehicle.

"Well, these tracks came from somewhere," Buck said, stating the obvious.

"Yeah, and did you guys see all the 5.56 lyin' around?" Josh asked.

"Yeah," Tony said. "There was definitely some kind of a fight here. But what happened to everybody else?" he asked.

Mike pointed to the tracks, showing the southern direction that the tracks made.

"It looks like they moved south. We gonna follow them or get outa Dodge?" They all looked at each other, looking for an answer to the question in each other's face. Buck spoke up first.

"I say we get outa Dodge. We are four guys against an unknown force. I say we head home."

"Okay," Josh said. "Let's head out."

"These guys don't look too bad. They move like they got some experience. They're not as good as we are, but damn, they look like they could do some damage if they wanted to."

The four-man team sat there and watched Josh, Mike, Buck and Tony move out. They picked up their gear and moved out, following the four friends.

"So, Top, how we gonna play this?" Al asked.

"Top" was First Sergeant Keith Jackson. He was the only African American in the four-man team and was also the team leader. Top had been a staff sergeant with First of the Seventy-Fifth Ranger Battalion before retiring. After finding a job as a bodyguard for high money CEOs, he got bored and joined the Pennsylvania Army National Guard in order to stay connected to his military roots. He was soon promoted to first sergeant.

About a week before the event had taken place, Top had been called into Alpha Company barracks on an emergency deployment training scenario. After a few days of mandatory equipment cleaning and weapons re-qualifications, the EMP hit. They had subsequently been told that they had now been reclassified as active duty and were required to stay.

Initially, everybody had been quarantined to the barracks, rechecking equipment and gear, making sure that it was in top working order. But within a month, they received orders to start patrolling the local area for intelligence on how civilians were handling things.

Top knew immediately what had caused the grid failure. What he couldn't figure out was how Alpha Company equipment and vehicles were still working. When he spoke to the Company Commander, Captain Altmont, about it, the answer he got was, "To not worry about it. They were working and that's all that mattered."

Once the intelligence started coming in, the company commander started receiving orders from Headquarters Company indicating that a Temporary Civilian Relocation Area (TCRA) had been set up and that all civilian personnel were to be rounded up and transported to the TCRA as soon as possible. Secondary orders were soon received, indicating that all relocation units were to confiscate all civilian weapons, food, and water, which was to be reallocated for government use.

Top had been deployed as a member of the TCRA relocation teams, but after the first trip, he immediately realized that what was going on was wrong. Team leaders were approaching civilians and telling them that martial law was now in effect and that relocation was mandatory. If civilians still refused to leave their homes, they were taken by force. If the civilians fought back, they were killed, citing treason as the reason for the military action.

Top decided that this went against his more civilized nature. He got together a few others that felt the same way, and he and his team went AWOL.

"Al" was Anthony "Al" Capone, no relation to the Mafia boss. He was the team medic and had seen two tours of duty in Iraq with the Tenth Mountain unit before returning stateside and taking a job as a medic on an ambulance. He had also joined the National Guard as a way to maintain his rank and status in the army and soon attached himself to Top.

"Let's just watch these guys for a while and see what they're up to. I don't want to make contact with anybody until I'm sure they're squared away. I don't want us to attach ourselves to a bunch of hillbillies." Top looked at the third member of his team. "Ben, keep that scope on them. Let me know when they're movin' again."

"Ben" was Kirk "Ben" Bennigan. He had been in the Ranger Battalion with Top and had been Top's unit sniper. When he found that Top was going back into the army, albeit the Guard, he decided to join up with him. When Top asked him what he thought about the relocation stuff going on, and if he would be willing to leave with him, there had been no questions asked. He rolled out with Top.

"Sure thing, Top. They're just sittin' eatin' now," Ben said as he brought the scope of his Remington Model 700 to his eye.

The last member of Top's team was Scott Ford. He was a little younger than the others and was extremely quiet. He had also seen action overseas in the desert in an infantry reconnaissance unit. His unit's job was hunting the Taliban in Afghanistan as a machine gunner on a Humvee. When he returned stateside, he missed the comradery and joined the Guard as a way to get some of that back.

His decision to go AWOL with Top and the others had been an easy decision to make when he saw how some of his fellow guard members were treating the civilians.

While Ben watched the four unknowns eating, Top and the others decided to take a break themselves. They were all dressed in woodland camo and carried standard issues large army rucksacks.

All members of the team were armed with M-9 pistols and M-4 rifles, except for Ben, who had the Remington and a sawed-off pistol grip shotgun to complement his M-9. After about a twenty-minute break, Ben spoke up.

"Hey, Top, it looks like they're getting ready to bed down for the night."

"Okay, guys, we'll do the same. If we all agree, we'll approach them in the morning."

The four friends set up a makeshift circular perimeter, each facing outward. As far as they were concerned, they were behind enemy lines, so light and noise discipline was a must. A lot of people didn't realize how far light and noise carried at night, but a cigarette or the knock of metal on metal carried forever.

They decided to alternate overlapping shifts for watch, with Buck taking first watch. First and last watches were the best. With either one, you got a full night of uninterrupted sleep. The middle shifts were horrible because your sleep was broken into two segments.

The night progressed with no issues. As night turned into day, each guy woke up at his own pace. Josh had been the last watch and was getting a breakfast of cold instant oatmeal and jerky ready for himself. As each person woke, they took turns keeping security while the others ate, switching so everybody got a chance to eat.

Buck and Josh were on watch when Buck heard a twig snap to his right. His AR immediately came up on target, which was a middle-aged black male in army camouflage and a black ball cap. His M-4 was slung on his back and his hands were up.

"Show me your fuckin' hands. You move and I'll drop your fuckin' ass. Keep them up."

Tony, Mike, and Josh jumped into action. Josh maintained his watch on their six, while Tony's AK was up and scanning the entire perimeter. Mike focused his attention on the wood line behind the black guy.

"I got another one. Hands, hands, hands. You reach for anything, you're dead!" Mike yelled at the second guy, who was dressed just like the first one. The black male spoke first.

"Easy, guys, we mean you no harm. We've been watchin' you. If we wanted you dead, you would be already. We just want to talk. By the way, I got a Ranger-qualified sniper and an infantry machine gunner covering you all right now. So I suggest we calm down and talk. I'm Top Jackson. This is Al Capone, no relation. His real name's Anthony, but we call him 'Al.' Can we talk?"

Buck, Josh, and Mike didn't say anything. They just kept their rifles up, scanning the wood line.

"What're we gonna do guys?" Tony asked, but nobody answered. The standoff remained silent for several minutes until negotiations started again.

"Okay, talk. But we keep you covered while you talk. And bring your sniper and spotter in," Buck said.

"No, if you keep your weapons trained on us, the sniper team stays out. It's up to you," Top countered, again sending the negotiations into silence.

Finally, Mike spoke. "okay," Mike said. "You bring them in, we keep you covered until they get here."

Top whistled and waited. A few minutes later, two more guys came walking in. They too were dressed like the first ones, but one was carrying a Remington model 700 and a shotgun, while the other had an M-4. Top made introductions.

"The sniper's Kirk Bennigan. We call him Ben."

Ben nodded his hello.

"The last guy is Scott Ford."

"What up?" Ford said.

Buck was starting to lose his patience. "Look, this ain't no fuckin' business meeting. Say what you wanna say."

Top smiled. Even though he had spent a lifetime in the military as a noncommissioned officer, he never understood the need to curse. But he did understand that under stress, people sometimes did.

"We've been watching you guys," He started. "You guys move pretty good and look like you got some experience. We need guys like you. We need guys that can maybe help us stop what's going on here."

Josh spoke for the first time. "What's going on here?" he asked.

"We saw you guys checking out that camp. What do you think happened there?"

"We don't know. Some scavengers got to them or something. We don't know," Tony said.

"Would you believe it if I told you it was your own military under orders from the president? Maybe not directly but an order through the chain of command."

None of these guys were fans of President Al-Buraq. They were at odds with most of his policies, both domestic and foreign. Domestically, he had forgotten about the working class and continued to take from them to give to the non-working class. He opened the borders to every foreigner that wanted in. He had continuously tried to take away the second amendment from the citizens, making it harder for them to protect themselves, while at the same time, he went easy on terrorists that attacked our people overseas. So it didn't surprise anybody that Al-Buraq would attack his own people.

Top started to explain. "Look, I don't want to use the word *conspiracy* because it didn't start out that way. This whole situation, the way it's being handled anyway, started during the Cold War. At that time, the country and its leaders—the presidency specifically—were deathly afraid that the Russians or a Russian ally would use nuclear weapons to attack the United States. They were especially afraid of an attack on DC, and rightly so in my opinion.

"The concern was not only the loss of life that would have taken place but the loss of government control. So in order to maintain a working government, a plan was put into place that would evacuate different members of the administration to separate locations around the country. These specific locations were set up in bunkers that would be able to withstand nuclear attacks. There's one in DC, one here in PA, a couple in the Midwest, and a few scattered out west. If one element of the administration was eliminated or contact was lost for an unknown reason, another would be able to step up and take over. They referred to it as Continuity of Government, or COG. Periodically, government officials would be sent to one of the bunkers and a practice run would be conducted. It's something that they continued to practice until recently.

"These bunkers are huge and can hold anywhere between three to five hundred people and the supplies necessary to house, clothe, and feed them all for extreme time frames. These bunkers are set up as small cities. So with this in place, the government will continue, in theory, to function.

"So, you ask, what about the civilian population and their well-being? Well, a number of executive orders were implemented and put into place. These executive orders each have a number and deal specifically with control of the civilian population. Each executive order permits the government to take control of some facet of our daily lives and needs. One deals with the seizure of any working transportation to include airways, waterways, seaways, and roadways. Any vehicle of any kind that works can be seized for government use.

"Another order provides for the ability of the government to seize all food resources. Farms and farming equipment, seed supplies, farm animals, anything used to supply food to the people can be seized. Others deal with heating and fuel resources, health and welfare functions, and they can even confiscate any and all weapons currently owned by the civilian population.

"Now, if that's not scary enough, there is an executive order that enables the government to mobilize civilians into work brigades under control of government employees. Think about that. They have the right to force you into slave labor, and if you refuse, any amount of force is authorized to get you to comply.

"I've heard that there are upwards of eight hundred camps in the United States. In the event that martial law is instituted, they come under the control and are supplied by FEMA. Each of these camps can hold approximately twenty thousand people and are completely self-sufficient with railroads, airports and roadways leading into the camps. It's rumored that the largest is in Alaska and can house two million people." Top stopped to let this sink in before he continued.

"I don't know this for sure, and it's just speculation on my part, but I don't think we were attacked by another country. I think we were attacked by our own government."

The guys all looked at each other. What Top was saying was not only scary but seemed a little far-fetched. Top could see the look of disbelief on their faces.

"Think about it," Top said. "This country has taken a shit. For years, the Democrats have made it harder and harder for the civilian population to purchase weapons, claiming that it's for their own safety. Mass shootings have fueled the presidency and the liberal administration to try numerous times to make gun ownership more difficult, yet all attempts have failed. The government continues to take away more and more rights from the people. Did any of you hear about the school in Texas that took the kids' freedom of speech? They wouldn't let them wear shirts that had the American flag on it during Cinco de Mayo celebrations. The Mexican kids could display Mexican flags, but the American kids were expelled if they wore or displayed American flags. Can you believe that?"

"What about this administration's decision to just forget about all the illegal aliens in the country and grant them citizenship. Who knows how many of them are criminals that fled here to escape prosecution? It happened in the eighties with the Cubans. Look how many of them were drug dealers, murderers, and rapists. In April 1980 after the Mariel boatlift occurred, it was found that the mass migration of Cubans, whom Castro had permitted to leave, had been released from jail and mental health facilities. If you talk to detectives that worked Miami at the time, they'll tell you, the bodies were stacked like cordwood because of the influx of criminals and drugs. It was a war zone down there. And it's happening again. This country cannot learn from its past mistakes.

"What about the refugees from these war-torn terrorist countries? How many of them were terrorists that this administration gave asylum? It's ridiculous.

"Well, the American population started fighting back. There were takeovers of government facilities and property. There were riots, demonstrations, and the demand for impeachment. When it looked like maybe something was gonna happen, an EMP hits, and now, due to COG, Al-Buraq has total control, and under a national security directive, his presidency continues indefinitely or until the crisis is over. And with the damage that the EMP created, it'll be a decade or more before this country is remotely back to any kind of normal. He got exactly what he wanted. He is now a dictator with complete control."

"Look," Josh said. "I wouldn't put it past the asshole to do something like that, but do you have any idea how many people had to be in on the conspiracy to get it to work?"

"Not that many," Top explained. "All that would be needed is a cooperative general that could get one nuclear launch pad unit to cooperate. One."

Top was an articulate speaker and had been easily able to grab everybody's attention. Ben, Al, and Ford had heard it before but were still mesmerized. Josh, Mike, Buck, and Tony were riveted to his speech but were at the same time skeptical.

"Where are the military units coming from?" Buck asked. He had been a combat engineer lieutenant, both active duty and as a member of the National Guard. He knew that as a member of the guard, you were more than likely serving in a unit close to your home.

"Right now, it depends on where you live. If you live in an area where a large military base is located, like Bragg, Benning, Knox, you're getting active-duty military. Here, they're using Guard units," Top explained.

"Look, Top," Buck said. "Josh and I are prior army. I spent some of my time in the Guard and I can't see a bunch of Guard guys, who more than likely live in the area of their unit, doing this stuff to their neighbors and family."

Ford spoke before Top could answer.

"You were army?" he asked. He looked at both Josh and Buck. "What were your MOS?"

"I was 12 Alpha," Buck answered.

"31 Bravo," Josh said.

"Nice, an engineer officer and an MP." Top looked at Buck. "I'm not salutin' you or callin' you *sir*," Top said as Buck smiled for the first time.

"That's fine," he said. Top continued with his explanation of events.

"Normally, I would agree with you, but what if your family and friends were promised the best food, facilities, and living quarters? Wouldn't you go? But people not connected to a unit member are forced into concentration camp-style barracks, surrounded by concertina wire-topped fences and forced to work crappy jobs." Tony spoke up again.

"So what do you need our help with?"

"We need help stopping this crap from going on. I can't stand by and watch a dictator kill his own people."

Mike spoke up first.

"Look, Top. We all got families back at our community that we gotta take care of. That's our main priority. We don't have the ammo or weapons to take on the army, Guard, or regular."

"He's right," Buck said. "I finally got the love of my life waiting back at our community. I'm not gonna risk losing her." He pointed at the guys standing around him. "These guys are my family. They're my best friends. I gotta help keep them safe. I can't commit suicide by taking on the army. Now if they come to our community and pull some shit, I'll do what I gotta do, but I'm not lookin' for it. And besides, how are we gonna stop something that's takin' place all over the country?"

"We can't," Top said. "But maybe if we stop it here, others will follow our lead."

"I get ya," Buck replied. "Top, can you guys give us a minute?"

"Sure," Top said. "But keep in mind that the army's searching for groups by breaking the area into a grid pattern. It won't be long before they find out where you guys live. They'll get to you before you know it."

Josh, Mike, Tony, and Buck stepped several feet away so they could talk in private. After spending the last hour talking with these guys, the friends felt that they were legit and didn't pose a threat.

After discussing what had been told to them, they decided that the best course of action was to let the entire community know what was going on. They would decide as a community what to do next.

"Okay, Top," Josh said. "We're goin' back home to let our families know what's up. We'll decide as a group what to do next. You and your guys are more than welcome to join us."

7

It took the better part of the day for the group to make it back to the community. Ned, Chip, and Jennifer were working the front gate. Mike approached the gate first to give Ned the heads-up. As Mike was talking to Ned, the others, along with the new guys, walked by, heading toward the community center.

Buck stopped at Ned.

"Hey, brother. How's Clark? He come to yet?"

"Yeah, maybe an hour or so ago. Doc Candy said he's still pretty bad, but at least he woke up."

"Any issues while we were gone?" Mike asked.

"No, nothing out of the ordinary," Ned answered.

Buck and Mike walked off, heading toward Doc Cathy's house. When they got there, they walked into the garage where she had set up her makeshift hospital, waiting room, and emergency room. If you didn't know any better, you would never know that it was a garage. It was set up with tables for surgery and containers of medical supplies and a couple of mirrors used to reflect light so that when the garage doors were open, sunlight would be reflected from the mirrors for any procedures that needed to be completed.

"Hey, Doc," Mike said. Doc Cathy looked tired and worn-out. She had bags under her eyes and her hair looked greasy and unwashed. Her shoulders were slumped, and she was shuffling around the room. He looked around the garage. "Where's Clark?" he asked.

"I moved him into the spare bedroom. He's awake and seems to be doin' better, so I moved him into a more comfortable bed."

"How you doin', Doc?" Buck asked. "You're lookin' a little rough around the edges."

"Thanks. You look like you're ready for a formal dinner," she said with a grin on her face. "I'm okay, thanks for askin'. I am tired. I got a cot set up in the hallway outside of his room. I'm gonna go lie down for a little while. How long are you guys gonna be? We both need our rest." They could tell by the look on her face that she was hoping that it wouldn't be too long.

"Not long," Mike said. "We just have a few questions. No more than ten or fifteen minutes."

Both guys walked into the house, walking through the living room to get to the second floor where the bedrooms were located. The house was a beautiful two-story with hardwood floors and beige walls. The furniture was tan leather, with pillows of forest greens and browns. The throw rugs and curtains matched and were a brown just slightly darker than the leather furniture. The beauty of the downstairs continued to the second floor where each room seemed to take on its own personality. Cathy had been single but had had a close relationship with her sister and her family who lived in California. There were several pictures of her sister and nieces on the walls, as well as pictures of Cathy in different places she had visited from around the world.

Clark was staying in the far bedroom that had been set up as a spare. When Mike and Buck walked in, it looked like Clark was asleep, but his eyes opened when he heard them enter. The initial look on his face was shock. He had never met either of the men, and when they walked in, they were both decked out in full gear with long guns and side arms. They were dirty and had a couple of days' beard growth.

"Who are you guys?" he asked as he pushed himself up farther in the bed.

"Easy, Clark. I'm Mike, this is Buck. We're friends. Doc Cathy told us you were here. You up for a few questions?" Mike pulled a small leather chair up to the side of the bed. Buck leaned against the wall by the door.

"I guess," Clark answered, still looking at both men with suspicion. Mike started the question-and-answer session.

"The guy you've been talking to about trades, Tony—well, that's my son." You could see in Clark's face that hearing that the two men were connected with Tony seemed to relax him. "Can you tell us what happened at your camp?" Mike asked.

Clark seemed to go to a different place. Fear returned to his eyes; uncertainty returned to his face. When he started to talk, his voice cracked. "I-i-i-it happened *so* fast."

"Look brother, you're safe now. Just calm down and tell us what happened," Buck said. He wasn't very patient and hated hymn-hawing around. He hated that when he was a detective in Maryland. When he would interview victims, they would always seem to get off track. Just tell what happened. If he needed more info, he'd ask for it. Clark looked at him and started again.

"We were out doing our thing. People were collecting wood, some had just come in from a hunt, you know—we were doing our thing. The same stuff we all do now. Well, we heard motors running. It sounded like big diesels. We couldn't believe it. Motors running. How was it possible when everything else couldn't work? All of a sudden, two of those big new army jeeps pulled into our camp."

"Humvees?" Buck interrupted.

"Yeah, Humvees. There were two of them and three big trucks." *Deuces and a half,* Buck thought but didn't want to interrupt again.

"We were all so shocked to see any vehicles that we all came out to see what was going on. A guy got out of the lead Humvee. He was in an army uniform, had a rifle kinda like yours," he said as he pointed at Buck's AR. "He had an eagle on his collar to. A bunch of other army guys started getting out of one of the trucks and the other Humvee. Eagle guy immediately yelled, 'Who's in charge here?' I told him that I was. As he was walking up to me, his men started to go around and take any guns that any of my people had. I mean, they even took .22 varmint guns.

"Well, he started to explain that the country was under martial law and that any gear, equipment, and food that we had now belonged to the government. He also said that we were all required to go with him, that we were now the responsibility of the government and that we would be placed into a secure, comfortable location. But the way he said it and the grin on his face made me hesitant to believe him. Before I could say anything, they started herding people towards the trucks." He stopped talking and closed his eyes. They remained closed as he told the next part.

"I don't know who it was, but a shot rang out. All of a sudden, all hell breaks loose. Eagle's guys open up on us with their rifles. My people start to run anywhere that they can to try and get away from the gunshots. I saw a couple of my people go down. It looked like they just exploded—they got hit with so many bullets. I went down pretty quick 'cause I was up close to the army guys, so I don't know what happened after that. The next thing I know is, I woke up here."

Buck and Mike looked at each other. Clark had just confirmed what Top Jackson had told them.

"Did eagle guy happen to mention his name?" Mike asked.

"I don't remember," Clark answered.

"Okay, brother, you rest. We'll get back with ya later." Buck said as he turned to walk out. Mike stood up and moved the chair back where he had gotten it.

"Do you guys know what happened to my people? I had family there, ya know." Clark looked broken.

"We don't yet. Not for sure anyway. We think people are being held in some kind of refugee camp. Like they had when Katrina hit New Orleans," Mike told him. "If that's the case, I'm sure they're okay." There was no sense in worrying him. Both men looked at each other again and walked out of the room.

8

After leaving Doc Cathy's, Buck and Mike immediately went over to Josh's. The situation seemed to be exactly as Top had said it was. The government had enacted martial law and was trying to imprison its population.

"Dude, what're we gonna do with these people?" Buck asked. "I'd go into battle with you and Josh any day of the week and twice on Sunday, but we can't hold off the army by ourselves and these people aren't trained for true battle."

"No, they're not, and we can't train them fast enough to get ready," Mike replied.

They opened the door to Josh's house and walked up the steps to the living room. Josh had washed up, and he and Heather were sitting in the living room talking about Top and his crew. Buck looked around for Mel, but she wasn't there.

"Hey, guys. Where's Mel?"

"She's at the pool house, helping to get dinner ready," Heather answered. "You guys seem to be doing quite well."

"Yeah. I really love her. It's good to have her in my life." He leaned forward like he was going to tell her a secret. "And the sex… wow." Heather smacked him across the shoulder.

"Buck. You are such a pig." They both laughed. Josh brought things back to the here and now.

"So, guys, how's Clark?"

"He's awake and seems to be doing okay," Mike answered. "Buck and I asked him a few questions about what happened. Brother, it's just like Top said it was. An army unit came to their camp and tried taking all their weapons and supplies and tried to force civilians to go with them to a camp. Somebody sent a round down range and set off a fight. After he went out, he doesn't remember anything. By the way, where are Top and his crew?"

"They're over at Chip's. He said he had a couple extra rooms they could use," Josh replied. "So since it seems that we are about to deal with a shit storm, what's our plan?"

Buck answered first. "Well, as I see it, we've got a few options. One, we pack up our gear and our families and get outa here, leaving everybody else to fend for themselves." Before anybody could say anything, he held up a hand, palm out. "I know, I'm not gonna do that either. Our second option is to stay here and fight it out with them. We don't have the resources or the knowhow for that. So the way I see it, our only option is to have everybody pack up what shit they need to survive and nothing more. Then we escort them someplace else, someplace safer. They only question is where."

Heather didn't look too happy about leaving. She and Josh had spent a lot of time and money on their house, and giving it up didn't sit well with either one of them. Heather spoke next. "How are you guys gonna move a hundred-plus people from here? That's a lot of people."

"Yeah, it is," Mike said. "But we really don't have much of a choice. Top and his crew can help of course. Logistically, it would be a nightmare. Moving enough food and water to keep these people living, not only on the trip to where we're goin' but also for the initial few days when we get there, will be nearly impossible. This ain't gonna happen tomorrow, but it'll need to be sooner rather than later. I say we talk to Top and his guys tonight and hold a camp meeting tomorrow morning to get the camps say on stuff."

"I agree," Josh said. "But right now, I'm hungry. Let's go eat." With that, the friends left the house and went to dinner.

Later that night, Mike and Mia, Josh and Heather, Buck and Mel, along with Top, Ben, Al, and Ford sat around a small fire and discussed the situation and what would need to be done.

Top told them that the reserve army unit that was causing all the issues was his old unit, the 786 Combat Infantry Unit. He told them about the commander, Colonel Lopez, who was a real SOB.

He and his crew had gone AWOL when they saw how the executive order was being interpreted and how it was being carried out. He said that when he had been activated, his initial thought was that he understood the order and that he understood the need to illicit help from the public. However, the interpretation and the severity of how they were handling things completely went against his moral and ethical ideals.

The 786, according to Top, was moving in a grid pattern through the county to accomplish their mission, and killing anybody that was not willing to cooperate or obey the executive orders. Top and his men had not been willing to participate in the administration's systematic order of assassination against its own people. They had not been the only ones to go AWOL. There were other unit members that had left to either defend their families or, as Top and his crew were doing, warn other civilians of the pending issues. However, enough had bought into the promises of better accommodations for their families, that they stayed and agreed to participate in the systematic killing and slavery of the American people.

As the discussion progressed, the conclusion was reached that the main priority was the safety of the community. They figured that the best way to do this was to move everybody to a place that was safer than their current location and out of the path of the 786. Essentially, they had to be moved to an area that had already been checked by the 786, affording them the ability to stay out of the path of the Army unit, thus avoiding detection.

The second safety concern was defendability. They needed to move everyone to a place that could be defensible if need be. Top knew that the 786 had cleared the southern end of the county up to at least the area called Saltlick, which was north of Blairsville, yet south of Homer.

Top stated that he knew of a waste management company that was a mile or two southeast of Blairsville that he believed would be perfect for the situation. He said that it had a two-floor office building and because repairs and maintenance of vehicles was done on site; they needed to keep vehicles in a secure location it also had a brick wall perimeter to keep people from messing with the trucks. He believed that it could be defensible if the need ever arose.

The next step was the planning of the move and the logistics involved. The ages of the people living at the camp ranged from teenagers up to people sixty-plus years old. The teenagers and middle aged would be okay, but the older people would need help with the walk and carrying their equipment. They would either need to find carts or build carts that could be used to carry supplies and the elderly.

Finally, what would be done about people that didn't want to leave? It was decided that there was not much that they could do. If people didn't want to leave, they wouldn't be forced to leave. It was their decision to stay.

The sun had set several hours before, and many of the community people had gone to sleep for the night. Mike stated that he would address the group in the morning at breakfast, at the camp meeting. As it was getting late, the group decided to break up to go to bed.

Buck and Mel stayed up and sat by the fire talking.

"Do you think we'll be okay?" she asked.

"I think so," Buck replied. "The biggest issue's gonna be the logistics. Getting everything ready to go, getting it all moved to where we plan on goin', and getting everybody on the same page. Moving a group this large, with the wide range of ages, it's gonna be a nightmare."

Mel was holding his hand and rubbing his arm with her other hand. She was staring at the fire, deep in thought. Buck had gotten to the point where he was able to read her mind.

"Don't worry about it, baby. We can make this work. All we need to do is get everybody on the same page. And I want you to know how glad I am that you're here with me. It really does make this whole situation seem better." He kissed her on the forehead. "Now let's go to bed. I'm tired." As she stood up, Buck smacked her on the butt, causing her to giggle. "Maybe you can show *me* how appreciative *you* are."

Mel turned around with a smile on her face, grabbed his hand, and walked him to their room.

The following morning, Buck and Mel got up at the same time. Buck was a firm believer that clean, serviced equipment would last forever and would work when needed. So when he woke, he decided to go over each piece of his gear, clean it, and make sure that it was in working order. Mel sat with him, watching him work and checking her weapons and equipment, asking him questions along the way about her weapons and what needed to be done to keep them working well.

Both his AR and 1911 were cleaned and checked. They were both in good working condition and had no rust or broken pieces. His ruck was loaded with his normal travel gear. He had ammo for both weapons, his gun cleaning kit, water, fire starting equipment, shelter, and some food. His battle belt had been checked and loaded with magazines for both weapons.

After finishing with their gear, he and Mel left for the meeting. They were late when they got there and found that everybody in camp was seated around the front deck of the pool house. Mike, Josh, and Top were up front. Mike was already in the middle of his speech.

"Clark is doing better," Mike said. "He is still in rough condition and is by no means out of the woods, so to speak. Buck and I spoke to him briefly yesterday. He told us some disturbing things. Some things that make us believe that the safety of this community is in jeopardy. He said that our own army came into his camp. They attempted to take supplies, food, water, weapons, and equipment. They then shot anybody that refused to obey the orders they gave. Our own army.

"Our main goal is to assure your safety and well-being. The army is moving north, searching for communities such as ours to force them into labor camps and taking everything you have to supply the government. Our options on what to do to keep you safe are limited. If we stay, they will eventually get to us. So we've gotta move you guys someplace that's safer and easier to defend."

There was a wave of protest before Mike could continue. People started shaking their heads and talking among themselves, causing

Mike to raise his voice. Holding his hands up as a way to get their attention, he continued to speak.

"Yes, I know. Our homes are here. But we can't defend you as well here." Top stepped forward and interrupted Mike, also yelling above the other voices talking back at him.

"Everybody, everybody. Listen. I know you don't know me from Adam. But I can explain to you what is happening and what will happen if you stay. You are not safe here." As the crowd started to calm down, Top continued. "When a disaster takes place, especially one of this magnitude, the POTUS has it in his authority to sign presidential orders that permit him and government entities the ability to move outside the scope of the constitution in order to maintain control. My old unit has been tasked with enforcing that order in this area.

"POTUS has signed a presidential order, making it law, that the military can use any and all means necessary to take your supplies, weapons, food, and water in order to keep the military going. Then in an attempt to 'help' you, the military can move you to a concentration-type camp and force you to work for your room and board. Any and all means includes deadly force if you refuse."

As Buck scanned the crowd of people, he saw the whole gambit of emotions on their faces. Some were worried, others were angry, still others showed fear, and some were a combination of several emotions.

"We only want you all to know what's going on," Top continued, "so you can all make an educated, informed decision about what you want to do. We will not force anybody to go anywhere that they do not want to go. But you need to know the truth so that you can make that decision with all the information possible."

Top stopped talking, and Josh spoke up next.

"Look, we aren't going to force anybody to leave if they don't want to. If you're willing to give up your supplies and let the government take care of you, then by all means, stay. When the army comes, surrender to them. They *will* take care of you. But keep in mind, you'll belong to them. You will no longer be free citizens."

Immediately, hands started going up, but people began talking over each other, shouting questions, voicing concerns, expressing fears.

"Where would we go?"

"How are we going to get there?"

"What happens if we run into the army on the way?"

All were legitimate questions and very real concerns. Many of them were questions that Buck had been thinking.

The leaders of the community answered as many questions as they could. If they couldn't answer them, Top and his crew answered them. Some of the questions went unanswered. The community would need to just wait and see.

9

The group knew that some of the community would want to go. How many, they didn't know yet. So after the meeting was over, they set out to plan the move.

As they saw it, they were going to have roughly fifty people to move. Maybe more. They figured that a lot of the older people would stay and people with younger children would also opt out of the move. So they would be moving the people and the supplies needed to support them.

Logistically, they would need to think about transporting as much food, water, ammo, weapons, and medical supplies as they could. They would not only need enough to get there but would also be enough to reestablish themselves when they arrived. And if need be, they would need to make two, or three trips to get all the supplies they would need.

Secondly, they needed to figure out how to deal with the elderly and children that did decide that they wanted to go. The young and old alike would slow the travel down, which would create a security issue. The longer they were mobile, the more of a risk that was created, and the young children did not understand noise discipline, which again caused a security concern. It would also be a health issue as older people and children wouldn't be able to handle the stress of the move as well. And stress did cause health problems.

The group also realized that their plan needed to remain fluid. Things would need to change and flow as the plan progressed, adapting to issues and problems that arose.

As the days wore on, their plan started to come together. Many of the house owners had utility trailers to use when working on their yards. Using these trailers, they were able to build carts that could be pulled by two or more people and could be used to carry the supplies. They were able to get eight trailers in all.

Next in the scheme of importance was water. They needed to take as much as they could carry. They began to collect and boil water. People were tasked with doing only this and, using any type of jug that they could find, storing water for the trip. One trailer would be used for just water.

Next was food. Each person was allotted a certain amount of food daily. That was the reason for group meals. Food could be made and distributed equally. Deciding what and how much to take would be complicated.

Jen, the woman in charge of cooking was pulled aside and used to figure out how to equally separate the food. As most of the food they ate was rice based, she was able to figure out how much rice each person would consume and how much each person would need for the trip. The other food was based on can and serving sizes. It was a difficult task but one that they were able to do as fairly as possible. Of course, the scavengers would continue to hunt and scavenge for additional food supplies.

Lastly was weapons and ammo. Each person could take whatever weapon and ammo they wanted, with whatever ammo they had for each. But each person was responsible for carrying their own weapons.

Once the carts were loaded, the group would move in a column, with the security personnel circling the group. Mike, Josh, Buck, Top, and his crew would move throughout the group, checking on progress, the group's constitution, and any security issues that may need addressed. The plan was looked at, revised, and changed as needed, addressing any problems that arose during the preparation and planning.

As the planning continued, the days turned into a week, then the week into two weeks. The scavenger group made more frequent runs in an attempt to build the needed supplies. Although the supplies available were scarce, they were able to find extra blankets, clothing, and jugs to carry water. And with a boatload of luck, they found an unmolested veterinary clinic in the basement of a house, which had an abundance of medical supplies which, of course, were confiscated.

Lastly, Top took Tony, Jennifer, Carl, and Jason, all members of the scavengers, to recon the waste management facility. The recon would tell them three things. Obviously, one was what kind of condition the facility was in. All this planning would end up being a waste of time if it was already inhabited or was not in an inhabitable condition. Secondly, it would give them an idea of the time and distance that they would need to travel. And lastly, it would give Top a chance to work with and teach the younger group some additional patrol skills and tactics.

It took them four days to get there. A four-lane roadway ran in front of the complex, on the north side, where the main entrance was located. Top and the scavenger group came in from the north end of the compound and stayed in the wood line across the roadway, looking for any sign of activity.

They then moved farther down the road, crossing into the woods, away from the complex. They worked their way around the wood line, skirting the perimeter of the compound. They found a brick wall surrounding the compound, which was about the size of a football field, sitting in a three- or four-acre lot surrounded by woods. A blacktop road led up to the front gate which was located on the north side of the compound. Beside the front gate, they saw a hole about the size of a school bus in the wall. It had been knocked in, but otherwise, the front wall looked okay. The front gate was a chain link fence, which provided minimum to no level of security.

Top broke the group into three two-man teams. Each team was given a corner of the compound to cover. They were to stay in the wood line and watch all four walls, looking for any movement or activity. They were prepared to stay for a few days if need be. Top didn't think it would take that long to decide what was going to happen next.

10

After a couple of hours watching the corners of the compound, Top called the group back together. Nobody had seen anything that reflected any type of possible danger.

"Okay, guys. We need to recon the inside. We're gonna check to see what's going on in there. I want you guys to see if you think it can be livable. I'll check out the security aspect of things. Anybody have any questions?" With no questions to be answered, Top issued orders.

Figuring the easiest point of entry was the hole by the front gate, Top moved forward, with the scavengers bringing up the rear. Knowing all about the fatal funnel philosophy, Top made sure to clear the hole quickly so as to provide security and cover for the scavengers as they entered through the hole.

Once inside, the small recon unit crouched down and scanned the area. There appeared to be no movement inside the compound. The open area of the compound was approximately a football field in size, with a grass courtyard in the center. On the right-hand side, at approximately the halfway point, stood a two-story office building with a large conference room attached at the back right rear of the building.

Along the left side of the compound were eight small garages. Apparently, each garage had been used to fix and work on different vehicles or for storing tools.

Top had Carl, Jennifer, and Jason move forward to check out the office building. He and Tony began a patrol of the courtyard and garages. The entire recon of the compound took approximately three hours. Once the recon was over, the scavengers and Top met by the front gate to discuss what they had found. Carl, Jason, and Jennifer reported first, with Carl being the spokesperson.

"Man, Top, that building is sweet. There's maybe thirty offices there. Each one's big enough to room three or four people. We'd need ta clean them out first, but the furniture in there's wood, so we could use it for firewood if we needed."

"Yeah," Jennifer chimed in. "And that back section of the building is a conference room of some kind. We could use that as a meeting spot or cafeteria. And there is a small kitchen in there. Of course, the water isn't running, but it could still be used to cook and serve food."

"Well," Top said. "The brick wall seems secure except for this spot." He pointed at the hole near the front gate. "The roof sections of the garages are high enough we can see over the wall for security measures. We could even put machine guns up there if need be... that's if we had machine guns."

The kids all started to laugh.

"You get my point," Top said with a grin.

Tony chimed in last. "That courtyard is big enough that we could plant a garden there come summer. I don't think we'll get a chance to plant anything there now, but next summer..."

"So?" Top asked. "Do we think this place is a go?"

All four of the scavengers gave Top a thumbs-up, indicating that they liked what they saw.

"Okay then," Top said. "Let's head back to the house and let them know what we found." By this time, the sun was setting. The group decided that they would stay the night and head back the next morning. Top took first watch.

The next morning, the day woke to a cloudy sky. It was not raining but had the dark clouds to suggest that it might. The small recon group gathered up their gear and maintaining proper patrol tactics, set out for home. With all their thoughts on the future, it was hard for them to focus on the tactical skills they had learned, but focus they did. All of them were excited to report back to the community what they had found, and how perfect they thought this place would be.

It took another five hours for the recon group to get back to the community, and fortunately for them, the rain had held off. As they approached the front gate, Mel and Buck were there working a security detail. Buck walked up to Top and shook his hand.

"Welcome back guys. Any issues?" Buck asked.

"No," Top answered. "Everything went smoothly. This is a good group here. They work well together, they get along great, and although a bit rough, their patrol skills are pretty good." He patted Jennifer on the shoulder. "The compound will work out great if that's what everybody chooses to do. I'll explain everything we found later. I'm beat, and I'm sure these guys are too. You think you could let everybody know we're back, maybe get a meeting scheduled? Preferably later rather than sooner?"

"Sure," Buck said. "Jennifer. You good to hang with Mel till I get back? I shouldn't be more than ten minutes."

"Absolutely," she said.

As Buck walked toward Mike's house, he could hear Mel and Jennifer laughing. The two of them had really begun to hit it off. Mel didn't have many friends and preferred to be a loner. But once she heard what Jennifer had been through with Buck, they became friends. Mel was thirty-five years old, and he thought that maybe Jennifer looked at Mel as a mother figure.

As Buck approached Mike's house, Mike and Mia were coming out the front door.

"Hey, brother," Mike said. "Everything good at the front gate?"

"Yeah. No issues. Top's back with the kids, and he seems to think the garage compound will work just fine. He wants to schedule a community meeting to tell everybody at one time what they found. You think we can make that happen? Later on, though, Top wants the kids to take a break, and he needs one too."

Before Mike could answer, Mia said "I got it" and took off.

"I guess that's a yes," Mike said as Mia ran off.

Mia had scheduled the community meeting for right after dinner. The rain held off for the rest of the day, keeping the temperatures down.

After dinner, everybody stayed at the field house and waited patiently for the meeting to start. There was a lot of chatter as everybody talked among themselves, speculating on what they were going to hear.

Eventually, Top hopped up on a picnic table and whistled for everybody to get quiet. “Hey, calm down everybody…calm down.” Top waited for everybody to get quiet.

“Okay. As you all know, a group of us went out to recon the site for a new living community. We checked out a garbage company in the Blairsville area. What we found is promising. It has a courtyard that’s about the size of a football field square, with a huge two-story office building with twenty-five to thirty offices that can be used as a dormitory. Apparently, the rooms are more than big enough to house four to five people per room. That’s room enough for a hundred, a hundred and fifty people.

“There is also a conference room area that is big enough to be used as a cafeteria, and it also has a small kitchen.

“The courtyard is surrounded by a twenty-foot brick wall. There is one section by the front gate that is damaged, but a repair of some kind can easily be made. There are several garage-type structures along the inner perimeter of the courtyard that are high enough that they could be used as security towers.

“I think this place is perfect for what we need. It’s big enough to house everybody comfortably and safely. It’s secure and can be defended if need be. I like it, and the scavengers that went with me like it.”

With that, Top jumped off the table and went and stood with Al, Ben, and Ford. Josh jumped up on the picnic table as the crowd of people started to talk.

“Listen up, everybody. We need to make a final decision on what we are goin’ to do. Are we goin’ to take our chances here, or are we goin’ to move? Are we all goin’ as a group, or are we goin’ to split up? Regardless of what we do, we need to make a decision so we can start doing whatever it is we are goin’ to do.

"Discuss among yourselves what you all want and take the night to think about it. After breakfast is over tomorrow, we can have a question session and then the decision will be made."

The following morning, after breakfast was over, the people had a lot of questions.

"What if the military finds us?"

"What about the people who can't move?"

"What are we going to do about food?"

"What if you don't want to leave your home?"

All the questions were valid and answered the best that they could be answered. Ultimately, it was decided that the community would be split. Those that wanted to move to the new location would, and those that wanted to stay would stay.

As was suspected when planning first started, the majority of the people that chose to stay were the elderly and families with little kids. They all believed that the move would just be too difficult.

Over the next couple of days, those that had decided to move to the new location began to pack their gear for the move. Two of the utility carts were used for necessities. One for water, one for food. One cart was then utilized to carry community items such as cooking utensils, blankets, spare clothing, and tools for gardening and ammo. The remaining carts were used to carry the people's belongings. They had been told to keep personal items to a minimum, with the group leaders having the authority to discard anything that was not deemed as essential. The only things permitted to be taken were those things that were necessary for continued survival. Personal belongings, other than a few pictures of loved ones, had to be left behind.

Buck had not come here with much, only what he could carry on his back, as well as his weapons and ammo. He repacked his ruck with his personal gear, and some other clothing, such as socks and a few T-shirts that he had been able to acquire during his stay at the community. It was the end of August. He knew winter would be arriving soon. During one of his scavenger trips, he found a green Carhartt jacket and a pair of tan Carhartt pants. They both fit him, so he had taken them. In today's world, you took stuff when you could find it. Without the need to carry food in his ruck, he was able to put them there.

Mel didn't have a whole lot of stuff either. The clothes she had she acquired over time, things that the scavengers had brought back for her. She was tiny and petite to begin with, but it was hard finding clothes small enough to fit her. Her Glock was hers and had been worn to work the day that the event took place. Her AR had been a department rifle, which she acquired when she decided to stay. Her clothes were packed in a box and placed on the community cart.

Jennifer did not have much to her name. Only the gear, weapons, and ammo that she had come here with, and a few items and clothing that she had acquired scavenging. As with Mel, her ruck was small, so her clothes were packed in a box and placed on the community cart.

Once the carts were full, they were ready to go.

Buck and Mel were both part of the security element. When not providing security, they would take turns helping to pull one of the carts, with Jennifer filling in when she could.

Mike, Josh, and their families also were packed and ready to go. The carts with food and water were checked and secured to ensure that none of the precious items were lost.

It was midafternoon. The sun was at its highest point, and it was hot. Final preparations were made. Top, Josh, Buck, and Mike discussed final security concerns. Al, Ben, and Ford were filled in.

The community members were all gathered together, saying their goodbyes. People were hugging and crying as friends and family were parting ways. Nobody knew what the future held or what would happen to each other, but everybody knew that more than likely this would be the last time they saw each other. Once goodbyes were over and the convoy was getting ready to leave, Senior walked up to Mike, pulling a small red utility cart. In it were several boxes of various sizes. Before Mike said anything, Senior spoke.

"Hey," he said, taking a long pause before continuing. "I'm not going. I decided I'm gonna stay."

"What?" Mike said, obviously shocked. The rest of the group started to gather around, anxiously waiting to hear what he had to say.

Senior looked at the ground as he explained his decision. "I'm too old to make this trip. My knees wouldn't hold up. I'd never make it. I would just slow you down. I'd be more of a hindrance than a benefit to the community." Holding up a hand to stop any arguments or protest, he continued. "I've made up my mind and that's how it's gonna be. I'll wait here for the military to show up. I'll let them take care of me. That's the least they owe me after all that money I've paid in taxes." There were chuckles from the group as he continued. "I told you that I've been loading ammo. I put a bunch in the community wagon, but I want you all to have this. It's all .223, .45, and 9 mm. Mike, I've put a box of 7.62 in there for that Socom of yours." He stopped to wipe an eye. "I love you all. Please be careful and take care of each other."

Top, Ben, Al, and Ford were limited to the gear they had carried on their backs, so they had agreed to help pull the community carts, while switching off to assist with security.

All total, there were eight carts and a total of sixty people, five of which were teenagers on the scavenger team, and eight children of adolescent ages. The rest of the community had decided to stay behind and take their chances with the military and the executive orders. The only bad thing was Doctor Cathy had decided to stay with the community, as the majority of them were elderly. Al was a Special Forces trained medic, so in the event of an emergency, the compound group would have a well-trained medic.

It was decided that the convoy would wait to move after it got dark. After the sun had set, the temperatures would be better and there would be less chance that they would be seen by any elements that wished to do them harm. The moon was going to be full and would provide more than enough light that the convoy could see what they were doing.

The scavenger team had taken five hours to travel cross country with only small packs, ammo, and weapons. During the logistic meetings, it was figured that it would take ten to twelve hours of travel by roadway to get to the compound. Breaks would need to be taken. People would need to eat and drink. However, security was paramount. Essentially, they were traveling into enemy territory. If things went well, they would be starting the first day of the rest of their lives. If not…

PART 3

THE COMPOUND

People can live free, talk free, go or come, buy or sell, be drunk or sober, however they choose. Some words give you a feeling. "Freedom" is one of those words that makes me tight in the throat—the same tightness a man gets when his baby takes his first step or his first baby shaves and makes his first sound as a man. Some words can give you a feeling that makes your heart warm. "Freedom" is one of those words.

—Davy Crockett

Our greatest weakness lies in giving up. The most certain way to succeed is to always try one more time.

—Thomas Edison

1

The night air felt cool and comfortable. The breeze was light yet refreshing, blowing through the leaves, causing a slight rustling noise. The birds were out, singing to each other, talking back and forth, trying to find a mate. The moon looked down on the group like a big white eye in the sky. The light given by the moon was clear and bright, providing more than enough help, guiding the travelers along the roadway.

The group was silent, not talking, or making any noise except for footfalls, breathing, and the sound of wheels and tires from the carts on the asphalt. The security element patrolled the perimeter of the group, with a point man stopping the travelers periodically to check around bends and to listen for sounds or any activity that seemed suspicious.

Al patrolled among the group, checking on everybody for dehydration or injury, ensuring that people switched off to get rest from pulling the carts. He encouraged periodic rests so people could hydrate or eat, making sure their energy levels stayed up.

Top, Buck, Josh, and Mike walked among the group to check on morale, knowing that in times of stress, and in unfamiliar situations, the mind began to wander toward fear, and morale would drop. Words of encouragement were passed along and shared with everybody to keep morale up and the fear of the unknown down.

Other members of the group, also stepped up into leadership positions, helping each other with whatever needed done. If carts were too heavy for one, some of the gear was moved to the cart of another, helping to keep everyone as healthy as possible and able to complete the journey.

Buck had always been an avid reader. It had been his way to escape reality and relax. As Buck walked security and watched the carts traveling along the roadway, he thought about the book *The Ghost Soldiers*. In 1944, the Japanese had held around five hundred American prisoners who had survived the Bataan Death March in a POW camp at Cabanatuan. The treatment that these prisoners were subjected to was brutal. The Sixth Ranger Battalion, under Lieutenant Colonel Mucci, conducted a daring raid and was able to liberate all the POWs before they were killed by the Japanese.

The book provided photos of not only the raid but also the aftermath as the rescued POWs and gear were moved from the POW camp to safety. As Buck watched the group of apocalypse survivors moving from one unknown to another, he couldn't help but see a similarity between these people and those POWs. They had what few belongings they could carry in carts. Everybody in the group had lost substantial weight from lack of food and the abundance of work needed to just survive on a daily basis. Both groups were moving from one unknown to what they hoped would be a better life.

Buck was both excited and a little scared. He was excited because he was proud of these people. They had worked hard to keep themselves and their families alive. He was proud because they had made tough decisions, all with the hope that they were the right decisions. He was proud because they had decided to take a chance on what they thought would be a better life. Buck just hoped that this was the right move. He hoped they weren't jumping from the frying pan into the fire.

After more than ten hours of traveling, the group was able to make it to what they had been referring to as the compound. It was around eight in the morning, and everybody was exhausted. The sun was up and shining down heat onto the heads of the weary travelers, heating the blacktop that they were walking on. Even the birds had stopped chirping, letting the world know "Screw this…it's hot."

As the group got to within fifty yards of the compound, they were stopped. The people were told to leave the cars on the road and to seek shelter in the tree line. They needed a break from the sun, and a security element needed to go forward to check the compound.

Top, Buck, Josh, and Tony moved forward, alone, to clear the compound and ensure that nobody else was there. Mike, Ford, Al, Ben, Jennifer, and Mel stayed back as a security element for the travelers. The four men moved forward in a diamond formation, weapons up and scanning for hostiles. Tony was at point, Buck and Top were on each side, with Josh was rear security.

As the sweat rolled off their faces and down their backs, the group reached the front gate. They cleared the fatal funnel created by the hole in the wall, entering the courtyard to find it clear of any threat. They cleared the garages that lined the left-hand wall, also finding them empty and secure.

Lastly, they moved to the main building which was along the right-hand side of the courtyard. By this time, the heat was beginning to hit all four men. Their shirts were soaked, and the sweat was running down their faces, into their eyes.

"Let's break here a minute," Top whispered. "Remember security and noise."

They maintained the diamond formation, taking turns getting something to drink, while maintaining 360-degree security. After a short break, the men moved into the building. It was warm inside. Without working air-conditioning, the temperature inside was not much different than it was outside. All the windows had been shut, creating a musty smell inside the building. After clearing the office space one room at a time, they found the building to be secure. It was okay for the others to come forward.

Tony and Josh moved back to the travelers and brought them forward to the compound, where Buck and Top stayed to ensure a secure arrival. Once the travelers were brought inside, everyone gathered in the courtyard area.

"Okay, listen up," Top began. "I know you are all tired—exhausted even—but we got a little bit more work to do. We checked the building where you all will be staying. Right now, there is enough office space for each family to have their own room." He pointed at two women, Sheri and Lisa. Jen had stayed back at the community to take care of those that stayed there. Sheri and Lisa had volunteered to be the food bosses at the compound. "I will show you the conference room, which we will use as our cafeteria and meeting room. It has a small kitchen, so it will work out nicely.

"As you can see," he continued as he pointed to the four corners of the compound, "we can secure this place with lookout towers on all four corners. It will take some work to accomplish, but it can be done.

"It's gonna take us some time to get this place where we would all like it to be, but with a little time and hard work, we will get it there, and it will feel like home. Does anybody have any questions?" When nobody said anything, Top continued. "okay then. We have the rest of our lives to get this place where we want it to be, so for now, get some rest. We will still need a security element for the night, so I'd like some volunteers. Chris, Bill, Tony, and Jessica will provide security for now. Carl and Jason, you rest a bit, then rotate them out. Once dusk hits, you will need to be switched out regularly. I want shorter shifts so people can sleep. It's been a long day."

With that, everybody broke off to look for rooms that they felt comfortable in. The security element each picked a portion of a rooftop to watch from. Buck, Top, Josh, Mike, Ford, Al, and Ben all began a walkaround, pointing out things that needed to be repaired or built. Things like the hole in the front wall and guard towers on the corners of the compound.

"I got some ideas for shower areas," Buck said as he pointed at some blue plastic barrels. "We can cut the tops off of those and put them on a roof to gather rainwater. We can run some hoses from them, down the side of a building. I'm sure we can find some hand tools around here we can use to build makeshift stalls and privacy areas.

"We will also need to either rig up some stuff in the kitchen or build a cooking area over by the cafeteria for Lisa and Sheri to use. Al, you'll also need to think about a medical station area," Buck said.

"Yeah, you're right. I want it on the ground level somewhere. I'd hate to need to carry somebody up a flight of steps if they have a broken leg or sprain…you get my drift? I'll look for a spot." With that, Al set out on his own, reconning the courtyard.

"Okay, guys," Top said, "let's get to work seeing what we have to work with here. Buck, check on tools. Ben, you and Josh go in and see who needs help getting moved in. Ford and Mike, take a look at that wall. See how much work we'll need to put into that to fix it. Me, I'm gonna walk around and get a better feel for this place and what's goin' on with it. If anybody needs anything or finds anything interesting, let me know."

With that, everybody set out to try to make this old garbage truck depot into a home for the future.

2

That night, while the group was asleep, the guys met back up to discuss what had been found. As the small buildings surrounding the perimeter of the compound were garages and work spaces, Buck was easily able to find all kinds of tools. Many of them were electric, which couldn't be used of course, but he was also able to find a plethora of hand tools that could easily be used to build just about anything they needed.

Mike and Ford reported that although the hole was pretty decent size, with the right equipment and tools, fixing it wouldn't be that hard.

"What do you think you'll need?" Top asked.

"Well," Ford replied, "we can drape chicken fence over the top of the wall, and tack it into the ground, so it will act as a containment wall. Then fill up the fenced in area with stones, cementing over the fencing, rocks and stones as we go. Once the cement hardens, it'll be good as new. So I guess we will need fencing, cement, and trawls."

"I saw some fencing and a couple of trawls when I was checking on the tools," Buck said. "I don't know how much fencing you'll need, but there's a few rolls in one of the garage areas. I didn't see any cement though."

Al spoke up next. "I found one of the garage areas that was clean and had a small office space in it. It'll work great as a triage/hospital area."

"Okay then," Top said. "Get your gear cleaned, get something to eat, and get some rest. Tomorrow we start working on this place. But for now, relax. Good job today, fellas."

The next morning turned out to be much cooler and overcast. The sky was dark and menacing looking. The birds were back out singing, and the breeze that was blowing was cool and refreshing. It hadn't started to rain yet, but it looked as though a storm was inevitable. As water was probably one of the most important commodities that the human body needed to survive, Buck decided that the first thing to do was take a few of those blue barrels he had found and get them ready.

Finding a pearl-cutting saw, Buck began cutting the tops off several of the barrels. He then carried them over to a wall beside the cafeteria. Cutting and reusing portions of the gutter system, Buck was able to rig five barrels to collect rainwater for drinking. The nice thing about gathering rain water was that it was essentially already potable. There was no need to boil it. It would need to be filtered to remove debris, but it was immediately drinkable.

Then he did the same thing to three more of the barrels. This time, though, he drilled a two-inch hole in each of the barrels approximately an inch and a half up from the bottom. Using several pieces of garden hose and epoxy he had found the day before, he was able to rig and glue the hoses to the barrels. Once the epoxy dried, he carried the barrels up to the roof of one of the garages. There was about a five-foot gap between two of the garages that could be used for showers. Once on the roof, he found an area where he could secure the barrels and drape the hoses over the side of the roof. It wasn't pretty, but it would work. Now all that was needed was the rain.

When he was finished, he looked out over the compound at the work being done. Everybody was hard at it, doing what they could to help make this old garbage depot a home. Top was supervising from the center of the courtyard. He had turned out to be a good leader. He cared about the people and had accepted them as family. His men were hard workers and took pride in what they were doing. They were loyal to Top and would follow him to the end of the earth. Even though they were new to the community, everybody in the group seemed to accept Top in a leadership role and were accepting of him and his men.

Buck took a minute to look outside the compound. At the main gate was a fairly large roadway. Cars were scattered at all angles, parked where their motors had stopped running. They were starting to collect dust and grime, remnants of what they used to be.

On the south and east sides of the compound was a forest, hopefully full of animals to eat and a place to gather water. He would need to go out there and recon to see what mother earth could provide them. Finally, on the west side was fields that he hoped someday could be fields of vegetables used to sustain the community.

As he stood there, looking at what was to become of what he hoped would be permanent home for him and Mel, he felt the first drop of rain.

It rained. And it rained hard for two days. Wind blew leaves, branches, and garbage all over the place, making the idea of even going outside an unpleasant thought.

Taking the opportunity provided by the rain, everyone took the time to set up their rooms. Furniture that was in the rooms was taken out into the halls to be broken down and used as firewood later. Some people, who had the ingenuity, figured out how to make beds out of some of the furniture and taught others how to do the same.

Once people had their rooms set up, they all worked as a group to organize and clean the cafeteria and kitchen area, again, moving furniture out of the room into the hallways to be broken down for firewood later.

That night, as the rain beat off the windows, Buck and Mel made love. It was passionate and long, kissing and holding each other into the far depths of morning. When it was over, they both lay there watching the rain and lightning through the window.

"Are you comfortable here?" he asked.

"As long as I'm with you, I'm happy anywhere," she replied.

"That's not what I asked," he said. "Do you think you could be comfortable here? You know, long term. Could you make this your home?"

She thought for a minute. "Sure, for now. Eventually, I'd like to have a place with a little more privacy, a place we could call our own, a place where the two of us could grow old together."

"I'd like that too," he replied. "Once things get set here, and things get organized, we can go out and see if we can find a place. Something abandoned. Something we could make our own." He lay there with a smile on his face. He had always wanted this type of love. Someone he could see himself spending the rest of his life with. They were then quiet, holding each other, watching the rain and listening to the thunder.

Over the next couple of months, the group worked and worked hard, making the compound livable. It was now October. The weather was getting colder, and the sun was setting earlier.

The scavengers made numerous runs, looking for anything that could be used for repairs or things that were needed for every day survival. The scavengers found a couple of gas stations/ convenience stores that had already been rummaged through. They had been pretty well emptied by either other people or the military, but the scavengers were able to obtain a few boxes of canned goods, some bags of rice, a few toiletries, and a few boxes of pasta noodles.

One thing they were unable to find was cement mix. Buck remembered seeing a prepper program on making bricks using mud. By mixing soil, water, sand, and straw, grass, or pine needles into a thick mud paste, you could create bricks. Buck thought maybe the same method could be used to make a cement-type paste to fix the hole.

Once the chicken fence was set in place, stones and pebbles were gathered and stuffed through the holes in the fence. Once a foot of stones were in place, the mud mixture was stuffed over and through the fencing. Over time, and with a good amount of patience, the hole was repaired. After baking in the sun for several days, the mud mixture became as hard as a rock. The same mud mixture was used for building a grill and stove outside the cafeteria.

A wooden fence was built for privacy between the two garages where Buck had hung the hoses for the showers.

Al, using some of the furniture from the offices, was able to furnish a pretty believable hospital room.

Using chairs found in the offices and pallets found in the garages or scavenged, guard towers were built on the four corners of the compound.

A dodge pickup truck was moved to the front gate for added security, and a pulley system was incorporated, making security personnel able to move it back and forth when needed.

Some people had primary duties that they worked all the time. These duties were based on previous skills or just preference. Lisa and Sherri liked what they called domesticated duties like cooking and cleaning, so they were placed in charge of the cafeteria. Mel and Tony were put in charge of the scavenger teams, while Top's crew, Buck, Josh, Ford, and Mike, were in charge of security.

Top, Ben, Ford, Josh, and Buck worked together to get everybody familiar and comfortable with weapons and weapons handling skills. Those that were unfamiliar with weapons and weapons skills were taught the basics first, then movement, transition skills, and cover and movement were taught. After a familiarity with weapons was learned, each person was taken on scavenger runs to practice squad formations and woodland and urban movement.

After a couple of months of hard work, the compound was coming together. The people developed an everyday routine. Each person took turns with each chore. Everybody took turns at security, scavenger runs, cooking, and general duties such as washing clothes and or dishes. The lifestyle of the Old West was in style again, and the community within the compound seemed to be finding a certain level of comfort with it.

One evening at the end of October, Sherri, a stocky brunette with a pleasant smile, approached Top and Buck as they were discussing upgrading some security precautions.

"Hey, guys, we need to talk."

"Everybody okay?" Top asked.

Sherri took a deep breath and placed both fists on her hips. "Yeah, everybody is fine, but we have a problem. Winter will be here before we know it. It's gonna start snowing soon. The scavenger teams have been doing a fantastic job bringing in what they can. Hell, Bill and Chris are out hunting every day. The gardens we planted got in late and just haven't produced enough to build any kind of substantial amount of produce. I've been rationing the food the best I can, but we will definitely not last the winter. If things keep going the way they are, we will have nothing by the end of December, beginning of January."

Top and Buck looked at each other. Buck had been afraid this would happen. After a certain amount of time, the scavenging just got harder. It was the nature of things. They had been unable to plant gardens until later in the summer.

"Okay, thanks, Sherri. We will get together and see what options we have available. We'll get back to ya later," Buck said. As Sherri began to walk away, he called after her. "Sherri, you and Lisa have done a great job with things. We'll get it figured out."

As Sherri smiled and walked away, Top looked at Buck.

"I hope so," he said.

3

The evening was cool and comfortable. A few birds who were late flying south for the winter were out singing. Grasshoppers and frogs were no longer out. October was that time of year where the days were still kind of warm, but the temperature at night was cool. The moon was bright and with no light from houses, buildings or cars, the stars were as clear as could possibly be.

After Sherri left and dinner was served, the guys all met to discuss the food shortage issue that was inevitable. There were really no options on what could be done. More frequent scavenger patrols needed to be completed, with more patrols into town to see what had been left in the stores and businesses.

"I think we need to hit town first," Top said. "We can clean out what's been left behind. Anything that is canned or bagged will still be good. I doubt we'll find much, but every little bit helps."

"Yeah," Mike said. "I was talking to Tony after they got back from a run. He said the store they hit had some stuff in it, but a lot of the cans had no labels. There was very little water, if any, and all the pop, chips, and bagged foods were pretty much gone."

"Well," said Ford, "we can check the convenience stores, pizza shops, any place you can think of that would have food products."

"We'll have the scavenger teams expand their radius and hit more houses," Josh said. "We gotta get as much as we can, as quick as we can. For the most part, the compound is done. It's secure, what needed to be repaired has been fixed, and we have the important creature comforts we all need. I say that we all focus on scavenging until we get the food issue taken care of."

They continued to talk, working out schedules, routes, plans, and directions. The following day, the whole scavenger group would take the carts they used to move here, into town. They would take the day searching as many buildings in town as they could, looking for food items, medications, and winter clothing. This was going to be an "early morning, late night" day. They had to work like their lives depended on it, which ultimately, it did.

The group woke up before the sun. They were all geared up and ready to go within a half hour. Gear was kept to a minimum. The only items that were being taken were weapons, ammo, water, and a few small food items for the day.

There were going to be three groups of four people. Buck was going with Top, Mel, and Jennifer. Josh, Ford, Heather, and Bill would be group two. Group three was Mike, Al, Tony, and Chris. Finally, there was Ben, Mia, Greg, and Jason.

Buck, Josh, and Mike, having worked for the sheriff's office, were familiar with the town and had drawn location maps for the only big store, convenience stores, pizza joints, and gas stations. The maps were broken into quadrants, with each group taking a quadrant. At the end of the day, each group would meet at the grocery store for a combined effort. It took approximately an hour to get into Blairsville, and once on the outskirts, the group split up into their teams.

Buck and Top took turns pulling the cart, with Mel and Jennifer providing security. The first building they got to had once been a Dollar General. There were a couple of abandoned cars in the lot, along with a couple of grocery carts. There was also an abundance of garbage littering the lot that had blown in during the storm or been dropped by other people who had been there scavenging.

The glass on the front doors had already been smashed in, so the quartet had no issues gaining entry. Buck and Top each had their ARs up and were scanning the store for possible threats. Mel had her Glock and Jennifer had her M9. Both had chosen to sling their long guns.

Once the store was found to be empty, Jennifer grabbed a shopping cart.

"Okay, guys," Buck ordered. "Whatever you can find, we take. Listen, most people don't think of vitamins in a situation like this. We are going to need those. If you find any, take them."

As they walked the aisles, they found pretty much everything had been taken. All they were able to get were a couple of rolls of paper towels, toilet paper, and a few boxes of protein bars. Jennifer did find a few bottles of multivitamins, which she placed into the cart. One thing that there seemed to be an abundance of were cans of dog and cat food.

Holding a can, Buck said with a grin. "You know, we might as well take these. If worst comes to worst, we can always eat it over rice."

"Are you out of your mind?" Jennifer blurted out. "Dog food? No fuckin' way. You'll get sick."

"Not really," Top answered. "In small amounts, it won't hurt. We couldn't eat three meals a day of it, but a meal a day wouldn't hurt. Besides, it's loaded with protein, which we will need. Let's do it."

Mel leaned over to Buck. "I can think of a few ways to get my protein consumption." With that, she pinched his butt.

Once the cart was full of stuff, they took it out to the cart in the parking lot. They then moved on to the next store. As the day progressed, things pretty much went the same. They checked a Sheetz, a liquor store, and a tobacco shop. A lot of the same items were found regularly, with a few lucky finds here and there. At one place, they found a family-size bag of Doritos. At another store, they found a couple of cans of mixed vegetables and a couple of cans of ravioli.

At the end of the day, they worked their way back to the main grocery store, which was a Shop-n-Save. They were the last group back.

"Well, how'd it go? Anything good?" Mike asked as they approached.

"Ah, okay, I guess. A lot of paper products, a few socks, and a shit load of pet food," Jennifer said with a scrunched-up nose.

"Yeah, we got pretty much the same," Josh said.

"Don't think for one second that I'm gonna eat pet food," Mia said with her hands on her hips. "I'll puke."

"Look," Mike said. "if it comes to starving, or eating it, you'll eat it."

"Yeah, he's right," Al added. "But we can't let the others know what it is. A lot of people will avoid it. But if it comes down to starving to death…" He let the sentence trail off. "Maybe Sherri and Lisa can tell everybody it's gravy."

"Well, let's do this last place and head back. I'm starting to get tired," Tony said as he walked toward the store.

Like all the other stores, the Shop-n-Save had already been broken into. Once inside, the store was checked for hostiles or any other threats. It had been hit a lot harder than the smaller stores. There was trash littering the floors. Some people had actually eaten in the store and discarded garbage and empty cans on the floor. The produce that had been left was all rotten and left a sweet, pungent aroma in the air. As far as edible food was concerned, it was virtually empty.

As Mike was checking the back stockroom, he decided he needed to use the bathroom. As he walked in, he could immediately tell that other people had also decided to use it. The smell of feces and urine was strong. He slung his long gun and focused his attention on his zipper. As the bathroom door closed on its own, he didn't hear the hammer of the large-caliber revolver being pulled back.

"P-p-p-put u-u-up your fuckin' hands or I-I-I-I'll blow your b-b-b-brains out!"

4

As the group began to load up the supplies that they could find, the double swinging doors to the storeroom opened up. Mike walked out of the storeroom with his hands up. There was a male behind him, with his hand on Mike's shoulder, and a large frame revolver pointed at the back of Mike's head. He was nervous. He was looking all over, his head turning in fast, short, jerky movements. It was obvious that he was unsure of himself. The first people he ran into were Tony and Buck.

The guy, with a shaky voice and obvious stress yelled, "Don't try nuttin'! I don't want any trouble! I just wanna get outa here and get home!"

Both guys had rifles slung, but Buck and Tony immediately drew their pistols.

"Drop the fuckin' gun," Buck said, his police training kicking in. "Drop the gun or you'll get dropped."

"I j-j-just wanna get outa here," the guy said, obvious nervousness in his voice.

"Then let our guy go. You can keep the gun and go, but let him go," Buck answered.

The guy maintained the hard grip on Mike's shoulder, backing up and away from Buck and Tony. By this time, the rest of the group, who had heard the yelling, came running from all directions to the sound of the noise. They, however, had their long guns up and trained on the guy.

"N-n-no way, you'll shoot me," he said. As the others arrived and started to surround him, he became more agitated and nervous. His voice got higher, and more stuttery. "S-s-s-st-stay away, I'll sh-sh-sh-shoot. I will."

Before anything else could be said, the guy slipped on an empty can of Spaghetti-O's left in the aisle by a former scavenger. He immediately fell backward, hitting his head on one of the empty shelves. His finger was on the trigger of his pistol. As a result of the pain from hitting his head, he inadvertently pulled the trigger.

The loud concussive blast of the pistol vibrated off the walls and ceiling in the store. The pistol flew from his grasp, more as a result of shock than anything. The round hit Mike at the base of his neck, right above his armor. The round exited his face, blowing off his chin and spraying blood, bone and brain matter all through the air. Mike never felt anything, collapsing to his knees then face first to the floor.

Mia screamed a shrill, piercing scream. Tony yelled, rage and anger flowing from his mouth as he pressed the trigger on his *Sig*. The guy took three rounds to the chest before anybody could react.

Mia and Tony immediately ran over to Mike. Frantic and emotional, they rolled him over, hoping that the worst wasn't going to be found. When she saw his face, Mia screamed again then just started to sob. Tony also started to cry but expressed his sadness by going over to the corpse of the guy, kicking it over and over again until he too collapsed to the floor.

The rest of the group just stood there, giving the two a chance to grieve, shock and sadness on their faces. There was nothing that could be done. Mike was dead. Top was the first to speak.

"We gotta get outa here in case somebody heard that cannon going off."

"Yeah," Buck said. "Ford, Ben, Mel, come with me. We'll go check outside to see if anything was heard."

Mel was surprised at Buck's reaction. He was hurt for sure. One of his best friends had just been killed. Maybe he was in shock. Maybe it had not really set in yet. Or maybe, she thought, he had just become calloused to this world and the death that it brought.

"Josh," Top said. "You and Al help them. Find something to wrap the body. We won't leave it here. We'll take it back to the compound and bury it there, have some kind of service."

"It…it…" Tony yelled, getting in Top's face. "He was my dad. His name was Mike!"

Jennifer rushed forward and put a hand on Tony's arm.

"Tony, Top didn't do anything," she said in a calm, soothing voice.

"Son. I know you're upset, and you have a right to be. But you best get outa my face," Top said, placing a hand on Tony's chest. "I understand your anger, but I didn't pull the trigger. And Mike is gone. This…" he said, pointing at the body, "was just a vessel."

Tony, either realizing what he had done or just not looking for an argument, backed off. He took Jennifer's hand and mouthed "Thank you," tears still streaming down his face.

The remaining group members began to clean things up and get the body ready to be taken back to the compound. A large tarp was found in the storage room. Josh cut it down so that its size was more manageable and, using 550 cord, tied the body up in the tarp.

The sun had started to go down. The bright light was beginning to fade, and purples, oranges and reds could be seen painting the sky. The temperature had begun to drop to more comfortable numbers, and the birds continued to sing. The sky was clear, and each star could be seen with complete clarity.

Once the body was secured, it was carried out to one of the carts. The food and supplies were moved around to other carts to accommodate the body. Buck, Ford, and Mel had set up a security perimeter as the supplies were loaded. Once everything was secured, Top, Ben, Greg, and Jason grabbed carts. The rest of the group provided security for the long trip back to the compound.

As the group approached the front gate, the Dodge truck blocking the entrance slowly moved out of the way as the cable was pulled. It was late, and the only people still up were the security element.

It had been decided that Mike's demise would be kept quiet until the following morning. Al, Ben, and Ford took Mike's body to a grassy area by the cafeteria and began to dig his grave. Mia and Tony stayed with Mike's body as the hole was dug. Heather, Chris, Bill, and Mel stood with them, providing emotional support for their friends. Greg and Jason then took the carts to the cafeteria where the supplies were unloaded.

Buck, Josh, and Top went around, checking the security element, making sure they had the supplies they needed and to check on the events of the day. Once all the work was done, the group went to bed. Mia and Tony stayed at the grave site.

The security checks took about an hour and a half to complete. After the security checks were finished, Buck had gone to the shower area to clean up and wash the events of the day away. He was exhausted and needed some time to himself. He needed to just crawl into bed and sleep until he woke up.

The sun that day had been hot and warmed up the water in the drums nicely. The feel of the warm water as it ran over his head, shoulders, and body felt refreshing, relaxing the tense muscles in his shoulders and back. He stood there, washing away the dirt, both literal and emotional, watching it disappear between the slats of the wooden pallet that they used to stand on.

After he had finished showering, he put on a pair of old sweatpants and a sweatshirt, wrapped his uniform into a ball, and strapped on his equipment belt. As he got to the center of the courtyard, he stopped. There was a light breeze blowing, which felt cool and refreshing on his still damp body. He dropped his dirty clothes on the ground and followed them down to his knees where he finally let go of the emotions that were attached to the death of his friend.

5

Buck was finally able to regain control of his emotions. He picked up his uniform and walked to his room. As Buck entered his and Mel's room, he tried to be as quiet as possible when he put his equipment on the floor. His rifle and 1911 always stayed close, so they went over by his bed, which was a sleeping bag on the floor. As he crawled into bed, Mel was there waiting for him.

"How ya doin', baby?" she asked as she rolled over to face him.

"I'm okay, I guess."

"Do you want to talk about it?" she asked as she started to rub his chest. She wanted to be there for him but knew that he was the type to keep things to himself. His response was what she expected.

"No. I'm fine," he said as he laid there staring at her in the moonlight coming through the window. "I just want to hold you." He took her in his arms and kissed her on the forehead, hugging her, smelling her, and feeling her warm skin against his body. Before he knew it, he was asleep.

Mel woke up first. *Woke* was a generous word. It would mean that she had slept, and she never slept. Her nights usually consisted of several one-hour naps, followed by bouts of staring at the ceiling.

She lay in her sleeping bag, watching Buck sleep. She loved him with all her heart. She had been single for a long time before he came into her life, often wondering if anybody could ever love the mess that she was. But he seemed to love her in spite of the mess, and that made him very special to her.

He had slept hard, snoring most of the night, which contributed to her sleeplessness. He seldom snored, except when he was utterly exhausted, and she could see in his eyes the night before that he had indeed been exhausted.

She rolled over and stared out the window in their room. The sun was just coming up, turning the sky from a deep black to beautiful shades of yellow and orange.

Mel didn't want to move. The nights were beginning to get cooler, which made sleeping even harder for her. Mel hated the cold. She wanted to stay here all day with her sleeping bag zipped up around her neck. She was petite, which made staying warm that much harder. But she knew there were things that needed to be done. In the new world, lazy days were nonexistent. She decided that she would let Buck sleep. He was still snoring, and she felt that he needed sleep more than he needed anything else.

Mel got up, wrapping a robe she had found previously around her shoulders. She shivered as she walked over to the corner of the room, where they had put a table with a bucket, water, a washcloth, and a bottle of vodka.

She washed her face and brushed her teeth. Toothpaste was in short supply in the new world, so they had begun using charcoal from campfires to brush their teeth. It was messy, but it worked, keeping the teeth as clean as possible. She first rinsed with water, spitting into the bucket, then she gargled and rinsed with the vodka.

Keeping up with hygiene was extremely important. The people of the old days were stronger and more resilient than their modern counterparts. They had built up tolerances to illness and sickness that modern man had lost due to cleanliness. Modern humans were more susceptible to illnesses than people in third-world countries, which the United States had now become, so making sure you stayed clean was important, even in the apocalypse.

Mel put on her gear and went outside. Buck never moved through the entire morning ritual; he had slept through everything.

As she approached the front door to the office building, she saw several people standing in the courtyard. As she approached, they turned and greeted her.

"Hey, Mel," several of them said at the same time.

"Hey," she replied.

"How's Buck doin'?" Top asked as she reached the group.

"He's exhausted. He snored all night and never moved while I was getting washed up. He's still sleeping," she answered, obvious concern on her face.

"Let 'im sleep, he needs it. Needless to say, yesterday was a rough day," Top replied. "I was just filling everybody in on what happened. A couple of people suggested and volunteered to go back to the community and notify Senior about what happened. You got anything?"

"No, I'm good. Anything special need done today?" she asked.

"No, not really. Just more of the same. We need security rotated out, hunting needs done, repairs on things need done…you know, more of the same," Top said with a grin. "Why don't you just be a jack-of-all-trades? Fill in where it's needed, then move on to the next job."

"Works for me," Mel said.

"Denny and Jenny volunteered to make notification," Top said as he nodded at two twenty-something community members. "Greg and Jason will be security detail. The rest of you know your jobs. Get ahold of me if you need anything. If nobody has any questions or concerns…let's get to it."

Before Mel could turn to leave, Top stopped her.

"Mel, hang out here a minute. I wanna talk with ya."

As the rest of the group broke off to cover their details, Top pulled Mel aside.

"How's Buck doin, really?" Top asked.

"I don't know. He showered before he got to the room. He was gone for a while. When he got to our room, he seemed okay, but he didn't want to talk. He fell asleep almost immediately."

"Okay, well, keep an eye on 'im. If he seems to be agitated, hostile, or feeling guilty or has trouble sleeping, let me know. It's a sign of issues in dealing with what happened to Mike."

"I will. Thanks, Top. How 'er Mia and Tony?"

"Well, as would be expected. Distraught. They were by the grave site all night. They both just went to their rooms. We have a ceremony planned as soon as Denny and Jenny get back."

"Do you think Senior will still be there?" Mel asked. "I thought the military was rounding everybody up?"

"They may not have gotten there yet," Top said. "Even with vehicles, it takes a while to do a town by town search and go house to house. You also have little communities outside of and between the towns. It'll take a bit. On the other hand, they could be gone. Either way, we'll have the ceremony when they get back."

"Okay, Top," Mel said as she patted Top on the shoulder. "Let me know if you need anything from me." With that, Mel set out to find a job to do.

Denny was twenty-six years old. He had been working at Walmart as a mechanic before the event and had no real purpose in what he wanted to do in his life. He had seen people work all their lives and have nothing to show for it. He had wanted to enjoy his life.

Then the event happened, and he was trapped in this new world with nothing to do but try to survive.

As he stood by the front gate waiting for Jenny, Denny tried to hide his excitement about this little trip. It had been a couple of months since he had moved here, and he had spent a lot of time working on the upgrades for the compound. When he told them he had been a mechanic, they compound leaders made it clear that his expertise was needed with a lot of the maintenance stuff. Because the compound had needed a lot of work to make it into what they wanted it to be, he had not been out of the compound for the entire time he had been here. Getting out for a couple of days would be nice. And besides, Jenny was going, and he kind of had a thing for her. He was shy and didn't have the nerve to say anything to her. He was hoping that this trip would bring them closer together.

He wasn't sure she was interested, though. He was kind of soft. Mechanic work wasn't real strenuous, and he did like to eat. But he had lost weight since the electric stopped—hell, everybody had—but he was still soft. He noticed that she paid a lot of attention to Ford. Why wouldn't she? These military guys were hard and confident. Who would pick shy and soft over hard and confident?

He looked up and saw Jenny walking toward him. She was of average height with blond hair. She was cute and chubby, with just enough meat on her bones to make her appealing to Denny. She was wearing khakis, a polo shirt, and carried a snub nose .38 and a shotgun.

"You ready there, sunshine?" he said as she approached.

"Yeah, I think I got everything I need," she said with a smile. "How 'bout you? You ready?"

He looked into her eyes, thinking about how pretty he thought she was. "Yeah, I got everything I need." And with that, they set out.

The gunshots sounded like cannon fire. Boom…boom…boom. Buck had his 1911 drawn, low ready, searching for the threat. He couldn't find it. No matter how hard he looked, he couldn't find it. He kept moving, kept looking. At first, he was in a room; it was dark. Not dark enough that he couldn't see, more like dusk. Boom…boom…boom. Then he was outside, in a forest. The trees went on forever. It was still dusk, but there was no moon. Boom…boom…boom. He couldn't find the threat. Boom…boom…boom…

Jennifer was knocking on Buck's door, but there was no answer. Twelve times she had knocked, so she decided to leave and check back later.

She turned to leave and got about halfway down the hall when she heard Buck's door open.

"Hey," he said, all groggy and half asleep. She could see he had that look in his eyes as though he was awake physically but his mind was still sleeping.

"Sorry. I didn't think you'd still be sleepin'."

"Yeah, me neither. What time is it?" Buck asked as Jennifer checked her watch.

"It's 11:05."

"Holy shit. I never sleep this late. Everything okay?" he asked as he stepped away from the door to let her into his room.

"Yeah, yeah. Everything's fine. I just wanted to check on you. See how you're doin'," she said as she sat down. "You know, I got a little experience with losing people in that way." She smiled, trying to be witty about the situation.

"I'm fine. It sucks losing a friend, but I can deal with it. I've got to. I've got a ton of people looking to me for guidance. I've got Mel, you, I've got these people… It's one of those 'It is what it is' moments. He's gone, it sucks, move the fuck on. Just like I told you when your family was taken."

She sat there a moment and looked into his eyes. They had become close friends over the past months. He had saved her life specifically and was partly responsible for keeping this group of survivors alive. He needed to be focused and had to have his mind right. What she saw in his eyes was a tired guy, but he was focused. She could see that.

"You know, I can see in your face you're good. But that doesn't mean you will be tomorrow, or the next day, or the day after that. If that day comes, when you aren't good, I'm here if you need me." She hugged him, thanked him for everything he had done for her, and walked to the door. "Mel's at the gate doin' security. I'll let her know you're up." She walked out, closing the door behind her.

Buck stood there a second. Jennifer had become like a sister to him. Her support was so important, and he was glad he had it. He smiled to himself and went to brush his teeth. Damn, he hated the taste of charcoal.

6

Denny had been walking point. He was trying to remember all the things that he had been taught by the other guys at the compound. Scan back and forth. Look for any threats. Watch where you step. Maintain noise discipline. Don't talk. Use hand signals. If you do talk, whisper. There was so much on his mind, and it all had to do with just walking. Soldier work was tough. Jenny was rear guard, and Denny assumed she was doing and thinking the same things.

Jenny was thinking, but she was thinking about Denny. She wasn't sure how she felt about him. He was a nice enough guy, and he doted on her every chance he got. *And*, she thought, *it's not like the selection of guys is endless.*

But Ford was good-looking. He was a bit older than she was, but what did that matter? He was nice, he was tough, and so good-looking.

Then again, should she really be thinking about any kind of relationship now? Who knew how long she'd be alive? She could die today for all she knew. Maybe that was why she should be thinking about a relationship. With things being so unpredictable, maybe getting into a relationship was the right thing to do.

She didn't know what to do. She felt like she was in high school again, which made her feel immature and stupid. She just needed to focus on the task at hand. Noise discipline, security, getting back to the compound alive, and making sure Denny did the same.

It took them five hours to get to the community. They had made good time. They stood just inside the wood line and watched to see if they could see any movement. Jenny had her binoculars out, looking from one house to the next, looking for anything from a curtain moving to people walking around.

"Do you see anything?" Denny asked.

"I don't see anything. There's no movement at all, but several of the houses are smoldering like they've been on fire…wait. I see a couple bodies. Not sure whom they belong to." She handed the binoculars to Denny.

"Yeah, I see them," he said. "What'd ya wanna do?"

"Let's go in on opposite sides," she said. "Do kinda like a grid search and meet up in the middle."

"Okay," Denny said. "I'll head left, you take right. Let's say a half hour. If either of us is not there, wait fifteen. If we're still not there, take off. You okay with that?"

"Yeah, sounds good to me."

Denny agreed, but he knew as he said it, he would not go without her.

They both stood to leave. As they got about ten feet apart, Denny called out Jenny's name.

"Hey, be careful. I don't want to lose you." He smiled as he turned and walked away.

Jenny moved at a crouch, checking between houses as she walked along the perimeter of the community. When she got to the middle of the perimeter, she stopped at a corner of a house, squatting down to just listen. She could not hear anything, but she could smell burning wood, smoke and what she thought was the sweet, pungent aroma of rotting flesh. At least that's what she remembered roadkill had smelled like.

She stood up and moved closer to the interior perimeter of the houses. She began walking through yards and checking individual houses. They were all empty. Deserted.

As she moved through her search area, the smell of rotting flesh grew stronger. It was maybe twenty minutes before she saw the first body.

It was lying on the porch to one of the houses. Old man Jenkins. He had been shot in the chest. He was such a good guy. Why would somebody want to kill old man Jenkins?

She continued to search around. Several of the houses looked deserted; however, it also looked as though they had been ransacked.

There was no food in any of the houses. Blankets and clothing had also been taken. It could have been a group of scavengers, but she believed that the army had been here.

She had heard what Clark said after he had been brought in to the community, stuff about the army shooting anybody that did not comply with their demands, killing anybody that didn't do what they ordered. She wondered what happened to him. He had been left behind when they all moved to the compound, still too weak to move.

Before long, she found three more bodies. All older people and found in front of their homes, shot and killed where they stood. It looked like they died trying to protect their homes.

She finally got to the center of what had been the community. She found Denny waiting for her there.

"What did you find?" he asked. "I bet it's not any worse than what I found."

"All the houses I checked looked abandoned, like the people had just left. But they had all been ransacked. No food, clothing, blankets...all gone," she said. "All gone. I also found four dead. All in the front of their homes. Like they died trying to protect them. Before you ask, it was old man Jenkins, Mr. and Mrs. Cline, and Mr. Willie."

"I found Ms. Connie and Ms. Williams. Same with the houses. Everything looked abandoned. I didn't find any live people. Everybody was gone," Denny said. "We need to head back and let the others know."

They moved back the way Jenny had come, reversing her route. When they got to the tree line, they stopped, looked, and listened. Not hearing or seeing anything, they headed for home.

Patrolling in the woods takes a lot of practice. Practice that Denny and Jenny had not had the opportunity to get. So it wasn't their fault that they did not notice the two camouflaged soldiers who stood up and started to follow them.

7

Colonel Tony Sanso Lopez sat behind his steel, green Army desk and read the reports brought in by his platoon commanders. Under executive order 12656, they had been able to search and secure most of the area his unit had been assigned to check. Approximately forty thousand people had been collected and sent to relocation camps where they would be utilized to help rebuild the country. There were still thousands of people out there that needed to be collected, but they would get the job done. He was sure of it. And if the civilian population didn't want to cooperate, then he would consider it treason, which was punishable, in his eyes anyway, by death.

Lopez was a strong representation of the modern American. He had been born in the United States to parents who had recently fled Mexico in search of a better life here. He spoke both Spanish and English and lived an American lifestyle, which was heavily influenced by his Latino heritage.

He lived in Arizona until the age of seven, when he and his family moved to the Pittsburgh area for work. He was small in stature, which led to his being bullied and picked on. He was also picked on because of his nationality. He found the population in the Pittsburgh area less accepting of his nationality than the people of Arizona. He wouldn't say they were racist, but they didn't like how "Mexican" he was, wishing he was more "American."

At that age, he didn't understand what they meant by being "more American." He ate cheeseburgers, liked football and baseball, and loved to go to the movies when his parents could afford the luxury. Yes, his parents still spoke Spanish, ate mostly Mexican food and celebrated Mexican holidays, but they also liked American stuff.

He grew up being very influenced by his parents and the things that they liked, which meant that he grew up being greatly influenced by the history of early Mexican politics and government. Because he was small in stature, he decided that he would expand his mind. As his education continued, he ran for school president, and was the president of several school-based organizations including "Future Leaders of America." Being a "brainiac" didn't eliminate him from being picked on, but it led to his being able to deal with bullying in a more educated manner.

Because of his childhood, he decided at an early age that he wanted to join the military, leading to him becoming a member of the Jr. ROTC program at school. He did this against his parents' wishes, who wanted him to pursue a career in sales. Trying to make his parents happy, Lopez enrolled at Carnegie Mellon University and majored in business management but also signed up for the college ROTC program, graduating from college as a second lieutenant in the army.

Due to his strong work ethic and level of commitment to education, Lopez excelled in his military career. He served in Operations Enduring Freedom, Iraqi Freedom, and Islamic State-Operation Inherent Resolve. He earned several medals and awards, working his way through the ranks and eventually reaching the rank of Colonel.

As adept as Lopez was in his career, he did have several setbacks. As is the case with many people who are small and bullied as children, he developed the chihuahua mentality. He would bark louder than was needed and would often bite at the heels of those around him. He was often reprimanded by his superiors for being too aggressive in the discipline of his own troops and for committing acts of mistreatment of prisoners or local civilians that his units ran into.

Due to his continued inability to change his manner in dealing with other people, his career stalled. He decided to use his business degree and continue his military career in the National Guard, which was what he was doing when the lights went out all those months ago. He loved it. He was back to his military career full time, and he was able to treat people how he wanted, with few (if any) repercussions.

Because this was a national emergency and the president had signed all those executive orders, he could pretty much do what he wanted, when he wanted, and there was really nothing anybody could do about it.

Lopez was interrupted by a knock at his door, which immediately opened a crack. Sergeant Wendy Athens stuck her head in.

"Colonel, Captain Almont is here to see you."

"Send him in," Lopen answered. Almont was a kiss ass, but he followed orders and got the job done. And in Lopez's mind, that's all he really cared about. Captain John Almont walked in and immediately snapped to attention and saluted. He was average height, with short-cropped gray hair and dark suntanned skin. His uniform was crisp and looked as though it had never seen any real duty.

"Colonel. How are you on this fine day? You look rested and chipper today, if I may say so?"

"Relax, Captain. Take a seat," Lopez said, motioning to a chair in front of his desk. "What can I do for you? I have a plethora of reports to read so make it quick."

"Well, Colonel, I came across some information I think you should know about," Altmont began. "Cunningham had a scout sniper team out reconning the area. He sends out teams occasionally to check for stragglers and to see if we missed anything. Kind of a follow-up precaution."

"Is your story going anywhere here?" Lopez asked with a sigh and obvious sign of annoyance.

"Yes, sir, it is," Almont continued. "Anyway, they were out for about a week. They just came back in and gave their report. Would you like to read it, or do you want me to paraphrase it for you?" Altmont asked with a smirk on his face.

"You can paraphrase," Lopez prompted as Altmont looked down at the report in his lap.

"To make a long story short, they reported that they saw a couple of people walking around one of the communities that we had already cleared. They followed them to the garbage company business located on 22, down in Blairsville. Apparently, they are living there with a community of about 150 other people. It's set up nice from what they say. Able to sustain the community with shelter, security, etc."

Lopez sat quietly at his desk, leaning back and placing his hands behind his head, staring at the ceiling in his office. He sat that way for several minutes. Altmont was starting to get nervous when Lopez finally spoke.

"How the fuck did you and your men miss this when the southern sector was initially checked?" Lopez asked without moving out of position.

"It wasn't missed, sir. That area was checked. When it was checked, it was empty. These people moved in sometime after it was cleared."

"Okay. Then what the fuck are you going to do about it now?" Lopez asked, finally sitting forward and placing his hands on the edge of his desk.

"Well, sir, that's what I wanted to talk to you about. I had planned on sending a small two or three squad unit down there to 'influence' their decision on staying. I just wanted your okay before I did it."

"Just do your fucking job, Captain. You know what we have been tasked with doing, and you know what we are permitted to do to accomplish this task. Get it done. Don't come back here again until you have done your job the way it should have been done in the first fucking place." Lopez said before Altmont could respond, "You are dismissed."

With that, Altmont jumped to the position of attention and snapped a salute.

"Get the fuck outa here," Lopez responded without returning the salute.

Altmont pulled the office door shut and shook his head. Lopez was an asshole. He treated his people with no respect. What did the old man expect him to do? The garbage place had been empty. How was he to know that somebody would move in there, let alone 150-plus people?

Once outside, Altmont placed his cover on his head and walked over to the officer's office building. He had decided that since

Cunningham's scouts had found the camp, his platoon would be responsible for bringing them in.

Once he got to the office building, he removed his cover and entered the building, heading immediately to the lieutenant's office. When he got there and walked in, he saw Lieutenant Beckum behind his desk.

"Lieutenant, where is Cunningham?" he asked as Beckum snapped to attention.

"I'm right here, sir," Cunningham said from behind Altmont. Cunningham was young. He looked like he was fresh out of high school. He was tall, well-built, and good at this job.

Altmont turned around at the sound of the young lieutenant's voice.

"Good, I need to talk to you about something. Lieutenant," Altmont said as he looked back at Beckum. "I need the room to speak to your cohort here. Please shut the door on your way out."

Altmont waited for Beckum to leave, which he did without saying a word. Once the door was shut, Altmont turned to Cunningham.

"Cunningham, we need to take care of that group of people you found in Blairsville. I'll leave it up to you how it's done, but get it done. I'm tired of the old man chewing my ass all the time. Are we clear?"

"Yes, sir," Cunningham replied. "Any suggestions on how you want it handled?"

"I wouldn't send more than two, maybe three squads. Sixteen, twenty-four, guys should be enough. Go loaded. The more intimidating you look, the more likely they will be to comply," he said as he stood to leave.

"Sounds good sir. First, second and third squads are transporting some supplies and gear to Anderson's platoon," he said, knowing Anderson's platoon was attached to a police department around Monroeville. There was a huge problem with a rebel group in that area. "I'll have them stop on the way. They can maybe put the fear of God in them, get them to comply."

"Whatever you think will work. Just get it done," Altmont said as he left the office.

8

The morning air was crisp and cool. It was turning into late fall, and it was the time of year when the nights were cold, but the days would still get warm. The birds were out singing, and the sun was just starting to peak up over the horizon.

Denny, Jenny, and six others from the group had been tasked with going out to scavenge for supplies. The usual scavenger team members had stayed behind at the compound to prepare for Mike's funeral. Since DJ, as Denny and Jenny were now being called, had been unable to find anybody at the community, the compound had decided to go ahead with the funeral. The news of the murdered community members was not a surprise as everybody knew what was going on and what was being done. Fortunately, the people who had been found murdered did not have any family members now in the compound.

The food reserves were low and were continuing to get lower. The leaders at the compound tried to hide it as much as they could so as to not alarm people, but the group knew. Portions were starting to get smaller at the dinner lines, and it had been decided a month ago that breakfast was no longer being served. Only lunch and dinner. So it was decided that a supply run would still be done regardless of the importance of a funeral. There were a lot of people who didn't know Mike or didn't know him very well. Those people had decided to volunteer for the run so his friends and family could participate in the funeral.

The group had been out most of the day. The majority of the area down in this part of the county was farmland, so the houses were farther apart and more secluded. The few houses that they did come across and search were empty, and they were only able to find a few cans of vegetables and a couple of jars of peanut butter.

The gas stations that they came to had already been ransacked, and there was nothing found other than a few small cans of green beans and a couple of bags of pork rinds.

They were on their way back to the compound and were maybe two miles from home, when Denny decided that it was time for a water break. He had the group stop, set up a secure perimeter, and get some water. Denny was no military tactician, and was definitely not a "warrior," but he had listened to the training classes that the military guys had put on and tried his best to do as they had taught.

They had been on a break for about ten minutes, when Chuck, one of the other team members, signaled that he had heard something. Denny got up to a crouch and moved over to Chuck's location.

"What you got?"

"I heard a motor—well, motors. Like a diesel-pickup-type sound."

"Where, which direction?"

"Over that way," Chuck said as he pointed.

Denny used his index finger, pointed in the air, and made a circular motion beside his head. Rally on me. The team moved at a crouch over to Denny's position.

"I need you guys to stay here. This will be the rally point if shit hits the fan. Chuck, Jenny, and I are gonna go check out the noise he heard. Any questions?"

Hearing no questions, DJ, and Chuck moved out in the direction of the truck noise. They got about fifty yards from their rally point, when Chuck, who was walking point, called a halt. Denny approached, and Chuck pointed out in front of them. Denny took out his binoculars and looked in the direction chuck was pointing. He saw four military vehicles. Three Humvees and a larger cargo style truck that looked like a five-ton. The vehicles had parked along the berm of a dirt road. The soldiers in the Humvees got out and set up a hasty perimeter. Denny couldn't hear what they were saying, but one of the soldiers was pointing and obviously giving orders.

The five-ton backed up into what looked like an old gas well road. Two soldiers got out of the five-ton and stood around, as the remaining soldiers got back into the Humvees and left. With the truck parked on the gas well road, Denny could easily see the cargo. It was loaded with fourteen pallets of MREs and two wooden crates. Denny couldn't see what was in the crates, but the MREs were of interest to him. Denny's mind began to race. There were two soldiers with the truck. The rest had left. The compound needed these MREs and needed them badly.

"Hey, Chuck. I need you to go back and get the rest of the group."

"Why? What's up?" Chuck asked.

"We are gonna take that truck."

"Are you nuts?" Chuck asked with obvious concern.

"Look, dickhead," Denny replied. "Do you see what's on that truck. MREs. We need that food. If not, we could starve. You understand that, right? Now do what I told you and go get the others." As Chuck left, Jenny approached Denny.

"What are doing?" she asked. "These are military people. We aren't trained to deal with this."

"Look. There are two of them. There are eight of us. We can overpower them, tie them up, and take the truck. We can hide it somewhere away from the compound and get the MREs by wagon."

"I hope you know what you're doin'," she said as Denny kept an eye on the truck. A few minutes later, the rest of the group showed up.

"Okay, guys, here's the plan."

Top was in the yard getting ready for the funeral when security at the front gate yelled, "Hey, Top, you need to see this!"

Top walked over to the gate and climbed the ladder to the top of the truck. One of the things done was that a platform had been built on the top of the truck so security elements could stand on top of it. When he got up there, he saw three Humvees approaching the main gate.

"Stay calm. Don't do anything stupid. You go get the others," Top said as he pointed at one of the security people, referring to Buck, Josh, Ben, Al, and Ford. The guys arrived just as the Humvees pulled up to the gate. All six of them stood on the platform as the Humvees pulled up and soldiers exited the Humvees.

"Lieutenant," Top said as Cunningham approached. "It's been a while."

"Yeah, it has." Cunningham said as the other soldiers fanned out in a security perimeter. "It's odd seeing you here, Top. What's goin' on here?"

"Nothin'. Just a group of people trying to build a life after the lights went out," Top said.

"Look, Top, I'm not gonna stand here playing games. It's hot out, and I got places to be. There are several truths here: One, you are AWOL. So is the rest of your squad standing there. Two, you know as well as I do that under executive decree, the military has all rights to take whatever food, weapons, water, and supplies you have in there, as well as relocate all indigenous persons to a safe and secure area."

"Well, yeah, but what about if the people don't want to be relocated and don't wanna give up those supplies? What about the Constitution?" Top replied, shrugging his shoulders.

"It's really quite simple, Top. It goes like this. You and I always seemed to get along okay. For that reason, I'm gonna be nice. I'll tell you what. I'll give you and your group here three days. Three days," he said, holding up three fingers. "That's seventy-two hours from right now to decide. We will be back. Now once we do come back, you have one of two options. One, comply. You give us what we want, and you all go to a nice, safe location. Now of course you and your boys will need to suffer some punishment for the AWOL thing, but everybody else will be fine. Two, don't comply. If that's your choice, then as you know, we are permitted under law to use force. It's that simple. It's your choice."

Without waiting, Cunningham ordered his troops back into the Humvees. As they were pulling away, Cunningham held three fingers out the window, mouthing the words "Three days," and then they were gone.

"Well," Top said after the Humvees left, "what do ya think?"

"Man," Buck said, "I believe what he says. We've seen what happens when people don't comply. They shoot people until they do. So the way I see it, our options are what he says they are. What kind of guy is this lieutenant?"

Ford spoke up first. "He's a douche."

The rest of the group laughed. Top spoke up next.

"Yeah, but he mimics the attitude of his commanders. If they're decent, so is he. If they're douches, so is he. That's what has me worried. The unit commander, Lopez, is an asshole. It's obvious that the way they've been treating people here is his doing. He's been known for this type of bullshit, mistreating indigenous persons is kinda his thing. Now, with no real law, he can get away with whatever he wants."

"So what's our play here, Top?" Josh asked.

"Top, keep something in mind here," Al said. "We have a bunch of civilians here with minimal to no combat experience. Do you really want to go to battle with Lopez and the army, or do you want to make sure these people are at least safe? I'm with you no matter how this plays out. I'm just playin' devil's advocate is all."

"Okay," Top said. "We have three days. Let's go do this funeral, then we'll have a community meeting once the scavenger team gets back. We can all decide how this is gonna go. All agree?"

There were a series of agrees, aye-ayes and yes sirs. The security element maintained his post, and the rest went to a funeral.

9

That night, as the sun was getting ready to set, and the darkness slowly began to move in, Mel, whose turn it was as the front gate security element rang an alarm. Buck, Ford, and Top responded, racing up the steps to the platform, seeing what looked like a Deuce and a Half army truck.

"Damn, Top, that was a quick three days," Buck said with a grin and a hint of sarcasm. Top looked at him with an "I'm gonna kick your ass" look on his face.

The truck started to slow down as it approached the front gate, coming to a stop mere feet from the gate. Denny hopped from the driver's seat with Jenny jumping out from the passenger side. The rest of the group jumped from the back of the truck.

"What the fuck!" Top yelled. "What the fuck did you just do?"

"Damn, Top, easy!" Denny yelled back. "This truck just may have saved our asses. It's got fourteen pallets of MREs and two pallets of something else. Not sure what. But it has MREs, and I know we need the food."

Buck turned and looked at Ford. Both men started to snicker, knowing that Denny and Top were both right but thinking the situation was kind of amusing.

"You two shut the fuck up!" he yelled. "It's not funny. This is some shit." Looking back at the truck, he yelled, "Get that fuckin' thing in here before somebody sees it." He turned and crawled down the ladder as the gate was moved out of the way. Buck and Ford stayed on top and continued to laugh.

Most of the people were crowding around the MRE pallets, obviously excited about having food. There were now 9,600 MREs to get these people through the winter. But a few had gathered around the other two pallets.

"Hey, Top," Denny said. "Look, I know we took a chance, but we need this stuff. They didn't see anything. We tied up and blindfolded the two guys guarding it then took it about three miles away and hid it. We thought they might be coming this way with the Humvees, so we made sure to hide it well. We took precautions."

Top just looked at Denny and shook his head.

"Holy shit, boss," Ben said. "Look what's in these two crates."

Top walked over and looked inside the first crate. It was full of different-sized pelican cases which held different firearms.

"We got like twenty M-4s, a bunch of *Sig* 320s, and check this out: two M-60s," Ben said. Buck was grinning from ear to ear. He always liked the M-60. "That crate, all ammo—.45, 9, 5.56, and 7.62 for the hogs. You name it, we got it." Ben stood and pulled Top aside. "I know grabbing this was probably not the smartest thing they could've done, but this is all the stuff we needed. It may not have been smart, but it was right."

"Son of a bitch," Top said. "I know, but if they suspect it was us, that three days may be lost, and option number one could very well go away, leaving us no choice. They just come in and start shooting." Top put his hands on his hips and started to pace in circles. After a couple of minutes, he called Jennifer and a guy named Marc over. "We gotta get rid of this five-ton. If they send a bird up to look for it and see it here, we're done. Take that thing as far from here as you can. Take it west. Park it in some outa the way place and set fire to it."

Jennifer and Marc took off to get their gear. As she was walking back from her room, she stopped and gave Tony a hug. They had gotten close over time, and a budding romance had started. She then went over to Buck.

"Hey," he said. "You be careful okay? Don't be stupid, think about what you're doin', and avoid people at all costs. You don't know what their intentions might be."

"I will. Be safe, big brother." Jennifer kissed him on the cheek, rubbed Mel's shoulder, and headed for the passenger side of the truck.

Marc came back from his room, loaded down with his kit. He hopped into the driver side of the truck and started it up, waiting for Jennifer to return with her gear. Even in the dark of night, black smoke could be seen billowing from the smokestacks beside the cab. Once Jennifer returned, the front gate was moved out of the way, and the five-ton took off down the road.

"So, Lieutenant, let me get this straight." Lopez yelled, getting louder as he spoke. "Not only did you not remove these people like I wanted you to, but you lost a five-ton M-939, fourteen pallets of MREs, and two pallets of weapons and ammo? Are you *fuckin'* serious?"

Lieutenant Cunningham said nothing but remained at attention in front of Colonel Lopez's desk.

"If it was strictly up to me, I would take you behind my office..." He paused and pointed out his window, to the grass on the other side. "And I'd put a bullet in the back of your fuckin' head for being just plain stupid. But it seems as though Captain Almont thinks very highly of you. He says that you aren't a complete fuckin' moron but that you just had a blinding flash of morondom. Is that the case, Lieutenant?"

Cunningham still said nothing.

"I asked you a fuckin' question, Lieutenant. Was this completely moronic display of soldiering a onetime thing, or is it your normal behavior?"

"It's a onetime thing, sir. I just thought..."

"That's the fuckin' problem, Lieutenant," Lopez interrupted. "You thought. I told the Captain what I wanted done. He told you. You were to do what I wanted you to do. This would have taken absolutely no thought whatsofuckinever, but you decided to think and loused it all up. Now get the fuck outa my office. I gotta think of a good punishment for you."

Cunningham rendered a salute, did an about face, and hurriedly exited Colonel Lopez's office.

"Captain Altmont. Could you please explain to me why he left the supplies intended for our sister unit in Monroeville out by itself while he went to 'talk' with the civilians?"

"He thought it best not to have supplies close to them when they were trying to intimidate the civilians. He figured that if something happened and they were overpowered, the civilians would now be in possession of food, weapons, and ammo. He didn't want that to happen."

"Well, we don't know who has our shit now, do we?"

"No, sir."

"Do we think it's the group we went to talk to? Fuck, that burns my ass. I should be looking at a report telling me we had to kill five before the rest gave in and surrendered." Shaking his head, he continued. "Do we think it's them?"

"He doesn't think so, but he doesn't really know. He didn't pass anybody on the way in, and the two soldiers that were jumped couldn't describe anybody. We honestly do not know who took the stuff."

"I want those two shot. I'm serious, Captain."

"Sir, with all due respect, some of the guys are already borderline on how we are handling this stuff. They are already thinking that we are taking things too far in our execution of our orders. If you go executing your own people, you will lose the rest of them and you won't be able to do the job you were tasked with doing."

"Fuck! I hate when you're right." He placed his hands behind his back and began to pace the room. "okay, lock them up. Indefinitely. No food, no water. Keep them locked up until they pass out from lack of food and water. Same for Lieutenant Moron, but only do him a week. Am I understood, Captain? And one more thing, Captain, fuck three days. Get the troops ready. We go tomorrow." Altmont jumped to attention and saluted.

"Yes, sir."

The following morning, a meeting was held. All personnel were pulled from all stations, even security, as the discussion of what the group should do was important enough to be heard by everyone at once.

Top stood on the front gate platform and addressed everybody, telling them what had taken place the day before and what he knew about Lopez and his methods. The whole talk took about a half hour.

"The decision is yours and yours alone. I can't tell you what to do here. If you choose to surrender to Lopez, fine. We will make sure you do that as safely as possible to make sure that neither you, nor anybody in your family gets hurt. If you choose to fight here, that's fine too."

Buck was on the platform with Top. Several of the people looked to him and Josh, asking what they thought should be done. Buck answered first. "Look, I'm gonna stay and fight. The way I see it is this. I have my ideas about what this country was, where it is now, and where it should go. You may not agree and that's fine too. But I'd like to think that each and every one of you has something, something that you believe to be so valuable, that you are willing to fight and possibly die for it. That's what this country was built on. The desire to defend what we value as important. Lopez wants to scare us into surrender. A surrender that leads to servitude and slavery. He thinks that anything has to be better than remaining in this place. But if he attacks…we may not win this battle, but by God we'll make it impossible for Lopez to defeat anybody else."

There were cheers. Top was smiling, and the men were patting each other on the back. To a person, everybody agreed to stay and fight.

PART 4

REBEL WARRIORS

Out of every one hundred men, ten shouldn't even be there, eighty are just targets, nine are the real fighters, and we are lucky to have them, for they make the battle. Ah, but the one, one is a warrior, and he will bring the others back.

—Heraclitus

1

As the morning progressed, the compound took advantage of their new found gifts. The MREs were taken to the cafeteria and stored to be dispersed to each person, one per day. The M-60 machine guns were placed on the roofs located in the southeast and northwest corners. M-60 classes were given to the security personnel, as the M-60 is an open-bolt fired weapon, and fed by a belt of 7.62-millimeter ammunition. It's usually a crew-fired weapon, but with the lack of people, security personnel would need to fire it themselves. The M-4s, pistols, and ammo were dispersed, and new security rotations were made.

The two best long-range shooters were Ben and Tony. They each found "sniper" blinds on the roofs, with Chris and Bill backing them up as spotters and secondary shooters. They selected fields of fire, and set small flags in the fields as range markers for easy recognition of yardage. They set up cover and concealment and placed ammo in the blinds to allow for quick and easy access.

Al set up his hospital area, making sure whatever medications and triage supplies he had were easily accessible, with Heather and Mia assisting as nurses when things started getting crazy. Litters were made from tarps and heavy tree branches to carry wounded from the field to the hospital.

Buck, Top, Josh, and Ford went to all the security stations and set up fields of fire, pointing out landmarks for each furthest right and left point, ensuring overlapping fire where they could. Riflemen, security personnel with M-4s, were placed sporadically along the walls in an attempt to provide overlap, and a heavier wall of fire. Boxes of ammo and magazines were placed in positions along the walls for easy dissemination.

Finally, fallback positions were selected inside the compound in case the walls were breached. The thought behind selecting fallback positions was to slow down an advance in the army troops, not stop them. It would buy the defenders time to possibly escape from rear windows in the main building, evacuate casualties to a safe area, if possible, and to cause additional casualties to the attackers. All the defenders could hope for in this situation was a little more time.

"Well," Buck said as they all met in the yard. "I think we've done all we can."

"Yeah," Top said. "We are pretty limited in what we can and can't do with small arms only. Boy do I wish we had explosives. I'd love to set up claymores and C-4 out in the fields." Ford had a thoughtful look on his face as Top was contemplating what they didn't have.

"Hey, Top, I think we could jerry-rig some pipe bombs using gasoline, nails and some other stuff in the garage." Ford looked at Al. "Do you have any Vaseline in the hospital?"

"Yeah, we do," Al said. "I've got quite a bit actually."

"Good," Ford replied. "I think we have enough stuff that we could make fifteen or twenty bombs. And since we don't need wiring in the dormitory, we can use wiring from there to rig triggers."

"Nice. You and Josh go to work on those. Get them done as soon as possible. I have a funny feeling that Lopez isn't going to wait three days. That asshole will cut that short, I'm sure." As Ford and Josh walked toward the garage he called after them. "Be careful. I can't afford to lose anybody." He then turned to Buck. "Buck, grab somebody and go pull as much wire as you can from the dorm. Keep the wires as long as you can. The more splices we have, the more chance for error and equipment malfunction."

Top stood with his hands on his hips and surveyed the compound. They had really done all that they could. He didn't think they were going to win. Hell, he didn't think for a minute that if Lopez showed up, that he would pull back. But he did think that they would be able to put one hell of a hurt on that asshole…no doubt about that.

By dinnertime, Ford and Josh had fifteen pipe bombs rigged together. Top directed Ford, Josh, and Buck, along with several others, on placement of the bombs and running the det wire to a control area at the compound, where a car battery and nails in a wood plank would be used as a detonator.

Digging holes at the selected spots, the defenders placed the bombs in the holes, covering them with dirt and grass. They then dug trenches to hide the wire, running the wire from the bombs to the detonator. The bombs were set in a grid of five bombs, three rows deep. The grid was a square approximately forty yards square.

Once the handmade claymores were set, there was nothing else to do but wait. The civilians in the group were suffering from apprehension and fear. Emotions which, if you were not familiar with them, you had a hard time processing. Although sleep rotations had been set up, nobody slept. The night air was cold, and you could hear the air move through the leaves, making you wonder if the enemy was moving into place, using the black night as cover.

The ones who had seen combat or been in stressful situations handled the waiting better. They were still trapped in their own thoughts but the thoughts were of the pending battle. Were the sentries placed in the right positions? Would the bombs work when they were needed? Was everybody informed of their jobs, and would they do their jobs, or would the gunfire scare them into giving up? All thoughts focused on tactics and possible strategy, not only for the defenders but the attackers as well.

The evening proceeded like this, everyone sitting, waiting, and wondering.

The sun came up the next morning as it did every day. The birds started singing, unaware of the potential events of the day. The camp slowly got up and started to move around. Security elements switched out, sending the night shift to get some sleep. Normal daily activity proceeded as usual…until.

"Hey…hey…we got somethin' goin' on here!" somebody yelled from on top of the wall. Before he yelled, even from inside the compound, you could hear what sounded like thunder, although there were no clouds in the sky. Top, Ford, Josh, and Buck ran to the wall and climbed ladders leading to the security stations. Once on top, they saw what was making all the noise.

The US Army was moving in. Humvees equipped with 50-caliber machine guns and TOW missile systems, as well as three Stryker troop carriers armed with MK-19 grenade launchers, and two M939s loaded with troops were moving into a circular perimeter around the compound. The M939s were sporadically placed, with men dismounting and taking prone positions, all facing the compound, approximately a hundred yards from the compound walls.

It took several minutes for the vehicles to get into place and for the troops to dismount and take up positions. There were roughly two hundred and fifty men with heavy weapons and explosive ordinance surrounding the compound. If you weren't standing in an abandoned garbage disposal facility, looking at the dangerous end of all their weapons, you may have thought it was awesome.

The guys moved down their ladders to the yard. Mel came running up and grabbed Buck by his hand, looking into his eyes, showing concern and fear. Nobody said anything. They just stood and looked at each other. Finally, Buck spoke first.

"Well, surrounding them's out," he said with a chuckle as everybody looked at him like he was a complete idiot. "Sorry, ever since I saw *Rambo III*, I wanted to say that."

"Well," Top said with a grin. "He's right. So the question is, what do we do now?"

About this time, other compound members started to run up, fear and uncertainty on their faces. They were yelling out questions, looking for some assurances.

"How do we fight that?"

"When are they gonna start shootin'?"

"How do we defend ourselves against that?"

"Maybe we should change our minds and surrender."

"Hold on, everybody. Just relax. No shots have been fired yet." Top said, trying to gain control of his thoughts and the group of people.

"All we can really do is wait," Ford said. "See what they do. I'm sure they'll try to negotiate with us first, get us to surrender, turn ourselves over. Let's see what their play is first then decide what we do."

About that time, the guy who had called out the initial alarm called out again.

"Hey, Top. One of those new jeeps is driving up to the gate." Top looked at Ben and Tony.

"Get up top on your rifles. Anybody does anything that even looks shady, whack 'em."

Top, Josh, and Buck went to walk out the gate. Buck turned to Mel. Go get someplace with cover. Shoot anything that gets close to you. I'll be right back. And I love you."

She hugged him tight. "I love you more," she said as she ran to a security position.

"Just for today," he said with a grin and jogged after the others.

Colonel Lopez exited the passenger side of the Humvee. His uniform was clean and pressed. He had minimal gear on but had a *Sig* 320 on his hip. He approached the group with the swagger of a person with confidence, real or implied.

"Top Jackson. I heard you were here. For what do I owe the pleasure?"

"Well, Colonel, I'm just here helping this group of people survive in this new world."

"Well, Top, you know I can't let that happen. I have orders to follow, and I will follow them. In fact, I'll follow them at any cost. You understand?

"I do, Colonel. But these people don't want to leave. They are happy here and want to stay here. They have a right to live how and where they want. At least I read that somewhere, in this little document called the Constitution."

"I'm sorry, Top. But the Constitution has been suspended and is no longer relevant. We are in a state of emergency, and I don't care what they want. Unless of course what they want is to turn themselves over to me and the US Government. If, however, they don't, then I will be forced to…well, force them.

"You see, Top, the country is trying to rebuild after this unfortunate event." Lopez paced with his hands behind his back, staring at the ground, as if the people in front of him posed no threat. "These people are needed for that. Their belongings, and belongings of mine that I can see you now have, will be used as supplies to help support that. And all that's really important is the rebuilding of this country. Don't you agree?"

Top stood facing Lopez. He looked him dead in the eye and said, "Veni, et sumam eam."

With that, Top turned to walk away, causing the others to walk away with him. Lopez, having never been disrespected in the open like that before, became irate, yelling at the top of his lungs, "Fuck you, you nigger piece of shit. How dare you turn your back on me? How dare you disrespect me in front of my men?"

But Top, Josh, and Buck had already walked back inside the compound. Lopez continued to scream obscenities.

Josh looked at Top.

"What did you say to him, Top?"

Before Top could answer, Buck answered for him. "It's Latin. Means 'Come and take it.'"

Top stopped and looked at Buck with a pleased look of surprise on his face. He patted Buck on the shoulder. "Well done, brother."

Lopez was furious. His face turned red and the veins popped out on his forehead.

"Fuck him. Fuck him and all those civilian pieces of shit. We'll just blow the place to shit. Kill all of 'em. Fuck them."

Altmont spoke up, trying to control the anger displayed by his boss. "With all due respect, Colonel. We have the advantage in more ways than one. We have the supplies, we have the weapons, we have the manpower, and we have time. They have none of that. I'm sure they are low on food, weapons, ammo, water…you name it. If we just wait them out, they'll surrender and you get credit for all of them. Trust me, it's the best course of action."

"Bullshit. They have our MREs, our weapons, and our ammo. I could see the M-60s on the roof when we drove up." Lopez thought for a minute. You could see the color change in his face and see the anger subside.

"Fine. We'll try it your way. But as soon as it looks like they won't give up, I'm turning up the heat. Do you understand me?

"Yes, sir, I do."

2
Day 1

As the first day after the warning began, nature acted as though nothing was different. The sun rose over the open fields; the frost on the ground began to steam as the sun warmed the ground and birds sang like it was any other day. But to the rebels, as the sun rose over the walls of the compound, it opened their eyes to the full extent of the military forces seen in a circular perimeter around the area.

The soldiers were set up in groups behind the vehicles, with campfires going and food and coffee being heated. They had unlimited supplies and knew that they could outlast the rebels during this siege. All it would take was time, and they could essentially sit here and relax.

But for the rebels, the first day after the warning was given was different from all the other days. Although the world had changed when the lights went out, many of them adapted to the change, even embracing it. They saw a future for themselves and their families. Albeit a harder future but a future nonetheless. Now those same people saw an end. Not a peaceful end to a long, hard life that they had built for themselves but a violent end to a life that they were forced to accept.

The day was hectic. People were running around organizing supplies, getting water bottled and ready for easy dissemination, loading magazines, and preparing for a battle that they knew would come. The leaders of the group were revamping and improving security and lookout positions, adjusting their defenses to the perimeter set up by Lopez and his men.

As the day progressed, some of the Compound inhabitants felt that they may have acted in haste and rethought their initial decision to stay and fight. Some of them approached Buck and discussed their concerns. Denny had been elected to speak on their behalf.

"Hey, Buck. I'm just here as a spokesperson, but some of the people here think that they may have answered too quickly. They were thinking that maybe they want to turn themselves over to Lopez, take their chances with the camps." Buck nodded, looking at the ground as he did.

"Okay. If that's the way they feel, we'll see if we can't work something out. Tell them to sit tight, and we'll get back with them. How many are there, Denny?" Buck asked.

"Oh, maybe twenty."

"Okay, I'll get with ya later, okay?"

"Yeah, Buck. I'll let them know."

Buck went to talk with Top about the situation and discuss possible options. Buck could understand how they felt. When a stressful situation just pops off and happens, when you don't have time to think about it, that's one thing. You just act. But when you have the actual time to think about all the possible outcomes and what might happen, apprehensions can begin to kick in. He didn't agree with their thoughts, but he wasn't going to begrudge them their right to make choices for themselves. That is why he chose to stay and fight, the right to choose for himself the direction his life went.

"So, Top, what do ya think?" Buck asked after he narrated the discussion with Denny.

"Well, they have that right. How do you want to handle it?" Top asked.

"Do you think we could still negotiate with Lopez? You know, let him know there are people that want to cooperate, see if he will still accept them. I was thinking that we could write a letter to Lopez. Ask him to accept the conditional surrender of these select few people."

"Okay, sounds good to me. I'll go ahead and write it."

"No," Buck said. "He has a pretty strong dislike of you. I'm afraid he may dismiss it outright if it comes from you. I'll write it."

"You got a good point. Go ahead with it."

To: The commander of the military forces
From: Citizens in the compound

As a former army officer, it is with much respect that I write to you to request the surrender of a portion of the citizens from our community. They do not wish to cause any problems, nor do they do wish to cause any harm to you or your forces. They only ask that they be permitted to leave, with no conditions, as they just wish to live a free life. A life of their choosing.

They are not combatants. These people worked as mechanics, secretaries, teachers…civilian jobs with no type of combat experience. Many of them have children and only wish to provide a stable and free life to and for their children. Please take their request into consideration.

Sincerely,
Lieutenant, Retired

After the letter was completed, Buck was preparing to go, to deliver the letter when Mel approached.

"Where do you think you're going?" she asked.

"Well, I was approached by Denny this morning. There are some people who want to leave. Top and I talked about it. I wrote a letter to Lopez, asking that he let them leave. I was heading out to deliver it to him."

"Not by yourself you're not," she admonished. "I'm goin' with you. And I think Josh should come too." Not wanting to argue, Buck complied with Mel's wishes.

"Okay, baby. If that's what you want," he said as she turned to leave.

"It is, and you're smart for not arguing. Just remember I'm always right," she said with a grin.

As he waited, Buck attached a white rag to a broom handle. The white flag was usually seen as a sign of surrender, but it is also seen as the universal symbol for a request for negotiation, and that's all Buck was requesting when they walked out to talk to the army troops.

Mel returned with Josh, and the three of them exited the front gate of the compound. Their pistols were on their hips, and long guns were slung on their backs. The flag was held high and was being waved back and forth so it was easy to see. Ben and Tony were on the roof, providing cover if things started to go south.

As they exited the front gate, they walked towards the center of the military perimeter. A military lookout, seeing them and the white flag, alerted his superiors that they were approaching. A group of ten soldiers ran forward with their rifles up, yelling, "Get your hands up! Get on the ground! Get on your knees!"

The three rebels complied, kneeling on the ground, keeping their hands up and the flag high.

"What do you want?" one of the soldiers asked.

"I have a letter for Colonel Lopez. I'd like to speak to him please," Buck said, trying to remain as calm and nonconfrontational as possible.

One of the other soldiers immediately left. The rebels and the soldiers just stayed as they were, staring at each other. Nobody spoke, and nobody moved. Buck began to think about the civil war and if soldiers on opposing sides felt as he did now. He was essentially preparing to go to war with his own fellow Americans. People from his own community. He may have even known some of the troops in formation in front of him. It felt surreal to him.

The soldier that left quickly returned.

"Colonel Lopez refuses to speak with you."

"Can you give him this letter please? We can wait here for his response," Buck said.

The soldier took the letter and again ran back to the rear of the perimeter. He was gone for about an hour when he and another soldier returned. The second soldier was in a pressed uniform. He walked with more poise and confidence. He was wearing silver bars on his lapels.

"Gentlemen and lady," he said with a gin and a nod in Mel's direction.

"Please stand up. How long have you been on your knees?" the new soldier asked.

As they stood up, Buck answered, "Maybe an hour."

"Well, my apologies to you. I am Lieutenant Robert Beckum. I have been ordered to give this to you. It's a letter from Colonel Lopez, a reply to your request," he said as he handed Buck a folded piece of paper.

"I saw the letter. Who wrote it?" he asked.

"I did," Buck replied.

"Can I ask you something?" Lieutenant Beckum asked.

Buck just nodded. "Why are you doing this? As prior military, you obviously understand what we are doing here. You understand that we were ordered to do this by a command much higher than any of us here. Why not comply?"

Buck thought for a few seconds before he replied. He wanted to be clear yet respectful. "Lieutenant, I understand that orders must be followed. How else can a military, or any organization for that matter, properly work if people don't follow the orders that they're given? However, I do not—and have never believed that I need or should—follow an order I believe to be immoral, unethical, or criminal. In this case, I believe that what you and Lopez are asking citizens to do is both immoral and unethical. Suspending the Constitution, regardless of the reason, does nothing but continue to destroy a country. The Constitution should be used as the cornerstone of rebuilding, not suspended as a way to rebuild. And your response to the refusal of American citizens to become essentially refugees in their own country, is criminal. Therefore, under my conscience, I will not, and cannot, comply."

Lieutenant Beckum just smiled.

"Okay then," he said. "I'll wish you good luck. I think you're gonna need it." With that, he turned and walked away, taking the other soldiers with him.

They did not read the letter until they got back to the compound. Top and Denny both came over to see how it went.

After a brief description of the conversation they had with Lieutenant Beckem, they opened the letter and read Colonel Lopez's response. The letter they received was not encouraging.

> To: The heathen criminal traitors
> From: Colonel Antonio Sanso Lopez
>
> I write this to you as a reply to your outlandish request. The American army cannot come to terms under any conditions with rebellious traitors and terrorists to whom there is no recourse left.
>
> If they wish to save their lives, then they can place themselves immediately at the disposal of the United States government, to be used to rebuild this beautiful country to the standard from whence it came. I can only guarantee that they *may* expect some clemency after deliberations concerning their traitorous behavior is taken into consideration.

After reading the letter to themselves, they just stood and looked at each other, not sure of what to say. Finally, Top spoke, saying that a community meeting needed to be held.

Josh went to get Denny and to pass on that a meeting was being called. Once everybody was present, Buck spoke. He explained that he had attempted to negotiate an unconditional surrender for anybody that may want to leave. He told them of his conversation with the lieutenant, and then he read the letter aloud to the compound. The letter confirmed the fears of many of the compound residents. There was no way out of their situation. They either became government-owned slaves or they died as free men.

As the weight of the letter sank in, members of the community returned to their duties, although there was little to no talking. Each person was deep in their own thoughts, the letter blanketing the compound with a somber feeling that lasted into the night.

3
Day 2

The following morning, Colonel Lopez awoke in his tent, which was about a hundred yards outside the military perimeter. He awoke feeling rested, alive, and in control. Today was a new day. A new day to turn the tide of success.

After brushing his teeth and washing, he decided that he was starving. He called in his assistant and ordered breakfast for himself. He was in the mood for pancakes, eggs, and bacon. As he waited for his breakfast, he got dressed in a new and pressed uniform. His breakfast arrived in a timely manner. As he ate, he again called in his assistant.

"Get me Captain Altmont. I want to speak to him."

As he waited, he thought about the traitors and how he wanted to handle things. He needed—no, wanted—to speed things up. He was not going to sit here and let the traitors decide how long this was going to take. He heard a knock on the frame of his door.

"Come in," he yelled. Captain Altmont soon entered.

"Captain. I've been thinking. We need to speed up this process a bit. I want some kind of action taken to either speed up their surrender or to speed up the need for some kind of decisive action being taken. I don't care what you do or how you do it, I just want something done. Are we clear?"

"Yes, sir. I understand," Altmont replied. He snapped a salute and left the tent.

Altmont understood the need to speed things up. They surely couldn't sit here forever and who knew the amount of supplies that the rebels had at their disposal. But at the same time, he didn't see the need to kill a bunch of people to get the others to surrender. Just putting the fear of God into them would work. So he had an idea. An idea that would limit the number of people killed, but he hoped, would scare the civilians inside enough to turn themselves over.

For the citizens trapped in the compound, the day started out much like the day before had ended. But the people had begun to come to terms with the idea of fighting. There was a more focused approach to their work and a more dedicated method to how they were getting things done. But then, the first explosion went off.

The western wall to the compound shook as brick dust, stone, and dirt rained down on civilians. Panic took over, and civilians began running for cover. They were screaming and yelling, shoving each other as they ran.

Top, Josh, Buck, and the others tried to keep them calm and orderly, directing them to fighting positions and security posts.

More explosions erupted as the MK-19s from the Strykers fired a salvo of 40 mm grenades, most landing a few feet short of the wall but a couple hitting the wall at its base. Pieces of the wall broke off and crumbled to the ground, but it held and did not collapse. As quickly as the bombardment began, it stopped.

Ben, Tony, Chris, and Bill ran to their sniper positions to see what the high-powered scopes could show them. Buck and Mel ran up to the south west corner to get a view of what was going on, while Top and Josh ran to the north west corner, Top reaching the security post before Josh.

As Josh crested the top of the ladder, Top was already there.

"What ya see Top?" Josh asked as he got there. Top was looking through a pair of binoculars.

"Well, those were forty mike mikes. I'm guessing the MK-19s."

Top heard a *zing* pass his left ear then heard the report of a rifle, followed by a thud. He turned and saw Josh drop, falling backward over the edge of the platform.

Heather, Bill, and Chris were frantic as Josh was rushed into Al's hospital area. Josh had blood all over his head, face, and neck. He was unresponsive. People had to forcefully hold them back as Al and Mia worked to see what was wrong with Josh.

There was blood everywhere. They used towels and duct tape as a brace to support Josh's neck. Al then used wet rags and started to clean some of the blood from Josh's head, looking for where the trauma was. He saw a large gash on the left side of Josh's head but did not see or feel any entry or exit holes. Al felt Josh's face and the back of Josh's head, feeling for deformities, or the presence of fluids like blood or brain matter. He did not feel anything. He then inspected Josh's nose and ears for deformity and fluids, checking his pupils for size and reaction.

Finding that the bullet had not penetrated Josh's skull, Al then proceeded to check for injuries related to the fall. He began checking each extremity for broken bones. Finding none, Al then moved to the abdomen and chest area. Not finding anything to make him believe there were broken bones, he established an intravenous line to administer fluids. The complete examination took close to half an hour, but now, all that could be done was to wait.

As Al was working on Josh and Top went to the roof of the dormitory and found Ben and Tony still watching the military activity through the scope.

"Hey, how's Josh?" Tony asked when he saw Top.

"We're not sure yet. He's unconscious. It looks like a bullet grazed his head. Al has an IV line in. We're just in a waiting game now. Ben, I need your expertise."

"Sure, boss, what's up?"

"I need you to take one shot. Take out somebody. I don't care who. Just drop one of those motherfuckers. We can't let them get this one. We need to let them know that they can't scare us."

Without saying a word, Ben got into the prone position. Stomach flat on the ground. His legs forming a *V*, with the insides of his feet flat on the roof surface. The stock of his Remington 700 placed just on the outside of his chest muscle, in the crook of his shoulder, with the support arm wrapped around the grip of the rifle with his support hand gripping his own bicep. He then sighted through the scope, searching for a good target, which he found as he saw a soldier feeding a grenade belt into one of the MK-19s.

Taking a deep breath and then letting half of the air out, Ben watched as his scope settled on the targets head. *Caarrrack!* The round went down range, hitting its intended target right below the left ear. Ben saw a mist of pink explode, and the soldier's head disappeared. There was no body movement at all, except for the body dropping straight to the ground. The other soldiers around him frantically ducked for cover; some of them grabbed the body and dragged it to cover as well. Ben looked at Top.

"Done, boss."

"Good job. Fuck them."

"Are you fucking serious?" Altmont yelled. "Who the fuck gave you the order to shoot at anybody?"

The soldier just stood there, unsure of how to respond.

"I asked you a fucking question?" Altmont screamed.

"I knew we were trying to scare them. I figured that if they saw one of their own go down, they'd comply with our demands," the soldier replied.

"Well, all you did was get one of your own killed in the process. You may have turned what could have been a potentially easy surrender into a real fight now. I hope you are happy. You may have gotten a lot of people killed today."

With that, Altmont left the soldier standing at attention and went to tell Lopez what had happened.

Once he had completed his explanation as to what had caused one of his own soldiers to lose his life, Lopez responded.

"Captain, we will suffer loss as leaders. One life in the completion of a mission is nothing. I am not concerned. Maintain our plans. Continue with what you have been doing. We will have the supplies we need from them one way or another. The choice is theirs."

4
Days 3, 4, and 5

The morning sun rose again over the rebel compound, a deceptive expression signaling the start of another day.

Heather, Bill, and Chris had not left Josh's side all night. His breathing had become labored, and the whole side of his head had turned a dark black and blue color. Al had been up periodically to check on Josh, believing that he had a concussion and quite possibly a brain bleed.

Al took Heather aside to speak with her.

"Heather, you need to prepare yourself. It doesn't look good. I think his brain is bleeding, and I don't have the tools or meds here to treat him properly." He let the gravity of what he was telling her sink in before he continued. "You need to get the boys ready and prepare yourselves for the worst."

Heather didn't say a word. At first, she just stared at him as though she hadn't heard anything he said. Then after a few moments, the news took hold and she just began to cry. She and Josh had been high school sweethearts and had only ever known each other. What was she going to do without him? How was she going to survive in this new world without his support?

Buck and Mel walked over to check on Josh. They didn't need to ask anything to know what was going on. Heather immediately grabbed Buck and hugged him, crying in his chest. Her tears were heavy and steady. Mia and Mel stood beside them, rubbing Heather's back, trying to console a grieving wife and mother.

Top walked over and tapped Buck on the shoulder.

"Hey, brother, we need to talk."

Buck leaned down and whispered in Heather's ear.

"Sweetheart, I gotta go. I'll be close if you need me." He hugged her tightly and turned to Top.

"Damn. I couldn't imagine," Buck said as he shook his head. "What dya got goin', Top?"

"They are starting to move the Strykers and Humvees around into more attack ready positions. They have a Stryker and two Humvees on each side of the compound. I'm sure that things are going to start heating up. We need to get the people ready."

"Damn, okay."

Before Buck could do anything, explosions erupted again, this time on each side of the compound. Grenades exploded, sending dirt and stone flying into the air. The rebel citizens ducked for cover, trying to protect themselves from the rain of stone, dirt, and debris. The grenade bombardment continued for approximately twenty minutes then stopped as quickly as it began. The birds had stopped singing, and insects stopped talking. The compound became deathly quiet. The citizens were in shock. They said nothing as they just sat there. There was no other action by the military.

As the sun set on another stressful day, the rebel citizens lay down to try to get some rest. Security elements took their positions, preparing for a long, hopefully uneventful shift.

Approximately a half hour after the sun had completely set, the explosions started again. There were only four or five—they were on the west wall—and lasted about ten minutes, then stopped.

Every hour on the hour for the next two days and nights, the explosions rotated sides. There would be five to six explosions, then they would stop. There was no real damage, as the explosions landed just short of the outside wall. Some hit the wall and did minor damage, but nobody was injured, and there were no breaches in the perimeter walls. There was no other military action except for the hourly grenade blasts.

The people in the compound attempted to maintain their normal rotations and schedules, but the explosions kept them awake at night and ceased work during the day. The fear and stress caused by the explosions, coupled with the lack of sleep, began to take effect, and during the times that no explosions were taking place they could still not sleep.

Exhaustion, depression, and weakness began to set in to the point where there was little to no movement in the compound at all. Many began to wonder. Would surrendering be all that bad?

By the fifth day of the siege, Colonel Lopez was in a great mood. Things at the compound were going as planned. He was sure that the constant, around-the-clock bombardment was beginning to take its toll. About this time, the traitors would be getting tired. They would be scared and unsure of the outcome of events. Fear would lead to exhaustion, which would lead to apprehension, which in turn would lead to an army victory.

And a victory is ultimately what he wanted. He was ready to finish this. He had other areas to finish checking and other people to round up for the rebuilding of the country. Playing with these traitorous heathens was starting to wear thin, and it was time to finish things.

He had called for Captain Altmont, who was now sitting in a chair in front of Colonel Lopez's field desk.

"Okay, Captain. I've done as you suggested and have given the traitors a chance to surrender to us, but they have chosen not to. It's time to put an end to this. We're wasting explosive ordinance, and our men are beginning to get tired. So tomorrow morning, we attack. Am I understood?"

"Yes, sir. Any suggestions on how you want to do this?" Altmont asked.

"Yeah. As a matter of fact, I do," Lopez replied. "Continue with the bombardment all night, however, increase it to every half hour. Wait until about 0400. Have the troops move into positions for assault. I want them about fifty yards from the walls. Then on my command, I want you to adjust the aim of the grenade launchers to actually hit the walls. Hit them all at the same time. Once a volley or two has damaged the walls, send a flare to signal assault."

"Sounds perfect, Colonel. And what do we do with survivors and those that surrender?" Altmont asked.

Lopez just looked at Altmont with disgust.

"What survivors?" Lopez answered. The look on Captain Altmont's face let Lopez know he was not happy with the decision. "Look, Captain. We need to make an example of these people. We need to let anyone thinking about refusing our orders to understand that refusal will not be accepted, and the result of treason will be death. We cannot have these citizens believing that they can fight the government. We need them to submit to our control so this country can be rebuilt into what it needs to be. Am I understood, Captain?"

"Yes, sir, you are."

"Good. Now go get the men ready. It's gonna be a long night."

5
Day 6

At midnight on day six, Lopez's military troops began preparing for their assault. Operations orders were given, weapons were checked, ammo was loaded, last-minute briefings were conducted, and squad leaders conducted final squad checks on their troops.

At 2:00 a.m., army troops began low crawling through the fields, trying to move into positions closer to the compound that would afford them easier and quicker movement to the walls when the assault began.

At approximately 2:30 a.m., one of the security elements for the compound ran into Top's room.

"Top…Top." Eric was a small guy, not too bright, and not any good at much of anything. But he had great eyesight, which was what made him a huge asset to the night watch. It took a few seconds for Top to get his bearings once he woke up.

"Damn, Eric, what's up?"

"Top, it's dark out, but I can see soldiers trying to crawl closer to the walls. What do you want us to do?"

"Go wake up Ford and Buck. Have them meet me on the walkway…where we have the detonators."

"Sure thing, boss." And with that, he took off.

A few minutes later, Buck, Ford and Mel came running up to the walkway, all loaded down with their gear. They had been told what was happening, so they all immediately began looking out into the night to see if they could detect any movement. Ford was the first to see it.

"Yeah, there those fuckers are," he said, pointing. "I can see them. They're gettin' close to the pipes."

"Okay," Top said. "When they get there…send them to hell."

Ford and Buck each picked up a detonator. Using binoculars, Top watched the army troops moving and crawling into position. Low crawling was an awkward movement. It was slow and time-consuming. Squads would crawl, get into a position, and wait for the others to get into position. They would then start crawling again. Top was able to watch and time the movement of the troops. When they got to the point where maximum effect would be reached, Top called it.

"Now!"

At the same time, Buck and Ford activated their detonators, setting off the first row of five bombs. Contrary to what was seen in movies, pipe bomb explosions are not huge night into day explosions. They do explode and cause a fireball, but the real damage comes from the shrapnel caused by the exploding pipes and the nails placed in them. The damage was devastating. The bombs went off one at a time in succession. Each explosion was a short crack, followed by a six-foot-diameter orange blast that sent pipe pieces and nails flying in all directions.

The army troopers were completely caught off guard. The pipe pieces and nails tore into bodies, ripping meat and breaking bone. The screams of the troops could be heard as the explosions shook the ground, one blast after another.

The troops not hit in the blasts retreated back to the safety of their perimeter, dragging the mangled bodies of their dead and injured friends.

Top, Buck, and Ford looked at each other and smiled.

"Well, hopefully that'll slow those bastards down," Buck said as he put his arm around Mel.

"Okay," Top said. "Watch them. They'll come again. When they do, hit 'em again."

"It'll slow them down, I'm sure," Ford said. "But we know now that they're comin'. It's just a matter of time. Once the pipes are done, we have nothing else to stop them. When they do get through—and they will—it's gonna be a fight."

"Yeah," Top said. "We need to get ready."

As the rebels knew they would, the army troops attempted a second time to move closer to the walls. As they got into range, the detonators were activated. The results were the same. Shrapnel moving at thousands of feet per second tore through the bodies of the approaching troopers, tearing flesh from bone and sending body parts raining down on the remaining troops. But this time, they did not retreat. A second wave of troops continued to move forward, forcing Buck and Ford to activate the third and final row of pipe bombs. The amount of death and carnage was frightening. After the last bomb was detonated, the troops finally retreated, dragging dead, lifeless body parts with them.

The rebels knew that the next movement forward would be it. The fight would be on.

In the tree line, Jennifer and Marc watched what was happening, amazed at the damage caused by the pipe bombs.

"We gotta get in there," Jennifer said as she attempted to run toward the compound.

"Hold on," Marc said as he grabbed her arm. "If you try to go in there now, we'll be killed, which won't help anybody."

"If we don't go, how are we gonna help our friends?" she yelled.

"Okay, follow me. We'll try to look for a break in the line, see if we can work our way through and sneak in," Marc said as they began to work their way around the perimeter, looking for some kind of opening in the lines that they could sneak through.

As they walked the perimeter, they became more depressed with each step. The lines were tight, not granting them any way to get in. There were soldiers everywhere and vehicles all over the place. There was no way that they could get into the compound.

Exhausted from the walk back from dumping the five-ton and despondent from finding no openings they could use, they collapsed to the ground, waiting to see what was going to happen next.

"What the *fuck* just happened?" Lopez yelled as he paced in his tent. "Why the *fuck* did we not know they had *fuckin'* bombs in the field?"

Nobody was able to answer the question. Captain Altmont and his lieutenants stood at attention in front of Lopez's desk as he screamed.

"I just lost thirty-five men because my officers failed to do their jobs! Failed to know all details about the capabilities of the opponent we were dealing with! You…" he said as he pointed at each of them. "You cost the lives of thirty-five good troops because you failed! Get out of my office! And this changes nothing in the timeline. We move this morning, so get your men together and get them into position."

Without saying a word, the men left. Lopez continued to pace, anxious to see an end to the fiasco.

It took a couple more hours for the last row of troops to move back into place for the assault, as the moon was nonexistent and the night was almost completely dark, except for the small fires created in the grass by the pipe bomb explosions.

As the troops got into their final position, the harassing bombardment began. Every hour on the hour, five or six grenades exploded, rotating from one side of the compound to the next.

Finally, at 5:30 a.m., Lopez ordered that the aim of the grenadiers be changed. The targets were now to become the center of the walls. On his command, the grenades were launched. Volley after volley were sent down range, striking all four walls of the compound simultaneously. The ground shook, and the dim morning light was brightened by the fiery explosions that ripped the night and the compound walls to shreds.

Colonel Lopez stood along the perimeter on the west side of the compound, grinning from ear to ear as the grenades exploded. This was a true show of his power: commanding the greatest show on earth. He had thought about using the AT-4s but decided that using them would be a waste of ordinance for this situation, ordinance that he may need later. No, the grenades were enough to do what he wanted to do.

After the last volley of pipe bombs had been set off and it was seen that there would be some time before the final assault would take place and that there was no immediate danger, Top went back to his room in an attempt to at least get some down time before the attack he knew was imminent.

At about 5:30 a.m., he heard a change in the volley of explosions. They were on all sides, and there were more of them. As with everybody, since the bombardment had begun, he had started resting in full gear.

Grabbing his M-4, he ran outside to find others already yelling that they were under attack and running to their posts. He saw Buck on the other side of the compound, directing people to positions and giving orders. As usual, Mel was by his side, watching his back, and helping him out. He was amazed at the love they had for each other. He was glad they had found each other.

Top saw a group of people running from the dormitory, and seeing him, they ran to him for direction.

He immediately began directing citizen soldiers into position, placing them where he believed they could do the most good.

The explosions continued to erupt, sending dirt, grass, and stone raining down on the rebels. As the rebels ran to their posts and took up positions, Top yelled after them, “Come on, people, the assholes are on us. Let’s give ’em hell!”

6

As the rebels ran to their posts on top of the garage roofs, a flare lit up the sky, bathing the compound in an airy, orange artificial light.

The rebels could see military troops jumping up from where they had been lying in the grass, running toward the walls and the holes that had been made by the grenades. The army troops were shooting at anything, laying down suppressive fire for their friends who were bounding forward. The bounding troops would drop and lay down suppressive fire for the next line to bound forward. Some rounds fired by the troopers found their targets, dropping rebels from the wall.

Once the army troops were close enough, fire shifted from suppression fire to concentrated fire on targets along the top of the wall.

The rebels posted on the southwest and northeast corners opened up on the soldiers with the M-60 machine guns. The *bup, bup, bup, bup* of the M-60 firing at 650 rounds per minute was impressive and deadly as it rained down on the army troops assaulting the walls. Every third round in the belts were tracer rounds, which caused a green laserlike arc from the M-60 to the target. Soldiers caught in the fire dropped as massive 7.62 plowed holes into their bodies.

"Cover those fuckin' holes! Shoot anybody that comes through there!" Buck was yelling as he pointed his AR15 at the holes in the wall, laying down fire as soldiers rounded corners. His SWAT training kicked in. Slow is smooth; smooth is fast. Take time to aim, press the trigger. Then he almost started to laugh. He couldn't believe a scene from a movie popped into his head…at this particular moment. It was a scene from Mel Gibson's *The Patriot*. "Aim small, miss small."

Meaning, aim at center mass. If you aim at something small, you'll miss it.

He continued to fire, firing until his magazine ran dry.

"*Reloading!*" he yelled. Mel ran over to him and stood over top of him as he kneeled down. She continued to fire, providing cover fire as he reloaded his rifle.

The Dodge truck that they used as the front gate exploded. A huge fireball erupted as the gas left in the tank exploded, the blast wave blowing Buck and Mel back toward the center of the courtyard.

Mel was up first, running to his aid, helping him up. As they both stood, they heard a loud coughing sound. They looked in the direction of the sound and saw the M-60 gunner on the south east corner take several hits to his chest and head, falling to the courtyard below.

On the roof of the dormitory building, the *boom, boom, boom* of the big bore sniper rifles shook windows and blew dust in the air as Ben, Tony, Bill, and Chris took long range shots at the approaching soldiers. The snipers would pull the trigger…*boom.* A soldier would fall, a hole in his chest or his head. *Boom*…another soldier would drop. The sniping continued as the fighting on the ground continued. Ben took a second to look at the melee on the ground, looking to see who of his friends were still left. He saw Buck and Mel in an active firefight at the front gate, and he saw Top on the other side of the compound, leading from the front, just as great Rangers do. Ford was on the wall, directing fire one second, and sending rounds downrange the next.

Ben knew that he would probably not make it and that the rest of these people would probably die this morning, but it didn't stop him from being proud to have fought at their sides.

Top was on the north side of the compound, directing citizen rebels. He ran up a set of steps to the platform on the north west corner and readied himself to fire, bringing his M-4 to his shoulder. Aiming at soldiers storming the wall, he'd press the trigger, sending three round bursts down range. A soldier would drop, he'd find another one and press the trigger.

He stopped shooting and grabbed a citizen standing at his side. Pointing at a group of soldiers that had inched forward, he yelled, "There…take them out."

He raised his M-4 again. He was able to discharge several rounds when his rifle jammed. Being in an active fight, he attempted to transition to his M-9. The pistol never cleared his holster. A single round struck him in the forehead, fired from an unknown soldier, random in its selection. His head snapped back. A second or two elapsed as Top just stood there. He was dead, but his muscles and body just didn't know it. Finally, he collapsed to the floor, the momentum of the fall sending him rolling down the steps, where he came to rest in a sitting position, leaning back at the base of the steps.

There was nowhere safe for the citizen rebels to fire from. Any position taken on what was left of the walls, exposed them to enemy fire from the soldiers, and the holes created from the grenade fire left openings too large to defend.

Buck was up and running, with Mel covering his back. They would both fire and reload, covering each other as the reloading took place. They would reload and fire, snapping off round after round at enemy soldiers. Working his way over to the fallen M-60 gunner, he slung his AR. He picked up the machine gun, lifted the dust cover hastily checking the belt. Slinging a second belt over his shoulder, he closed the dust cover, charged the handle, and turning to the hole in the wall began to fire.

The *bup, bup, bup* of the M-60 and the recoil of the big machine gun sent round after round down range. The heavy 7.62 rounds found their targets as soldiers attempted to gain entry through the hole in the main gate. The bodies fell like cordwood as Buck laid down a continuous wall of 7.62-millimeter lead.

Buck heard a huge explosion. He turned to see what had exploded and saw the roof of the dormitory building erupting in a huge cloud of dust and debris, the cloud billowing into the sky, silencing the steady booms of the sniper rifles that had been providing the long-range cover. Windows in the dormitory blew out, and dust was exhaled from the holes as if the dorm was taking its last breath of air.

Things began to move in slow motion for Buck. He looked around and saw his fellow citizen rebels dropping. Some were taking hits from gunfire, while others dropped in hand-to-hand battles with more seasoned and experienced soldiers. The enemy soldiers were making headway. The citizen rebels were fighting hard, but there were just too many soldiers, who were better equipped, better trained, and more experienced at warfare.

"Fall back!" Buck yelled, ordering the rebels to their fallback positions. "Fall back!" Dropping the now empty M-60, he reached for the AR on his back.

Mel, always at his side, ran out of ammo for her AR. Transitioning to her Glock, she began to lay down fire.

"Go!" Buck yelled. "Get to the cafeteria! *Go!*"

"What about you?" she yelled back.

"I'll cover you! *Go!*" he yelled as she began to run toward the cafeteria doors. As she ran, she could hear his AR cracking. Round after round until it too ran dry. She turned to see a large group of enemy soldiers storm through the hole at the front gate and rush Buck's position. She saw her lover and best friend transition to his beloved 1911. Buck stood in a two-handed fighter stance, the 1911 bucking in his hands. She saw the pistol fire, cycle, and fire and saw the enemy soldiers fall from the big .45 round.

As the pistol ran dry, Buck was charged by a force of soldiers. Gripping the 1911 by the barrel portion of the slide, she saw him use his 1911 as a hammer. He began cracking soldiers in the head until the number of enemies became too much and he was overtaken.

Tears formed in her eyes as she watched her lover, best friend, and soul mate die with a pile of dead enemy around him.

7

Al was in the courtyard running from injured to injured, attempting whatever lifesaving medical help he could provide. Tourniquets and pressure bandages were applied to those that needed them. Mia, who was also running from injured to injured, was triaging who she could. Using a Sharpie marker, Mia would place an *E* on those who were expected to die, an *I* for those who needed immediate care, and a *D* for those who could wait. Al, who was following behind, would do what he could.

The battle continued all around them as the rebels attempted to hold back the seemingly endless wave of soldiers. Mia, seeing a rebel fall, ran to her side. Bending down to apply pressure to the wounded woman's leg, Mia felt a sharp pain at the base of her neck. She thought it was odd. Everything got really heavy, and the initial pain went away. She couldn't hold herself up. The ground seemed to rush toward her face, but she was unable to put her arms out to stop it.

Mia hit the ground. She couldn't move her head, so she just stared straight ahead. As she lay there, all she could see were feet running past and around her. Soldiers and rebels continued to fight as the sight in her eyes slowly turned black.

Al saw Mia go down and rushed to her side. He could immediately see that she was dead. As he was checking on her, Al saw an army soldier take aim. He pulled his M-9 and fired, dropping the soldier before he got off a shot.

As Al bent to close Mia's eyes, he felt something hit the side of his leg. It didn't cause any pain, so he knew he hadn't been shot. Looking down, he saw a small round object, green in color, lying in the dirt beside him. He knew what it was. Having seen and used them a hundred times, he knew that his time on earth was over.

The explosion sent shrapnel screaming through his body, literally blowing him in half. Blood and intestines blew everywhere as Al's upper body flew through the air. He was dead before he hit the ground.

As the battle continued, and the citizen rebels began to fall, the enemy soldiers were able to gain entry into the compound. Some of them stormed the infirmary, where they found Josh unconscious and in bed with Heather at his side, having never fired a shot during the assault. Regardless, the army soldiers showed no mercy. They shot them both in the head and dragged their bodies into the courtyard, throwing them in a pile of other dead citizen rebels.

The surviving citizen rebels continued to fall back to the cafeteria where a meager defense was attempted. The rebels fought as long as they could, but eventually their ammo began to dwindle, and the gunfire became sporadic. Enemy soldiers rushed the darkened room. With rifle, pistol, and knife, the enemies fought. The rebels fought with everything they had, but the experience of the soldiers enabled them to outfight the rebels. The enemy soldiers moved through the cafeteria, taking out one citizen rebel after another, showing no quarter or mercy.

Finally, the only resistance left from the rebels came from the kitchen. Several enemy soldiers, deciding to limit the chance of injury to themselves, threw in grenades, blasting apart the last remaining defenders.

As the fighting died down, the enemy soldiers moved through what was left of the compound. Bullets and knives were used to finish off the wounded. The bodies of the dead were piled together into a heap in the center of the courtyard, where they were doused with gasoline and the bodies set on fire.

A small group of rebels in the kitchen were able to bunker down behind heavy appliances, and those who had survived the grenade blasts were captured and taken prisoner. Mel was among them.

The prisoners were brought before Colonel Lopez. He stood in front of them, hands behind his back. He had a smirk on his face, letting the captured rebels know that he thought they were worthless, lower than scum individuals. As he paced in front of them, chastising them for believing that they could win, Mel stood there in defiance of the colonel, staring at the wall in front of her…until she saw an opening.

One of Lopez's soldiers was following behind him. As the soldier turned, his pistol was right in front of her. She reached for a soldier's pistol, getting the 320 free of the soldier's holster. As the other soldiers in the room reacted, she was able to get off one shot before she was shot in the back of the head and killed. But during the fray, she took one last soldier with her but was unable to get to Colonel Lopez.

Captain Altmont asked for mercy for the remaining rebels, arguing that showing mercy at this point would show that he was willing to work with the population, causing the other citizens of the area to believe that the actions of the rebels is what caused their demise. Colonel Lopez's only answer was a smirk, ordering their execution.

The remaining prisoners stood their ground, never uttering a word. As the soldiers stood behind them, preparing to place the execution bullets into the prisoners, one of them yelled, "*I go to God!*" then the shots rang out.

With those last shots, the battle ended. It was 11:00 a.m. To the best of Lopez's knowledge, there were no survivors from the compound. He ordered that the bodies of his troops be removed from the compound and taken to a quiet field where they were to be buried with military honors. The bodies of the citizen soldiers he ordered to be burned, with the corpses to be left where they were.

EPILOGUE

As the battle raged on, Marc and Jennifer, unable to help or do anything to turn the tide of the fight, watched in horror as their friends and family were slaughtered at the hands of the military.

They stayed hidden in the wood line until the military had finished taking all the guns, food, and equipment that the rebels had been using to survive.

After the military was gone, they worked their way into the compound, where they found piles of charred and burning bodies. They stood and cried as huge plumes of smoke rose into the sky.

Jennifer walked the compound, looking for any sign of Buck or Tony, but she could find nothing to indicate that they had survived.

Eventually, she and Marc gave up and left the compound, heading for some other unknown place where another new life could be started.

Approximately a month after the battle, Colonel Lopez, continuing to slaughter and imprison American citizens, found another group of rebels that he had surrounded and was preparing to eliminate. As he was berating his men, belittling them, as he was famous for doing, he stopped in midsentence and dropped to the ground as his head burst into a mist of bone, brain, and blood, a rifle shot echoing through the air moments later. No other shots were heard, and no other soldiers were killed.

Altmont took over command, and although he continued to fight and conscript citizens into government-sponsored slavery, he no longer murdered or killed those who did not wish to surrender. They were permitted to leave, allowed to go wherever they wanted, as long as they left all food, clothing, and weapons with the military.

Unless fired upon, Altmont's soldiers were ordered not to engage citizens in a firefight. He believed that Lopez had been far too brutal and that under his command, the brutality would stop.

Word of the rebel siege and massacre began to spread across the country. Small pockets of remaining citizens who heard what had happened, heard about the bravery and dedication to freedom that the rebels had displayed, began to create rebel units of their own, eventually joining together and becoming an army of citizens.

Verbally and actively supporting new and different methods for rebuilding the country, an individual named Samuel McAllen emerged as a leader among the rebels. Having served as a major in the US Marine Corps, the rebel army soon elected McAllen to lead them in their fight against the slowly emerging dictatorship in the country.

The siege, as the battle was to become known, was the location of an important battle for citizens who fought for continued freedom and independence in a damaged and newly healing country.

Knowing how badly the rebels had been defeated, McAllen's army reinstituted the tactics of the Native Americans when they fought an invading army in the west. Hitting quickly then retreating to safety, they were able to avoid heavy casualties and were able to prepare to strike again. In doing so, McAllen and his army began to win quick and decisive battles, winning and surviving against the American Army forces at Somerset, Shanksville, and Johnstown. Soon, other rebel armies began to appear, and independence for Pennsylvania soon followed.

Due to McAllen's spectacular leadership and decisive wins in the fight for freedom, life, and liberty, Mc Allen was elected president for the New Territory of Pennsylvania. The state capital was moved to Indiana, Pennsylvania, the county where the rebel fight for independence began. McAllen remained in Indiana until his death in 2045. A twenty-seven-foot-tall statue of him now stands in front of the Indiana Courthouse, towering over a damaged and neglected statue of Jimmy Stewart.

In 2030, it was decided that a monument should be placed at the site of the first rebel battle to make sure all who came after would know about and remember the sacrifice of those that died for freedom and independence.

The monument stands fifty feet high, with the likeness of a soaring eagle on top. The names of the rebel leaders are engraved on the monument, given to the sculptor by a beautiful young woman named Jennifer. The plaque, which is placed underneath the names reads…

> This memorial was here as a tribute to those heroes who bravely gave their lives on this location, October 15, 2024, in the defense of America. In the defense of Freedom. In the defense of Liberty. Their choice to fight, instead of surrender, thrust their lives and deaths into the flames of timelessness, securing that the memory of their actions would lead to the continued democracy and freedom of this great country.

About six months after the monument was erected, an unknown person snuck onto the grounds and painted the following on the monument:

RIP BROTHERS

There was no name given as to the writer.

ABOUT THE AUTHOR

Robert Ciancio is prior military and is currently a twenty-five-year police veteran that has worked in both suburban and metropolitan areas. He has a background in patrol, investigations, and tactical operations. After retiring from the city department that he worked, he began working for a suburban sheriff's office where he met his fiancée, Melissa. He currently lives in Indiana, Pennsylvania, and hopes to retire from police work to pursue a full-time writing career. His spare time is spent with his fiancée, their children, and their two dogs, Alvin and Durga.

CPSIA information can be obtained
at www.ICGtesting.com
Printed in the USA
BVHW031137290720
584942BV00004B/15

9 781646 546053